THE DESTROYERS
DOC PRUYNE

MOUNTAIN SPRINGS HOUSE
INDIANAPOLIS

This book is a work of fiction. With the exception of recognized historical figures, the characters in this novel are fictional. Any resemblance to actual persons, living or dead, is purely coincidental.

Copyright 2013 by Doc Pruyne

All rights reserved. In accordance with the U.S. Copyright Act of 1976, the scanning, uploading, and electronic sharing of any part of this book without the permission of the publisher constitute unlawful piracy and theft of the author's intellectual property. If you would like permission to use this author's material work other than for reviews, prior written permission must be obtained by contacting the publisher at abruning@mountainspringpublishing.com. Thank you for your support of the author's rights.

Cover Art: Tamara Sands, Pixalpod.com
Editing: Lee Porche
Print Formatting: Lynn Hubbard

ISBN-978-1-940022-59-8

DEDICATION

For Leon A. Pruyne Junior.
Dad, rest assured, you were a damn good builder.

FOREWORD

This isn't a whodunnit. I did it. Killed somebody. Might as well get down to brass tacks. All told, I killed seven somebodys.

Not that I'm proud of it.

Fisher Pangbourne was the first and he died on a Thursday night, but don't go thinking I planned it or wanted it. Me? I'm a workin' man, I build houses for a living, pound nails all day. As a matter of fact, I was finally working on my own dream house, way out in the country, finishing the foundation for it, and I was feeling pretty good that evening.

I was in such a good mood that my old friend, Vince Catalone, knew he could break my horns and get away with it. He waved his green can of cream ale and pointed. "Darryl, you missed a spot."

I slung gravel. "You old fart, gimme a break."

I was down in a ditch, covering drainpipe with pea stone, dirt to one side of me, a fresh concrete wall to the other, and Vince was there to inspect it all. He was a code enforcement officer for the town. He shrugged and said, "You don't cover all the drainpipe, puppy, guess what? I can't pass the foundation."

"Slack off? On my own house? What am I, a knucklehead?"

"Slip me a hundred and I'll tell you the truth. Then I might pass the foundation too."

He grinned and took a gulp. Me down in the ditch, him up there against the blue sky, he couldn't help but feel superior, so he sniggered at me. "You call yourself a home builder? That spot, right there."

"Where?"

"Right down there, it's as bare as a baby's ass."

"At the top of your form, I see. Have another beer."

"Of course. Will Rogers never met a man he didn't like. I never met a beer I didn't drink."

I laughed. I didn't know I was gonna kill someone that night. But to tell the truth, what I did—well, truthfully, what my son and I did—I don't know if it was murder. I don't know what to call it. But I was still enjoying my old friend, it was still September sixth, the hot day was settling down into a warm evening, I was working on my own dream house, and so for once I liked the tangy acid smell of newly poured concrete walls. Standing deep in the ditch, I followed Vince's glance, dug the shovel in, and heaved pea gravel down onto the bare spot on the drainpipe because he was, in fact, the building inspector.

For another four days. Then they shot him.

But I can still see him standing up there among the dirt piles above the ditch, smoking his coffin nail, his gold cufflinks gleaming, the crease in his pants still sharp as a knife edge at the end of the day. Down in the ditch, sweaty, tired, and filthy, with holes in my tee-shirt, shoveling gravel, I glanced up when Vince tossed his empty can and it clattered along the scabby base of the wall. He was entering the seventh heaven of a good beer buzz. He said, "Yes, I'll have another. Want one?"

I sleeved the sweat and dirt off my face. "No thanks."

I glanced around, my eyes level with his black dress shoe as he ground out his cigarette in the dirt. My cooler sat by a track of the bulldozer. I stocked it for him, he liked to drink, but I was already satisfied because it was gonna be a fine house for me and my kids and Carla, soon to be my second wife. We hadn't set a date yet, but she had the glittering rock on her finger and so I figured it was a done deal.

Except for my divorce.

Vince cracked open a beer. "I know you got the papers from the lawyer. Did you send them back yet?" My boots were so old the steel toes gleamed through the leather. I smoothed the gravel with a gleaming toe and pretended not to hear. Vince said, "Lynn was a shit. She took off with another man and left you with the kids. Do yourself a favor and send back those papers."

"I hear you, all right!" Over three years later and it still hurt. I stood up and looked at him, dressed in a pinstripe monkey suit, his hands clean and dressy with gold rings. I jammed my shovel into the wet hardpan at the bottom of the ditch and glared up at him. He didn't flinch. He got divorced, went through it, he was right and he knew it, and he also knew I was a reasonable guy. I kicked a rock, dirt was dirt, I couldn't deny it, so I sighed. I said, "Here, gimme a can of that green death."

He handed me a dripping can, I cracked it open and poured cold beer down my throat. It was bitter, like me. I sighed.

"Yeah," I said, "I know, don't tell me. The goal."

"And what's that?" We did a little exercise, him and me, and it got me through some rough times after she left. He said, "What's your goal, puppy?"

I drank a gulp and said, "Marry Carla and have a nice place to live for us and the kids. A place without a lot of memories."

I tossed away half the beer. Vince said, "And?"

"And be a damn good home builder. And make good money while I'm at it." He chuckled, so I squinted up at him. "What's so funny?"

"Not a thing." He gazed down at me, amused, like a dad whose son won the school science fair, and I knew that's how he felt about me, like I was the son he never had. He said, "You're already a damn good builder, everybody says so, and the foundation looks fine. I'll leave the approval on your windshield."

"Well...thanks bud."

I looked up at him. It wasn't often he gave me a compliment like that. I watched as he turned and headed for the cooler. "And I'll take a beer for the road."

He ambled toward the road, sidestepped a big rock, but already half drunk, tripped on a track print churned up by the bulldozer. He looked back at me, half smiling, and stopped. Maybe from thirty feet away he saw a bigger view of me and felt the need to expound on it.

"Puppy," he said, "it's been a grinder for a few years, but now you're coming out the other side."

"And feeling like burger meat. Slap me upside the head with a pickle."

Lame joke, I know, but he chuckled. "Carla will loosen you up. See you at the Pine Inn?"

I shook my head. "Too tired."

I'd already worked nine hours that day on someone else's house. He toasted me, drank, and started walking. He didn't run much risk, passing the foundation before it was done. I wouldn't cut corners on my own house, so he fluttered a certificate before he put it under the windshield wiper of my "Codger," my old Dodge truck, and settled in behind the wheel of his Cadillac. He drove off honking his horn as I kept on doing what I do best. Work.

I covered the drainpipe with pea stone all the way around to the back, to where the pipe followed a ditch down toward the septic tank. The tank sat in an oval field of gravel, then an old growth hardwood forest sloped away and down to a creek spilling through mossy boulders. I'd bought the land because it had a serene feel to it, and that's what I wanted in our home. Calmness.

I trudged uphill to the Codger. I pulled a long-handled slop brush and two heavy cans of tar foundation coating out of the bed. I glanced up to the ridge. The sun hit the field beyond the dirt road, the long rippling grass glowing like a platinum blonde. After I bought the plot I cut a gap in the trees just wide enough for a driveway, cleared a patch just big enough for the foundation and thirty feet of dirt on each side, so the house was gonna feel as snug as a bug in a rug of spruce trees, oaks, and elms.

The six o'clock news was about to come on. Hungry and tired, I gulped a beer while I pried open the cans of tar. I thought about my kids. Patty, my seven-year-old sweetie, was already with the babysitter across the street from our house, but Paul could fix his own dinner. He was sixteen, I thought he was a good kid, resentful about his mother being gone but not much trouble for a teenager...or so I thought.

I dipped the long-handled brush in the black foundation coating and slopped it thick over the concrete walls. I've always hated that job, coating a foundation, and tried to keep the tar off my jeans so I could still wear them out in public. The trees went dark. I sleeved the dirt and sweat off my face. My stomach growled, I was starving by then, so I drank another beer.

The sun went down. I finished that awful tar job, tossed the cans into the bed of the Codger, and dragged sheets of pink foam sheeting down to the foundation. It was almost full dark.

I was down in the ditch, pressing the foam sheets against the tarred walls, the last step before I hopped on the bulldozer and backfilled the foundation, when lights swept across the trees. A car turned in off the road, headlights low to the ground. Too low for a truck. Too low for Vince's Caddy, so I thought, who's it? I was tired, four beers on an empty stomach, so when I tried to claw my way up out of the ditch I stumbled back against the wall, "Dammit!" and ruined my jeans with tar on the back.

I grabbed the shovel and used it to climb the dirt bank. I squinted in the glare of headlights. It was a low gleaming sports coupe, the real thing, the engine humming quietly until the driver shut it off. Car doors opened and two guys stood up. Silence. The headlights stayed on. I couldn't see. It irritated me. I was a little drunk.

I recognized my son's walk. "Paul? That you?" He shuffled up and shoved his hands into his pockets. His brown hair messy in his eyes, teenager skinny, clothes baggy, he looked nervous. I was still holding the shovel. "What's up? Where's Patty? At the Kavidge's?"

He wouldn't look at me. "Dad? I...uh..."

He shuffled his sneakers, eighty bucks a pair and the laces untied. I said, "What's the matter?" I looked at the other kid. He was older, nineteen or twenty, curly dark hair, good looking, a diamond stud glinting in his earlobe, black leather vest. He nodded to me and grinned, real friendly, but now I wish I had noticed the bump under that vest. I said, "Who are you?"

"Hi, I'm Fisher."

"Fisher what?"

"Pangbourne, Fisher Pangbourne. Paul told me all about you, Mr. Jones, how you're a successful homebuilder, a good businessman." Fisher had a charming smile, very genuine. "He says you're an all-around good guy. Pleased to meet you."

"He told you I'm a good guy? I don't believe it."

"No, he did." The kid stuck out his hand to shake. "Being in business, it's hard, I can appreciate it. Glad to meet you."

I shook half-heartedly. He smelled like smoke and something didn't feel right. I looked at Paul. He looked away. I said, "What's going on?"

Paul crushed a dirtball with his sneaker. "Uh...Dad? I..."

I leaned on the shovel. "I'm too tired for this. Spit it out."

Paul looked up from the dirt, a pleading look in his eyes. What the hell? A pang of anxiety made me stand up straight. I looked at Fisher Pangbourne and suddenly I didn't like him. "Is there some problem?"

"Yes, Mr. Jones," Fisher said, "there is. I don't want you to get too excited, but Paul owes us five thousand dollars and we have to be paid."

I snorted. "This is a joke, right?"

Fisher shook his head. "I'm afraid not."

"Five thousand dollars? You're serious? For what? Paul?" Paul ran his hand through his hair, something he learned from me, so I looked at Fisher. "I asked a question. Five thousand dollars for what?"

Fisher opened his hands. "Just like you," he said, "we're in business, Paul and I. We're partners, but, well...he suffered some losses."

"What are you talking about? What business?"

"The pot business."

"What business is that?"

"The pot business. You know, marijuana. I front him weight, he breaks it up into smaller amounts and sells it for a profit. Lots of profit, Paul, don't you."

"For real? I mean, you and him are dealing dope?"

"That's right." Fisher nodded as if to apologize. "I'd like to forget about it, but five K is five K. We have people to pay too so..."

"So...what? You've been fronting dope to my son?" My face went hot and it wasn't sunburn. I looked at Paul. "You've been smoking it too, I suppose. That's what you're telling me?"

"It's mostly because he had what you might call an 'interpersonal' problem," Fisher said, looking at Paul, "so it's not like he's been smoking much. Have you, dude?"

"And you sold it to him?" I had the shovel, I flipped it up and jabbed it at Fisher. "I heard enough. Get the hell out of here, you punk."

Fisher turned defiant. "Yeah, I'll leave when you pay us."

"Why you little—"

I jabbed at him, caught a button on his vest and jerked it. He slapped at the shovel and snapped, "You got it, right in your safe."

"No, I'm calling the cops!"

"Just pay us!"

"Get outta here!"

I jabbed at him, nailed him in the ribs. That's when he stuck his hand under his vest. He pulled out a pistol, a chrome revolver.

"He owes us!"

Paul shouted, "Fish!"

Things happened. I jabbed with the shovel, it hit Fisher's hand and the gun fired, crack! Fisher cringed in shock. He'd obviously never fired it before, but it was already in the dirt, the pistol, and the rage was roaring through me. "Why you son-of-a-..."

"A gun?" Paul has my temper. He gave Fisher a shove. "I can't believe you. A gun!"

"He owes us!"

"A damn gun!"

Paul gave him another shove. Fisher stumbled back, startled, but I couldn't see his face. He couldn't see either. His heel caught on a ridge of dirt, he tripped and fell backwards, toward the bulldozer. Clunk! He flopped down among the pistons and hoses behind the blade of the dozer and lay there.

"I'm calling the cops!" I smacked the bottom of his sneaker with the shovel. He lay behind the blade, half lit by his car headlights. His foot kicked. He was staring, eyes open, I saw them glinting in the shadows. Nobody home, I didn't realize, I shouted, "Get up!" His leg quivered. His hand twitched, but then he didn't move, so I stepped closer, leaned over him and said, "Hey. Hey, kid? Get up."

Silence.

"Fish?" Paul whispered it. "Fisher?"

Fisher's nostrils turned dark with blood, it thickened and broke in a dribble down his cheek. Blood? I lost hold of the shovel, it clanged in the hardpan. "No!"

I grabbed Fisher by the ankles and dragged him into the open. The back of his head left a trail of dark blood in the dirt, blood running out of his nostrils, down his cheeks.

Paul freaked. "Dad, stop it, he's bleeding. Holy shit!"

"My god, oh my god!" I dropped to my knees, ripped off my tee-shirt, and clamped it to the back of his head. It was a big hole punched in Fisher's skull, blood on my hands, my shirt soaked in it. He was staring up at me, not blinking, blood streaking his cheeks, and all I could say was, "Paul, how could you... Oh my god, kid, I'm sorry. I'm sorry!"

"Dad, I..."

Pressing the wound, I felt the wet bone fragments, blood flowing, and Fisher didn't blink. Oh god, I thought, please no! But the blood flowed and Fisher kept staring. He was gone, gone as hell, so I pushed back off him and sat in the dirt, stunned, looking at him.

"Oh christ, oh god, he's dead. Dead as a doornail, what the fuck!" I jammed my hands into my hair. "Wasn't our fault! Somebody's boy, it wasn't our fault!"

Paul thought otherwise. "I killed him. Dad, I killed Fish. I killed him!"

"No, he fell and you...we didn't. It was an accident!"

Glaring headlights, dead Fisher, my son lost it and shouted, "I did! I can't believe it, I killed him!"

Suddenly I knew how it would look to a cop, to anyone, a judge and jury. Guilty. Paul owed him money, murder, guilty, plain and simple. Guilty, cut and dried.

What'll they do to him? I stood up, my hands shaking. "Paul?"

"Look at him, Dad, he's...oh god, I can't believe I..."

"Paul?"

He looked at me and froze, reading me. He looked at Fisher, looked at me. "They'll think we...we wanted to?"

What'll they do to him? I wasn't worried about me, honestly, I was looking at him, Paul, and I couldn't let it happen to him, my son, my only son, so I blurted it. "We have to get rid of him. Now."

My stomach hurt. I heard someone moan. It was me. I hurt like a big hole got punched in me, my life, someone's life. All over America drugs were punching holes in people's lives, dead kids, dead neighbors, dead parents...but how could I know that? Fisher just lay there dead. Oh christ, God help us, what now? What?

What now? It was over. Life as I knew it.

CHAPTER 1

Fisher Pangbourne died Thursday night and Friday morning I totally lost my senses. I got up and went to work as if nothing happened.

I had to take my kids to school, the usual routine for Patty, my little blonde sweetie, but for Paul, well, we had to have a little talk. I leaned into Patty's room where she was hopping around in her paisley panties and a tee-shirt. She held up two jumpers and asked, "Which one, Daddy, the pink or the blue?"

"Uh...the pink one."

"Mommy sent me the blue one. I'll wear that."

Ouch. Mommy ran off to California with Mister Spinach the artist with green hair. I rubbed my eyes to hide my wince. "Breakfast? Count Choconuts?"

"Yumma yumma." She laughed, showing tiny white teeth. "With the big spoon!"

I shut her door and turned to Paul's. Closed. I didn't want to remember what happened. I let my breath out slowly, raised my hand, but it took three tries for me to get up the nerve and knock.

I listened a moment and opened the door. Curled up in bed, messy hair in a nest of sheets, all he said was, "Don't you knock first?"

"I did."

"Two seconds ago."

"Dammit! Don't you..." I was in his room by then, smelling his teenage b.o. and the bag of potato chips on his desk. I exhaled and dug my fingers through my hair, got myself calm, then said it evenly. "I'm taking you to school. Get dressed."

"Stevie's coming for me."

"No, I'm taking you. Get up."

I went out to clear off the jump seat in the Codger. I stowed a three-foot level and a couple of tape measures in a toolbox in back, and because I didn't want the bed to get sticky I lifted out the empty cans of foundation coating and lined them up along the edge of the driveway. Big mistake, but what did I know? Then I stuffed a few rolls of blueprints behind the front seat and wadded up all the burger joint bags and foam coffee cups.

The garbage collects when you work eleven hours a day building houses and keeping the books. I stacked up the old newspapers that ran my ads, sample books of cabinet knobs, catalogs for house plans, vinyl siding, and bulldozer parts, and shoved the stack under the seat. Under a packet of hacksaw blades and a menu for a sub shop I found a utility knife I'd lost two weeks before and stuck it in my pocket. Patty giggled every time she spotted grass growing on the floor mats but Paul just stomped on it. It was growing there again, a few green sprouts where I spilled some seed, and I thought what a trial it must be for Paul to have a dear old dad like me.

Dear old dad. My accomplice in murder.

I went back into the house. Patty had a bowl of Choconuts spilling on the table as she tried to eat it with the big spoon clicking on her teeth. Paul shuffled out of the hallway with his hair looking like dozens of sharp little brown prickers. I said, "You're going to school with your hair greased out like that?"

He rolled his eyes. "It's mousse."

He ate, I couldn't, but I had to act normal for Patty. I gathered her school books into her dinosaur backpack. "Did you get your homework done, sweetie?"

"Uh-huh. Did you?"

"Not last night. Let's go."

We walked outside. Blue sky, warm air, and all of a sudden, oh my god, my gut clenched. Mud was all over the driveway, all over the truck. River mud. I grabbed a hose, turned the spigot, and started rinsing down the Codger, Paul looking at me like I had three heads. I shrugged for Patty and explained the obvious. "Daddy's truck is dirty."

"I love your truck when it's dirty. All the other trucks look like they're right out of the box."

I couldn't say it: the dirt balls in the driveway, sweetie, might link me to a murder.

That's when the door opened on the house next door. Oh great, it's Binks. No neighborly waves, him or me, and not because I went tight with fear. He was a detective with the State Troopers, a hard egg who didn't like me or the kids. He gave us a gimlet eye, like a crocodile before it dives under water, and though I pretended not to see him, as Binks adjusted his suit jacket

I spotted the snubnose pistol belted to his liver. Typical cop in demand, he jumped in his blue copmobile and zoomed away.

I backed my truck out of the driveway and drove down our street. Verna Drive lay half up the hill to Snob Knob where the doctors and lawyers lived. Small houses stood well maintained on lawns that were getting crinkly dry after six rainless days in September. The little box houses built in the sixties were well taken care of, cleanly painted and shuttered, but getting old.

We hit the dead end at the playing fields and I turned down Pruyne Street, a big hill that sloped past the side entrance to Homer F. Brink Elementary School, built of brick when it was still cheap, Patty humming a kid's tune and Paul looking glum.

"Sweetie," I said, "you have a good day at school."

"Bye Paul. I love you, Daddy."

"I love you too."

I kissed her cheek, Paul let her out, I shifted into neutral, and we coasted down Pruyne Street toward Hooper Road. I glanced at him. He looked out the window. I thought, We got a problem, don't we? Great, yeah, he's dead, so now what are we gonna do? Five grand? How much were you smoking?

I could think it, but I couldn't say it.

The air in the truck grew tense, or maybe I got angry and squeezed the wheel until my knuckles whitened. I told myself not to shout at him, so I let my breath out slowly and asked, "Paul? What are you gonna do today?"

Belligerent. "About what?"

"Dammit!" I tried not to shout, "I mean...well...yeah, dammit, that's what I mean. What are you gonna do about your buddies, those 'friends' of yours? Your suppliers? You're gonna stay away from them and everyone else who had anything—I mean anything!—to do with that junk. You hear me?"

Hooper Road wound up a hill where I took him sledding when he was a happy little kid. Not anymore. He said, "You don't get it. Me, Dad, I'm the supplier, everyone comes to me. What am I supposed to tell them? Fisher didn't come last night? They'll know I'm lying. What do I tell them? That I—"

"No! Don't! Don't say anything!"

I turned the truck into the high school driveway, kids tramping down out of bright yellow buses. I stopped by the curb, threw it into park, squeezed the wheel, and looked at him.

"Paul, you don't get it. It was an accident, but does it look that way?"

His face turned red, he was about to cry, but he didn't. He whispered, "He was a cool guy."

"He was a damn dope dealer!"

"Yeah? So am I!" He jumped out, but before he slammed the door he shouted, "I should've gone to live with Mom!"

I stuck my head out the window. "As if you had a choice!"

He was already gone among the kids crowding the sidewalk. I hung my head and thought, What am I gonna do? He doesn't get it! The fear clenched my throat, I choked, freaked out, hit the steering wheel, tried to breathe, suck in the smells of tractor grease, dirt, and old papers that filled the truck. I dug my hands through my hair. I had to talk about it. Mudgie, Carla, Vince, only them, they were the only ones who wouldn't freak out and call the cops.

Death penalty. That's what we'll get, the electric chair. Holy Hannah.

I shoved the gear stick and pulled out, drove past the long curving line of yellow school busses, so scared I was barely able to think. I drove up Farm to Market Road, past the Endwell Middle School. We lived in Endwell, a big misnomer. That's what Lynn called it when we were splitting up, a misnomer. Lynn and me, classy and clunk, no wonder we didn't make it. Misnomer, what's that? Latin, a mistake in naming, something she learned at the state university across the river. I paid for her master's degree and she hit me in the teeth with it, so that's what Endwell was, damn straight, the biggest misnomer in upstate New York.

A failure at marriage and a murderer. Yeah, Carla's gonna dump me like a dead cat.

That kind of thinking and I was feeling real chipper when I pulled into Green Meadow Way, my subdivision. I drove up the street of beautiful houses I'd built, French Mansards with sloping roofs, raised ranches, shuttered colonials, English Tudors. One of those Tudors had a real slate roof, a rare and expensive frill; but I sweat bullets over all those houses, built them with quality, had to be proud of them, so the buyers always waved when they saw me because they knew they'd make a wheelbarrow full of money when they sold out. I drove by Mr. Radziwill with his perfect hair, red tie, and blue blazer. He waved, but it didn't help, I was on the verge of throwing up when I got to the house we were working on.

I stopped the Codger at the curb. Mudgie's truck was already there. We had that house to work on through October, then I'd be paying him to work on my own house, so he was happy. His wife was an Amway distributor, twenty years or so—they didn't have to worry about money—but he had a new half-ton with extended cab, a hefty nut to make every month, so I fretted about keeping him busy.

Not that day. I climbed out of the truck and trudged through the churned up bulldozer tracks, shipping bands, dirt, and wood splinters to where Mudgie stood filling the front door opening. He wore big new tan boots with his pants bunched on top, the knees of his jeans worn to white, a leather carpenter's apron strung under his big gut. He grinned and slurped coffee from a metal cup steaming in his pudgy fingers.

He said, "You look like hell. Where'd you and Vince end up?"

"Mudgie, I..."

His eyes narrowed, he saw I was in bad shape, real bad, right away. "Bud?"

"I...I screwed up, big time."

He stepped down from the doorway, wincing when he spilled coffee on his hand. "Darryl, what? What's the matter?" I motioned for him to come. "What is it?" I led him out to the weeds at the back of the lot. He watched me all the way and then he said, "What's the matter?"

"Mudgie, I'm in deep shit."

"Why? What happened? Carla catch you bangin' somebody else?"

I shook my head. "I killed somebody."

He blinked. "Say what?"

"A pot dealer from New York. I killed him."

"The hell are you talking—"

"By accident."

"When? Last night?"

"No, last fucking Christmas!" I jammed my hands in my hair and turned in a circle. "I was out at the house, and Vince okayed the foundation, and I was about to jump on the tractor and backfill it when a car pulls in, a sports job."

"And?"

"And Paul gets out with this kid, Fisher, a slick salesman type, diamond stud earring, the whole nine." My face started to hurt. "He...I..."

"Who was he?"

"He's been fronting pot to Paul."

"Oh. So Paul's been dealing reefer?"

"And something happened, so Paul owes him five thousand dollars. When I realized what the guy was saying I went ballistic. I had a shovel, and this guy jabbered how Paul's not smoking too much product but I still gotta pay him five thousand dollars out of my safe."

"What safe?"

"In my office, petty cash, that's all. So I lost it and...kind of...killed him."

"No shit? How?"

"Well...you know Vince, he likes to drink, and I had a few with him. No supper though, so they hit me pretty hard."

"Yeah?"

"So I started shouting at this Fisher punk and I scared him. He pulled out a pistol, a chrome-plated revolver, and that's when I knocked it out of his hand with the shovel."

"And what? Killed him with it?"

"The shovel?"

"No, the pistol."

"You think I could shoot somebody? Hell no. I smacked him with the shovel and he stumbled a bit, but then..." I don't know why, but I made it sound like Paul had nothing to do with it. "He tripped in the dirt, fell and hit his head on the blade of the tractor, on the corner of it. That broke his skull. Then he died right there, kicking in the dirt."

He silently mouthed the words, No shit. He said, "It was an accident. He fell."

"But my kid owes him five grand, we get in a ruckus and he ends up dead. Does it look like an accident? See what I'm saying?"

"No kidding. I see what you mean."

We both looked at the pond. There was a stump, a pond, and empty fields beyond, an overgrown golf course gone to weeds. I looked at Mudgie, he looked at me. He remembered the cup in his hand and gulped coffee, his jowls shaking as he wiped his mouth on his sleeve. All he said was, "Holy cow."

I felt like a scared little kid. "What am I gonna do? The governor just reinstated the death penalty. What am I gonna do? Mudgie?"

"Where's the guy now? The body?" I dug my hand through my hair hard enough to hurt, but I still couldn't think. Mudgie poked my arm. "Where is it?"

"I can't tell you."

"Why not?"

"Because I can't! I don't wanna think about it. I just...can't...think about it. Okay?"

He looked confused. "What about the gun?"

"In my truck. I couldn't get rid of it."

"Why not?"

"I thought I might need it."

"For what?" My hand turned spastic, so I grabbed a handful of my tee-shirt and bunched it up. He said, "What about the kid's car?"

"In the Susquehanna. Paul followed me down in the truck, to River Road, and I...I don't think anyone saw us. But what am I gonna do? What?"

He gazed out over the rippling grass of the abandoned golf course—I bought three or four holes of it for a song—and the gears were turning in his head. Mudgie was smart enough, but none too motivated, and not much for breaking the daily routine. That was his answer.

He lay his big calloused hand on my shoulder. "You know what you're gonna do? Work," he said. "Work your ass off and forget about it, almost, if you can, like it never happened."

"Are you serious?"

Mudgie squeezed my shoulder and leaned so close I smelled the java on his breath. He said, "About ten o'clock, after all the suits go to work, we're gonna bury that gun right over there, by that stump." He nodded to the stump sticking up out of the weeds by the pond. "We get rid of the gun and there's no evidence, then you act natural, work your ass off, and forget about it. Nobody's gonna catch you...unless you were so dumb you buried him in the next door neighbor's yard."

"Binks? He's a state trooper, he hates me."

"I know." Pudgie Mudgie turned me around and we started back. He shook his cup out, keeping his other hand steady on my shoulder. "Carry on, like normal, no evidence, nobody'll find out, they won't find you. Right? Right, bud?"

"I don't know, I just..."

We walked out to the front of the house. The managers and bean counters were pulling out of their driveways, droning off in their BMWs and Acuras. Nine-to-five, the routine carries on, bigger than anybody. Mudgie, stunned, must've been thinking something similar.

"Don't matter who's dead," he mumbled. "Off to work we go."

CHAPTER 2

He, David Allen Binks, having sworn to uphold the laws of the State of New York, closed his detective's badge in the leather flipcase and slipped it into the chest pocket of his dark blue blazer, his favorite. He was a civilian until he stepped out of his own house, or so he liked to think. He shrugged his shoulders into the blazer and walked away from the mirror.

Forget his job? With a .38 snubnose belted to his hip?

He strolled out of the master bedroom, past the bedroom they used as an office—evidence: no children—into a spotless living room. Deep creamy shag rug, chrome tubular furniture, leather sofa, big screen TV, and his wife, Sheila, still as beautiful as a magazine cover. Flowing straight hair, lean feminine shape, legs firm after running twice around the Earth on a treadmill. Binks slid his arms around her from behind and kissed her shoulder, savoring a memory of their sex in the night, damp skin, salt tastes, rhythms, gasping.

Sheila rubbed his wrist but was already in day mode, looking out the window.

"That's a first," she said. "Darryl Jones is washing his truck." Below their bay window, below their front yard sloping down to Verna Drive, Binks spotted Darryl Jones, scruffy-haired, lean in his worn jeans, hosing down his old beater truck, his kids standing there watching. She said, "I hope he doesn't leave those cans there."

Four black sticky-looking cans stood along the driveway. Odd, Binks thought, the kids watching him like that. He said, "Darryl loves his truck the way a cowboy loves his horse."

Sheila chuckled. He inhaled the smell of her perfume as she leaned against him, but he let her go when his cell phone chortled. He raised it, "Binks here," and Sheila turned and walked behind him, trailing her fingers along the top of his butt.

Emma's voice. Morning, Dave. "Morning, sweets. Got something for me?" New and unusual. A car in the river. Binks watched the remnants of the

Jones family, Darryl washing his truck, its rusty fender dribbling water. "Where?" The end of River Road, in past the burger joint. "Fifteen minutes." He cut off the call as he strode for the door. "See you tonight, hon."

"Sic 'em, tiger."

Binks stepped out the door, amused, and glanced over at Jones, water dribbling onto his work boots, boots so old the steel toes showed through the leather. The kids watching, again it struck Binks as odd. Seeing the kids always made his mouth clinch. The doctor said he was shooting blanks. Sheila had no kids, it hurt, but it was an old pain and his mouth unkinked as he slid behind the wheel and fired up his cruiser. The V-8 hummed, the cabin shivering as he turned on the scanner and pulled out from the curb.

Binks drove down through Endwell to George F. Johnson Highway. George F. was a shoe tycoon, but long after the man was ashes and dust the highway still ran through the bottom of Endwell, where it flattened out on the flood plain of the Susquehanna River, four lanes of blacktop laid and stripped into the heart of Endicott. Endicott was also the birthplace of IBM, but now the downtown stood empty. E.J. Shoes went belly up, IBM poisoned the aquifer and jilted the place, so now Binks had to deal with the workmen left standing on the altar. Drunkenness, drugs, wives bouncing off walls, school kids with black eyes, an epidemic of B&E's.

This was a different puzzle, interesting. Binks took the dogleg before the burger joint and drove slowly through a neighborhood of little houses. River Road. He cruised past the Washington House, one of the oldest in the county, the river glistening through the sycamores on the other side of the road and below. Binks passed modest homes owned by retirees, well maintained, and near the turn-around at a dead end saw the red lights of a cruiser flashing, a tow truck flashing yellow, and Cummings was stringing caution tape over the dirt ruts.

He parked on the turn-around, got out, and looked at the pavement. Road sprinkle, nothing unusual. Binks strolled down the gravel that led to river dirt, scanning the ruts. Moist soil, rich black tire tracks. Cigarette butt, used condom, stones, chewed toothpick, then he reached Cummings' black shoes and looked up his legs. Mid-thirties, trim, quick eyes below his flat brim hat, Cummings said, "Didn't find any other tire prints, I checked."

Always covering his ass.

Cummings lifted the tape for him. "Thanks." Binks scanned. Paper soup cup with a dead fish worm hanging out, a butt with a red-stained filter, cream ale cap, an old wrapper for a pair of pantyhose. Nothing...yet. Binks walked up beside the tow truck, its winch creaking as the cable quivered, the back end of a car breaking out of the river. The operator in greasy coveralls watched him flip open his cell phone. "Who found it?"

The operator pointed to an old man with a fishing rod and tackle box. Emma's voice out of his cell phone. What can I do ya? "Run a make on a Dodge Viper, license 1-John-Nancy-dash-644. 1JN-644. Thanks."

He pocketed the cell phone, walked over to the old man and nodded. Hunched by age, the old man puffed his words out through his thick white mustache. "Hooked something bigger than I expected."

"See a body in the water? Anyone around when you got here?"

"Nope, didn't see a thing. Sorry."

Binks turned to watch as the tow rig winched the Dodge out of the river, a glittering candy apple red convertible shedding water, the seats awash in gray bilge. Cummings stepped in and said, "Watch your shoes," and opened a door. Water cascaded onto the mud and sluiced back into the river.

Binks walked around the car, scanning the paint. Not a scratch. Beautiful finish. He stepped between the open door and the passenger seat. White leather buckets, five speed stick, no hanging tags, stickers, knickknacks, or gewgaws, and certainly no plastic Jesus. Something black over on the driver's seat, four inches up. Keys in the ignition, no pendants on the ring.

"Suicide?" Cummings asked.

"Don't think so." Binks pointed around the cockpit of the Viper. "No personal effects, it means one of three things. The car's a rental, it was cleaned out before it was dumped, or it was owned by someone who's self-effacing."

"Self-effacing? What do you mean?" Cummings asked.

Binks opened the glove compartment. Owners manual, sodden papers. "Someone who doesn't have a big ego, doesn't like to take up space. Easy to get along with, friendly. Someone who might pick up a hitch-hiker."

His cell phone chortled. "Binks here." Dave? The car is registered to High Performance Rental and Lease in Scarsdale, in Westchester. I'll connect you. "Thanks."

He glanced under the dripping seats. Nothing. The cell phone in his hand began to buzz the number and Binks lifted it to his ear. A woman's voice. Good morning, High Performance. "Hi. This is Detective David Binks of the New York State Police." Oh...good morning. I'll put you through to Mr. Walters, the manager. "Thank you." Binks waited. A crow flew overhead. He turned to look out over the river. Water rippled around a tree stump, the current rolling smooth and fast in the deep channel ten feet from the bank.

THE DESTROYERS

Binks realized it: a local dumped the Viper. He knew it dropped off deep.

A voice trying to sound deep and masculine. What can I do for you, detective?

"We have one of your cars here, we're just pulling it out of the Susquehanna River, upstate, outside Binghamton. A Dodge Viper, plate number 1-John-Nancy-dash-644. 1JN-644. Who's got the lease?"

We're not required to release that information...but since it's you. Binks rolled his eyes. What a nice guy. He waited. Traffic droned on the highway a few hundred yards behind his back. Up the river the chimneys of Gowdy Station belched smoke into the sky, the odd mountain in the middle of the flood plain standing dark against the pale blue sky.

The man on the other end lit a cigarette, the knash of steel on flint clicking through. Here it is. A three-year lease to...Fisher J. Pangbourne. Address is...268 East 238th Street, the Bronx. "I see. Occupation?" A chuckle. Stripper. Telephone number? "Give it to me." Binks scribbled the information into a pocket pad. Any damage? "No damage, just soggy, but it's being impounded. What's the monthly?" Four-sixty, it's loaded. "Income?" Sixty thousand a year. Not bad for a kid of nineteen, and his credit checked. "Uh-huh, thanks."

He pocketed the cell phone, stepped over the cable hooked under the back bumper, and circled to the driver's door. He looked carefully at the handle plate, an oval flush with the body—no prints, no marks—and with one finger pulled it up and popped the door.

He leaned in beside the steering wheel and looked at the leather bucket. Black smear four inches up the backrest where a driver's lumbar curve would match the cushion. Binks touched the gunk, rubbed it between his fingers. Black, viscous, too thick for oil. Tar. Tar on the back of somebody's pants.

He turned to Cummings. "Tow it to impound and call Walt at forensics. Tell him to sample the gunk on the driver's seat and call me with the work up. Tell him the current was pretty fast, he probably won't find much else."

"No kidding," Cummings said. "Washed clean."

Binks walked to his cruiser, looking at his notebook. Nineteen-year-old male stripper making sixty thousand dollars a year and driving a candy apple red convertible. Kid must feel on top of the world. He slid behind the wheel and started the engine. Unless he's at the bottom of the river.

Binks drove into a parking lot behind a converted elementary school, a four-story box of faded bricks, a sign over the back door: ENDWELL SUBSTATION, NYS POLICE. They leased the bottom floor, a holding cell just inside the back door, a counter across the aisle, desks, a water cooler, offices, and, of course, old Emma. "Morning, sweets."

Grey-haired, wrinkles around her mouth and eyes, Emma was his mother's age, though his mother had passed away some years before. She said, "Morning, handsome. Anything exciting?"

"Maybe." He walked into his office, sat down, dropped the pocket pad onto a blotter calendar and noted the little x's by some of the dates. Sheila's fertile days, it'll be this weekend. They were going away. A baby-making trip, don't give up hope. He picked up the phone and dialed the numbers on the pad. Those little x's, Binks had it. Performance anxiety.

Four rings before a woman said, Hullo? Hm. A blunt edge. Binks said, "Is this the Pangbourne residence on East 238th Street?" Yeah, who's this? "Detective David Binks, State Police. I'm calling about Fisher." A test. "Is he your husband?" No, he's my son. Why? What's the matter?

Binks doodled on the blotter as he said, "I'm calling because we found your son's car in the Susquehanna River this morning, up here in Endicott. When was the last time you spoke to him?" He wasn't in it, was he? "No, and there's no reason to worry. Have you heard from him lately? Why would he be upstate? Was he performing?" Performing what? "He's a male dancer. Isn't he?" A snort of ridicule. Hell no. He's a student at Binghamton University. Are you really a policeman? You sound awfully dumb to me.

Binks drew uppercase letters, BELLIGERENT, and said, "That's the occupation he listed on the lease application for his car, Mrs. Pangbourne. Your first name is?" Dorothy. I...I talked to him Sunday. He calls me every Sunday, about noon. He's a good kid, everybody loves him, he's really sweet. He's doing good in school, straight A's, so...any idea what happened?

"Not yet. If he's not a performer, Mrs. Pangbourne, how can he afford to lease a convertible sports car?"

I hope he's all right. "Mrs. Pangbourne?" Uh...I gave him some money. But his brother, Blake, he gave him some, and Fisher got a little from when his father passed. Any idea what happened? Binks said, "As I said, not yet. What's his address and phone number up here? Any friends you know of?"

Binks got off the phone with Mrs. Pangbourne and dialed Binghamton University. A woman's voice. Registrar's office. May I help you?

Seven minutes later he was cruising up George F. Highway. The Pangbourne kid was a marketing major scheduled to be in his required humanities class, The Epic Novel, for another fifty minutes. Binks arced through the traffic circle and drifted over the bridge over the Susquehanna, warm September wind combing his hair pleasantly.

Those little x's on his calendar preyed on him. He felt himself sink into one of those moods. How do you boost your sperm count? He fidgeted, rubbed his smoothly shaven cheek. Powerless, he thought, that's what you are. A victim of biological determinism.

He made the end of the river, the buildings of the university that climbed the southern side of the river valley ahead of him. College kids. Citizens in training. Doctors, dentists, computer programmers. Words were too specific, but maybe he felt the doubt. Will kids make her happy? Is that why you have kids? To make yourself happy?

He parked outside Campus Security but didn't bother to go in. Instead, he climbed stairs to the quad and strolled the sidewalks and grass toward the tower at the center of the campus. He was forty-one. The college girls looked young, healthy, and stripped nude they'd look like peaches molded into human curves, fresh and dripping with life. The boys hadn't lost anything yet, laughs spiked the air, gleaming smiles, white teeth, experimental whiskers on their chins. He watched a Frisbee skip on paving stones and connect with fingers that flicked it spinning away again.

He pushed open glass doors, into the humanities building. Echoes, coeds, fluorescent lights, a blue pall on the floor dispelled around the doors and windows by daylight. Binks felt the blue pall in him and didn't like it.

He knocked on a door and it opened too quickly. An old professor with bifocals, a white goatee and stringy throat glared at him, clutching a fat paperback copy of Crime and Punishment. Even his monosyllable was sonorous. "Yes?"

Binks leaned into the room and said, "Fisher Pangbourne?" Sixteen peaches and college boys taking a test. No one looked up. "Fisher?"

A chubby teenager wearing a Metallica tee-shirt, curly dark hair, glasses, very Jewish, raised his head, startled. Odd, Binks thought. Not a Dodge Viper type. The professor said, "Fisher? Go ahead."

The kid slid out of his desk, the top creasing his gut, and trudged his expensive sneakers toward them. The professor closed the door and they were alone in the hall. Binks measured him: an inch shorter, curving cheeks, jowls, a creased throat, forty pounds too heavy. The kid wouldn't look at him.

"Fisher," he said, "I'm Detective Binks, with the State Police. We found your car in the river this morning. What happened?"

The gas must've been percolating inside the kid during class because when he bolted he also farted. "Hey!" Binks got after him, the kid's tee-shirt hiking up, a thick roll of fat jouncing on his hips as he ran. Daylight, an exit sign, the kid barged into a door and Binks caught him, grabbed him by the shoulder and slipped an arm around his throat. He levered the kid, wheeled him around and shoved him up against a plate glass window.

The kid croaked, "Wait! I'm not Fisher, I'm not!"

College boys stopped to watch, girls hugging books to their chests. Binks grabbed a fistful of the kid's shirt. "Who are you then? Where's Pangbourne?"

"I don't know!"

"Who are you? Answer me!"

"Harvey! Harvey Epstein! I didn't do anything!"

Binks shoved the kid back against the glass. "Were you driving his car?"

"No, I haven't seen him." Epstein had his hands up, clutching at Binks' hand that was full of his shirt. "I do his homework, that's all, I swear it!"

Binks let go of his shirt and stepped back, Harvey Epstein, flushed and sweaty, pulling his shirt down over his belly fat. He said, "Do I have to cuff you?"

"For what? I didn't do anything!"

"You tried to run. Do it again and it'll be six months in Broome County lock-up." Binks exuded his strength and the kid's hands got jumpy. Binks gestured to the door. "Let's go."

CHAPTER 3

The South Bronx. The good family folk of Davidson Avenue hurried to begin their daily business, unaware of the killers plotting among them.

The traffic drone and smog of the Major Deegan drifted over the rooftops as the sunlight of a new morning pleasantly warmed the windows overlooking the street. The buildings along Davidson were built of orange and pale red brick, warmer than brownstone, that echoed the efflatus of engines, vehicles sputtering over the pavement, the gutters all but hidden by parked cars. Old women slouched on stoops, smoking cigarettes, while teen mothers let their newborns suckle beneath their shirts. A parade of school kids, clerks, secretaries, shoppers, and businessmen scraped past their toes.

Blake Pangbourne, good-looking with dark messy hair and dark brows, muscular in a white tank top, plugged coins into a pay phone as the sneakers, shoes, pumps, and work boots of the locals tramped past his heels. A backpack bumped him, three boys hurrying for P.S. 91, but Blake didn't mind the little people and the sheep. He was about to have some fun.

He listened. Ring ring ring, clatter-clunk, a voice on the other end. What? Better be golden, you callin' this early. Who is it?

Blake chuckled. "Keeshon, it's Blake Pangbourne. How are you this fine morning?"

Blake the blade, ma main juice man. Hold a minute, I gotta... Keeshon grunted, mumbled, a woman's voice in the background. Whassup, brotha?

Blake's pleasure lightened his voice. "I called, big guy—bro, brutha, blood o' mine—to tell you that your mama's already out doing the morning shopping."

Keeshon chuckled. Yeah, she make the best grits. But...how'd you know? Where are you? Blake let him hang. Juice man? Somethin' wrong? Whaddup?

"Keeshon, we do have a problem. Our mutual friend? Mr. P.? You shot your mouth off about him to the wrong people. Didn't you."

Naw, Blake, not me, we in the biz together so I'm be cool. Blake glanced away. He noticed patterns. He noticed the pattern of pigeons strutting around the filth over a manhole cover. Patterns in a telephone conversation, speech, and silence, how the tension increased when he let the pattern lapse. Keeshon turned defiant. Mr. P., fuck, he outta hand. So what? You sidin' with his sorry ass? So you—

"So so so." Blake rolled his eyes. "So, Keeshon, you have to pay. Your momma, she with the little piggy tail at the back of her head? She won't finish her shopping. Look out your window. She's wearing a curly black wig—we know she doesn't have any hair, just a little piggy tail at the back—and that dress she's wearing? That nice blue dress? It's about to turn red."

A hundred feet up the street Keeshon's head poked out of a third floor window, a silver ankh, the symbol of his gang, swinging on a chain around his neck. His head swiveled north, then south, and he squinted toward his mother, a short chubby woman shuffling along the sidewalk across the street from Blake. She stopped by a Korean kid loading a bin with cantaloupes, puffed a cigarette, picked up a leafy peach, and smelled it. A Korean guy swept the walk behind her with a broom, teenagers bustling out of a donut shop next door.

Blake, at the phone booth, waved to Keeshon, who saw him and shouted, "Ma! Ma!" He pulled his head back inside. Blake hung up the pay phone, noticing how odd it had become to use one, and as if to prove it he unclipped a cell phone from his belt. He thumbed a single button and squinted.

He noticed things other people didn't. Blake saw how the early morning sun painted a rectangle on the street with a platinum patina that highlighted the grain of the tar. Interesting.

Escobido's voice. Kee-mo-sabe? That you?

Blake chuckled, he already liked the new guy.

"A son's love for his mama. How touching." He said, "Wait until he's right by the fire hydrant, the no-parking zone, so I can see him. Unless he tries to shoot me." He glanced up, shielding his eyes, the glint of a rifle barrel poking out from the top of a building. He looked down at Keeshon's chubby mom. "Look at her. Fat as a burnt pork chop."

A beep on the line, call waiting, but Blake let it go to voicemail as Keeshon, a black man with a head of red-beaded pigtails, burst out of a doorway. "Ma!" Muscles lumpy all over him, pistol in hand, Keeshon stumbled down his stoop and ran down the sidewalk shouting, "Ma! Ma!" Keeshon's mother shuffled ahead, exhaled tobacco smoke, and peered into a shop window. She was thirty feet from Blake. She lifted one Chinese slipper to a threshold, into a shaft of golden light, and squinting, Blake made out the blue of vericose veins scrawling down to her thick ankle. She paused, Keeshon shouting, "Mama!"

Scooby's voice on the cell phone. I not gonna wait.

"Not yet." Keeshon knocked over a high school kid, dodged between commuters munching donuts. Blake said, "Not yet."

Keeshon shouted, "Get in the store! The store!"

"Scooby," Blake said, "take him."

A chuckle. Naw, I gotta wait.

"Take him!"

Keeshon swung up his pistol and fired, the piece hazy behind the discharge. Blake felt bullets punch the phone booth. He didn't duck. Pandemonium. Screams, stampeding people, Keeshon's piece cracked again. For an instant Blake felt it. He felt like the calm eye of awareness in a storm of terrified people. For an instant.

From the rooftop: the crack of a rifle. The gunshot echoed as Keeshon fell. He slammed on the walk, kids screaming, running, the new mothers hunching over their babes. Keeshon's mama screeched over him, the cigarette falling out of her mouth. Two boys in front of the donut shop, one boy stood frozen, staring wide-eyed at Keeshon, while the other darted into the street. A car swerved to miss him, plowed into a parked taxi, windshields burst, glass, plastic, and headlights shattering across the pavement.

Keeshon struggled onto his hands and knees, blood dribbling onto the cement walk, his mother wailing. Keeshon crawled toward her, she was screaming, but he was staring hatefully over at Blake. Blake shrugged—I told you so—and said into his cell phone, "Again."

Crack! Keeshon slumped, his mother screaming as he coughed blood onto the sidewalk. Her cigarette, still smoking, rolled across the concrete as she lost her only begotten son, lost control, sank to her knees, wailed and cried out in the pandemonium, "No! My baby! My baby!"

Blake glanced up to the rooftop and said, "A quick wipe and leave it. Move."

Blake snapped shut his cell phone and stopped. A man with a briefcase dodged into the street, dropped a foam cup, and Blake noted the triangular pattern made on the tar by the spatter of coffee. He glanced to the roofs and clipped the cell phone to his belt.

As casual as a farmer in his barnyard he walked among the screeching, stampeding sheep, strolled around the corner onto West 182nd Street, the slicing screeches of Keeshon's mama fading as he left the dead man's turf behind. He murmured, "Not a bad neighborhood." He strolled past a long line of parked cars, the chaos falling behind, sirens calling from somewhere. He popped the locks on his SUV, sitting cool in the shade of a maple, slid in and pulled out.

He drove West 182nd to Jerome Ave. and took a left, beneath the elevated tracks that let the sunlight hit the street in long rows of yellow squares, turned left on West 183rd Street, and cruised up to the corner of Grand Avenue. Scooby, looking like any other twenty-something Hispanic in sneakers, jeans, and a polo shirt, jogged out of an alley and hopped in.

"Anybody see you coming down?"

Escobido shook his head, three locks of carefully greased black hair quivering in front of his forehead. He lit a shaky cigarette, his voice husky as he looked out the window. "Nada, nobody see me. Nice rifle to leave though, huh."

Blake gunned the SUV out onto Sedgwick. The butt shook in Scooby's hand, smoke scribbling in the air. Blake said, "First one's the hardest, but now you're in the Org."

"Yeah, even before breakfast I prove I a toro muy mal, huh."

"Very bad bull all right, and soon you're going to be a rich one. Cock of the walk, you'll see." Scooby rolled down his window as Blake unclipped his cell phone. He thumbed the button for voicemail and listened. His mother's voice. "Shit."

Scooby's hand jittered nervously. "What's up?"

Blake thumbed a button to speed dial his mother. One ring and she said, Hullo? "Ma, what about Fisher?"

Angry. The state police called from Binghamton. No, it was some place called...uh... Endwell. They found his car in the river there. "They know where he is?" No, they asked if I knew. He loved that car. "I know. You call his apartment?" What do you think?

Blake rolled his eyes. "Don't worry, the jughead probably went out partying last night and got his car stolen. Don't bother calling, I'll find him. Okay?" Okay, Blakie, but I'm still worried. I'll call his house too. "Fine, do whatever the hell you want. You always do." He snapped the phone shut and looked at Scooby. "They found my little brother's car in the river, upstate, in Binghamton."

Scooby sucked his cigarette, his arm cocked, a barbed wire tattoo stretching around his upper muscles. "You brother? He runnin' a group all away up there?"

Blake's hand rose to his throat. The tip of his thumb found a delicate ridge against his skin, a fine gold chain that led down to a golden cross.

"Troopers scared my mother," he said. "That's not easy, she's a class A bitch." He squinted. "You should see her. She beats her dog, a little dachshund, so now it's mute, not even a peep, just hides under the table."

Scooby flicked his butt out the window. "Try his home number. He prob'ly in bed with some brown-eye susan."

"Hope so." Blake thumbed button #2 and listened. Ring-ring-ring-click. Hey, this is Fisher's answering machine. Do it now. Beep. Blake said, "Fisher, where the fuck are you? You don't call your big brother anymore? Do it now." He cut off the call and thumbed button #3. "He always picks up his cell phone."

Ring-ring-ring-click. You have reached 607-966-. Blake's forehead creased. The muscles tightened around his eyes, then he snapped the phone shut, clipped it to his belt, and lit a butt. He scratched his upper lip, inhaled deeply. The smoke seared his throat, the tobacco taste distracting him from an inkling of fear stirring under his anger. He mumbled, "I got a feeling."

Scooby, smoking another menthol, blew smoke rings against the windshield. "We going to grandma's house? You got a feeling about what?"

"We got a shipment last night, ten kilos, so Swain's expecting us to help with the cooking." Blake unclipped the cell phone and said, "One more."

His lips in a donut, Scooby snapped his jaw to send a perfect ring of smoke to the windshield. He was getting back his cool face. "One more to who?"

Blake looked over at him. "You're in the Org now so I can tell you. We have a number of powerful stakeholders." He pressed eleven numbers and listened. A voice with an Arabic accent. Yes? Blake said, "Mr. P. That problem you mentioned. Taken care of." Good job. You're quite the exterminator, aren't you. "Yes sir, I am. Keep me posted on any new developments with our main business and I'll continue to do what I do. Okay?"

Blake cut off the call, dropped the cell phone and punched Scooby's barbed wire bicep. Covering his fear he said, "Time for a Scooby snack!"

Blake pulled over to a liquor store, went in and came out with a bottle of Irish crème liquor. Scooby cracked open the bottle, lifted it, and let slugs of thick brown liquid jerk his adam's apple as it went down cool and sweet. Blake lit a good cigarette and pulled out onto the Major Deegan southbound.

"It's better cold."

"Is better in my stomach," Scooby said. A jag of nervous laughter. "How come you don't snuff Swain and take over the Org? You a gladiator, I can tell."

"Because he does all the crap I can't stand. He built the Org so now we have protection, communication, contingents all over the place. I like to execute, move, slice and dice, chop chop. What Swain does is important, the connecting, building the network, the payoffs. But me," Blake said, "I wield the sword. You're right, I am the blade around here. Don't you forget it."

Scooby nodded. "You got the ice water veins, I see that. So who the supplier? Where we buyin' all this junk?"

"Offshore, the Muslims. They hate us." Blake gunned down the expressway and took the ramp onto I-95 east, the Throgs Neck Bridge just visible in the distance. He said, "One thing I have tell to you, Scooby."

Glug glug, Scooby lowered the bottle and burped. "What's that?"

"Don't smoke the product. You get hooked, you try to stop, it'll kill you. Our suppliers add an extra ingredient."

Scooby smoked so he wouldn't think. "Comprendo. Nothing to worry about."

They all say that, Blake thought. Even Fisher.

He pulled off the expressway at the last exit before the bridge, in Throgs Neck, drove into the side streets and pulled into the driveway of 362 Revere. Scooby left the bottle in the SUV.

They climbed the front steps of grandma's house. Roses twined into the slats of a trestle-fringed porch, leafy jigsaws of sunlight dancing over a swing hanging by a door with an old-fashioned marble knob that ruckled in its socket when Blake twisted it. Inside the house it was quiet and the smell of cured pine boards and musty rugs greeted them. Blake saluted a tiny video camera staring out from a potted plant. They strolled across creaky floorboards into the kitchen where sunlight burned on the ceramic tiles. Blake motioned to a jar. "Cookie?"

Scooby grabbed a chocolate chip cookie as Blake jerked open a door, the basement stairs below. The smell of butane. As they skipped down the stairs Scooby burped. He said, "Don't smell like ham 'n' eggs, joebro. What you got cookin' here?"

Bare cement floor, workbenches, gridboard with tools hanging on hooks, it looked like a hundred other basements in small old houses. Except for the camp stoves, cocaine, and men. Ganz, dressed in moccasins, boat shorts, and a tee-shirt with a tequila logo, stood by a four-burner camp stove. Two pots burbled, full of thick white gruel, crack in the making. Chewing bubble gum, Ganz cracked a bubble and nodded to Blake. "Hey dude."

"Ganz, this is Scooby."

Scooby nodded and looked at the man tending the other camp stove. Swain wore a stockbroker's cut of taffy-blonde hair, a tangerine colored polo shirt, and a gold watch with no numbers, just hands and a diamond at twelve o'clock. Swain glanced at them, stirring a pot with a wooden spoon, and Scooby noticed he wasn't fat but he had wide hips, like a girl.

"You take care of that problem for our friends?" Swain asked.

Blake leaned over the camp stove and looked into a pot. "Had a little fun."

Scooby wanted to impress him. "I told you I a good shot. Basic training, I kick ass before I get kicked out."

Scooby liked that story but didn't tell it. Instead he glanced into the pot bubbling on the camp stove, white gruel sputtering, crack oil gathered like a veneer on top. Two large bags of cocaine lay on the workbench by the stove, ten boxes of baking soda standing in a line.

"This how you do it, huh? Baking soda all it take?"

Swain ignored Scooby and glanced at Blake. Blake felt his lips tighten against his teeth. Swain saw it and said, "What's the matter?"

"They found Fisher's car in the river, in Binghamton, and he's not answering his cell phone."

"They?" Swain's brows rose over an ice blue gaze. "They who?"

"State Police called my mother. He's been keeping you posted, hasn't he? With the e-mails?"

"Sunday was the last. Nothing unusual, but I'll check it again."

"I'll call him again."

Blake flipped open his cell phone and speed-dialed. No answer. He dialed every fifteen minutes, Fisher's apartment or his cell phone, no answer, every half hour, no answer, and they started another batch, another batch, batch batch batch. First they refilled the pot with bottled water, brought it to a boil, filled a measuring cup with white powder, refined coca, quarter pound, dumped it in. Four ounces of coke, two ounces of baking soda, splash, stir it in, just enough water to dissolve it. Turn the knob, the flames danced higher. Scooby sniggered and chanted, "Boil, boil, toil, and trouble."

Swain said, "Shut up, you spic fuck head," and Scooby lost his chuckle.

Still no answer. Blake went out to smoke. Back inside, another batch. Boil, boil, toil, and trouble, he added water, Fisher's Viper in the water, white crud sticking to the pot. Swain was watching him. Oil on top, he shut off the flames and Swain dropped in the ice, ploop ploop ploop. Swain's a cube of ice, Blake thought, and he wished Fish would surface. Dump out the ice and there it was, a solid plate of crack cocaine. He dropped it on wax paper and it broke into chunks.

"How much for a plate like this?" Scooby asked, broken plates drying on wax papers all over the bench, all around the basement.

Blake slipped a butt behind his ear and flipped out his clamshell phone and dialed. He watched Swain watch Scooby break a tiny crystal of crack off the edge of a plate. Swain whispered, "Ten thousand. Escobido."

Scooby looked up and Blake knew how he felt, the phone ringing, no answer, a new danger, the feeling of a threat. Scooby didn't know Swain. He said, "Yeah?"

Swain leaned over Scooby, who took a step back. Scooby backed into a corner as Swain leaned into his face. He whispered, "This is a business. Don't smoke the product. Ever."

"Yeah, no problem, relax. I see what crack do so I not gonna start. I don't do no heroin, just a little reefer, and I buy it. Comprendo?"

The phone rang, Blake wanted to smoke, but he watched Swain branding Scooby. Branding him with fear. Scooby nodded, scared, the phone rang, and Blake whispered, "Pick it up, Fish. Pick up."

Click. Hello? "Fisher? That you?" No, this is Dave. Who's this? Blake tensed as Swain looked at him with those ice blue eyes. "Dave who? Where's Fisher?" Not here. I'm Dave, Fisher's friend, he must've told you about me. "If he's not home what are you doing there? Fuck!"

Blake cut off the call. God dammit! The fear spiked through him, stiffened him, he didn't want them to see and turned away. Fuck! Fisher? Boxes of Christmas tree ornaments glistened under the stairs. He was panting, his stomach clenched, he was almost sick. Business, people die all the time. God dammit! Fuck! If he...

"Blake?" Swain's quiet cold voice. Blake squeezed the cell phone until the plastic housing creaked in his grip. Swain asked, "Who was it?"

Blake turned and looked at Swain. "It damn sure wasn't him. Something's wrong."

Swain, always methodical, spoke to one problem at a time. "Stop and find out what happened to him on your way up to do that thing in Buffalo."

Swain turned his icy gaze back to Scooby. He lay a heavy hand on Scooby's shoulder, the locks of black hair shivering against Scooby's clean copper-colored forehead. Swain whispered, "I'm telling you: you smoke even a pinhead of product, you little spic fuck, and I'll send Blake to rip your eyes out."

"Jeez Christ! What you say that for?"

"So we're clear about it. He'll rip your eyes out and then you'll stumble around in the dark for a while before he takes you out with a knife. Is that clear?"

Scooby swallowed and looked up at Swain. Nothing funny now, he was in the Org. He whispered, "Yeah. Real clear."

CHAPTER 4

Like I said I would, I went to pick up Paul at the high school at 2:30; but as I walked through the front doors I felt strange, as if I was walking back into my kid self. *Darryl Jones, please come to the principal's office.* Uh-oh, they found out I killed somebody. Then the adult me, if there was one, pushed open the door and stepped into the principal's office for real.

A row of chairs, a counter and the same old battle ax, Mrs. Lindbergh. Her cheeks looked like too much white latex paint slopped on her cheekbones had sagged into wrinkly pouches. "Darryl Jones," she said. Her eyes still glittered like ten-penny spikes and nailed me the same way. "Have you finally come in for a parent-teacher conference?"

"No, I needed another one of your doses of industrial strength guilt. My son, Paul, can you page him?"

"I can," she said, not a gray hair on her head moving. I'd long ago figured she sprayed it with aerosol glue. She asked, "But will I?"

"Will you, please? It's important."

She picked up the old steel microphone mounted on a pedestal and I heard deja vu over the loudspeaker: *Paul Jones, come to the principal's office. Paul Jones to the principal's office please.*

I said, "Thank you, Mrs. Lindbergh," and sat down to wait.

Drrrrring! The bell rang to end the class period and kids flooded the hall outside the office, looked in, hurried past, herding, babbling, giggling, shouting, and holding hands, exactly how it started with Lynn and me twenty-some years ago. Damn. Sadness stirred in my chest because it always seemed to be right below the surface, the hurt.

The door opened and Paul leaned in, saw me and said, "Oh, it's you."

Mrs. Lindbergh looked over her bifocals. "Paul? Are you done?"

"Yeah, Mrs. L., that's my last class, I'm outta here. Tell Linda I said hello, okay."

Mrs. Lindbergh looked down at her papers, half smiling, as if he was flirting with her instead of her granddaughter, and then I had to hurry to catch up with him in the hall. The herd filled the air with the thunder of sneakers so I almost had to yell, "Mrs. L.? Since when?"

"Since I like her and she likes me," he said.

Everybody liked Paul, the phone rang all the time. He barged out into the warm day as if he owned the place, spotted my truck, and led the way toward it. Where'd he get so much confidence at a time like this? I gotta admit, I was envious. He followed a bee-line through clusters of kids, the girls checking him out, and I could tell they thought he was cute and cool. Then again, I thought, maybe he gives them a good deal on weed.

"Where are we going?" he asked.

"To meet Carla."

He stopped. "Why?"

"To get some legal advice." I unlocked my truck. "Hop in and don't give me a hard time. She can help us figure out what to do."

I pulled out, the engine rumbling, truck parts clattering, and he hunched low on the seat, embarrassed by the Codger. I drove, he bit his thumbnail, reached and turned on the radio, but turned it off again when he couldn't find any rap junk on it; and that's when I noticed it. He smelled of smoke. I didn't say anything. After pounding nails and hauling sixty-pound bundles of shingles all day, all the way up a twenty foot ladder, all the time expecting a squad car to pull up, I didn't feel strong enough to fight him. And who wants to think their kid smoked dope at school?

I drove and he sulked.

I parked in front of a low stucco building painted Pepto-Bismol pink, with a sign that said FRANK J. PAGANETTI, ESQ. Frank was a real classy guy who stank up his reception room with cigar smoke, even the plastic palm tree in the corner. Zelda, his receptionist, was also Mrs. Paganetti, who at fifty-eight showed lots of wrinkled cleavage and lots of scalp through her bouffant. She lit a filterless Camel and croaked, "How's business?"

"Fine. Is Carla here?"

Carla walked out of a hallway. "There's my hunk," she said.

Short brown hair, clear eyes, white smile, slim, and I don't know if anyone else called her drop dead gorgeous but when she appeared like that, looking professional in a blue pinstripe dress, I wanted to take her in my arms and drop to the floor right there between the coat tree and water cooler. She touched my hand. I felt the edges of her red claws, but the soft print of her fingertips sent tingles of pleasure up my arm.

She squeezed my hand and turned toward Mrs. Paganetti. "Zelda, this is Paul, Darryl's oldest." Zelda squinted at him through the smoke of her burning Camel. Carla glanced at me. "This way."

We followed her. She closed the door on a hushed room filled by a twelve-foot oval table with a dark glowing top. Paul looked nervous. We sat. Carla clasped her hands on the table and looked at us. Waited. Raised her eyebrows. Paul stared down at the table. When she looked at me I said, "Well..."

She looked at Paul. "Is this about college? Your father did ask me to help do some research."

Paul's face hardened. "I'm not going to college."

"You're not?" News to me, so I asked, "Why not? You wanna grub around in the dirt for a living like your old man?"

He looked at me deadpan. "I'm going to be a guerrilla film-maker. I'm going to make movies about people killing each other with garden tools."

"Funny. Very funny."

Carla switched into lawyer mode, though she was only a paralegal. "What's going on? Boys? Get to the point."

I took a deep breath and managed a mumble. "We, uh, had a little trouble last night. I...well..." I looked at Paul, he looked at me, and right then I decided: nobody had to know about him, that he did the pushing. I said, "I killed somebody."

She put her hands on the table and leaned forward. "Come again?"

I told her what happened, the basics, with a few of the minor details a bit, well, modified. She blinked. She raised her hands to cover her mouth. She blinked again and sat back in her chair, as if she needed distance, needed to get away from me, and that really scared me. I hurried to say, "But I got rid of the gun, Mudgie and I buried it today."

"Making him an accessory after the fact." She couldn't keep the irony out of her voice. "I'm sure his wife will be pleased."

I leaned on the table. "Carla? It happened, I didn't mean it to, it just did, and now all I want is to keep Paul out of the newspapers and me out of the electric chair."

"You'd have to shoot a policeman to get the death penalty." I could see her drawing back inside herself like people do when they take a hard shot and start to panic. She exhaled slowly and looked at Paul. "How did you meet this Fisher character? How long have you been selling this stuff?"

He shrugged, staring at the table. "Not long. A couple months."

"That's all?"

"Darryl, quiet." She leaned over the table and touched his hand. "Go ahead. How did you meet him?"

"And how did you start dealing it?" I asked.

He crossed his arms, still staring at the table.

"He showed up at a fire we had in the woods. We were having a few beers, smoking some, and Fisher showed up with Samantha Williams' older sister, Cassie. He had a case of micro brew and passed it out, and then Cassie told me she wanted to show me something." He glanced up from the table. "She's, like, off-the-scale hot. So we went out in the dark and I smoked some of Fisher's stuff with her...but then, while I was smoking it she...you know."

"No," I said, "I don't know."

Paul rolled his eyes. "She smoked...me."

"Gave you oral sex?" Carla glanced at me. "Quite a combination. When did you see Fisher next?"

"I went out with Cassie another time, just us, and after you smoke Fisher's dope a couple times it's all you can think about, getting more. But the night you and Dad celebrated your one year anniversary..."

"July twenty-eighth?"

His hand spasmed on the table. "That night I was really...I don't know...but Cassie called and I went to meet her at a sorority house in Johnson City, one for Binghamton U. Anyway, Cassie wasn't there, only Fisher and one of his other groupies, but he said I had to buy some. After that I had to keep buying it, and then my friends wanted some, so I bought it and sold it and made enough to pay for my own stuff. It happened kind of fast. I knew it was getting crazy a few weeks ago, out of control, but I couldn't do anything about it."

Carla kept up her cross examination. "How much have you been dealing?"

Paul plunked his elbows on the table and covered his face with his hands.

"Not much," he said. "Not until Fisher started fronting me product. Then he took me over to meet people at J.C. High and down at Union Endicott, so last week I made...like...I got a lot of people high, but I still made three thousand."

"Dollars? Three thousand!"

He gave me a mixed look, amusement, pride and something else. Loathing. For me. He said, "I knew you'd be impressed. But—"

"But Paul, you're not telling us everything." Carla waited until he looked up. "That's not everything, is it?"

I caught her cue. "Yeah, I wondered. You owe him five grand? Isn't that an awful lot for pot?" His mouth tightened. I tightened. "So? Spill it. What else is there? Come on, spill it!"

He spat it at me. "Coke!" I slammed the table and slumped back. "Yeah," he snapped, "coke too! Is that what you want to hear?"

I covered my face and groaned. Oh god, too much, it screwed me up, but Paul snapped off my groan. "Because everybody wanted it. Do I need tons of money? For me? No, I don't, but...but it's your fault anyway, Dad."

"My fault? What are you talking about?"

"Darryl—"

"But I don't want to do it anymore." Paul flushed red, his fists clenched. "I took stuff, some real weight, over to dump on some guys in Binghamton, but they put a gun to my head and ripped me off. So now I don't want it anymore, don't want to smoke it, sell it, nothing. But I can't stop. I can't!"

Crack in his voice, he started to cry, and for a second I didn't know what to do. Then I got up and kind of put my arms around him. It's really bad for a man when his son is bawling in his arms and he realizes he hasn't hugged him in years. Not that he would've let me. I looked across the table. My eyes met Carla's and she saw her chance, came around the table and put her arms around Paul and me both. Patty loved Carla already but Paul wouldn't even talk to her, so while she had a chance she stroked his hair.

"Everything's going to be all right," she said. "It'll be all right, Paul." The three of us rocked like that a second before he started to sniffle. She kissed his forehead, wiped off the red print of her lips, and looked him in the eyes. She said, "Everything's going to be okay. Understand? I promise."

He sniffed, wiped his cheeks and wouldn't look at us. My voice came out gravelly. "Can you wait out in the truck? For a minute? Please?"

He sleeved the tears off his cheeks, slipped on a pair of sunglasses, and walked out the door. Carla and I stood there in the hushed room. I slipped my arms around her and felt so much relief just holding her. She stroked my hair, it felt good, and I said, "Can't deal with this, I'm going nuts. I just want it to go away."

"It won't," she said. "And the first thing is to get him into a rehab."

"Why? He's only been at it a couple months."

"You heard him, it only takes a couple weeks. He won't be able to stop by himself. I'll make a few calls, okay?"

I touched her cheek. "Do you still...still want to...?"

"Get married? Oh, Darryl." She kissed me. I stroked her hair and kissed her, and when we parted she wiped lipstick off my mouth with the end of her pinkie. "I'll schedule a time," she said, "with one of the big law firms in Binghamton. After the weekend."

"Why?"

Her hand went still on my chest as she gazed at me. "You'll need counsel."

"For what?"

"For when you and Paul turn yourselves in. You killed someone, Darryl."

"That's why I shouldn't tell anybody. Let them find me. If they don't, I won't worry about it."

She snorted. "You think they won't? There'll be an investigation, they'll find you, and then it'll look even worse."

"Maybe, maybe not. But why should I do the work for them? If they find me, fine, I'll get a big shot lawyer, pay through the nose, the whole nine. All right?" Disbelief pinched her brows, a wrinkle formed over her nose. "I don't want to pay legal bills with the money I saved for us, for our house, unless there's no other way around it."

God forbid I call them wrinkles, but they tightened around her eyes. "Have it your way." She yanked open the door. "It's your life."

"Carla, wait!"

I followed her out into the waiting room, into the watchful gaze of Zelda Paganetti, and when Carla gave me the benefit of the doubt and looked back at me I took her hand, led her to the door and pulled her out into the sunlight. There was a beautiful blue sky and I was still a free man. Aware that Paul was watching us, no doubt disgusted, I led her around the corner of the building and kissed her beside the pink stucco. She was scared, which made her angry, so I stroked her hair.

"Carla, please, I'm sorry." I whispered it. "I love you. Please don't worry. Everything will work out, just like you said."

Holding her, I rubbed the small of her back. She sighed, her forehead sank to my chest, it almost worked; but then she pushed me away. "I hope so. For his sake." It was the best I'd get, so I let her go and got in the truck.

I drove through the heart of Endwell, past a Video King, drug stores, a pharmacy and gas station, and at the second traffic light I turned right, drove up Pruyne Street to Verna Drive, and drifted down our strip of middle America. I stopped the Codger in front of our house and Paul slid off the seat and out the door.

"Patty's coming home," I said, "so send her back over to the Kavidge's. You stay close to home too. Hear me?"

He said, "Yeah yeah yeah," and slammed the door.

I drove through Endwell, up past the high school, up Farm to Market Road to the junior high, took a left up Hillside Terrace and down Twist Run Road to my subdivision, Green Meadow Way, a single row of houses to either side of me as I drove up the street. Useful artwork, that's what they were, houses for people to live in and dirty up. I parked in front of the half-finished colonial, Mudgie already gone off home to wrap his arms around his wife and a six-pack, and the shell of the house peacefully waited for me.

I trudged upstairs to the second floor and went to work carrying rolls of tar paper up to the roof. I rolled it out over the sloping plywood, zipped it off at the edge with a razor knife, and stapled it down. The work calmed me, I could see what I got done. The familiar glue-and-pulp smell of plywood reassured me that most of the world was still the same. The sun warmed my back, cranky in the morning, and I didn't bother hooking up the hydraulic nail gun because swinging the hammer felt good, familiar, satisfying in the simple way I could bang nails through the shingles and into the wood.

I quit after a couple hours. The stuff in my head wasn't so loud anymore as I got into the truck. I knew what I wanted, a beer and a minute to think. I drove down Green Meadow Way, downhill through the swerving gorge of Twist Run Road, along Route 26 toward Endicott until I turned in at the gravel parking lot of an old time honkytonk.

I walked into a place that hadn't changed in forty years. The Pine Inn had a big dance floor to the right, scuffed by cowboy boots on Friday nights and sneakers on Saturdays when a rock band drove out the shit kickers. A half wall separated the dance floor from a game area, then an aisle of splintered floorboards lay between the pool tables and the bar. The afternoon crowd looked over at me, Phil the plumber, Electrical Joe, Skanky Hank the wood butcher, ditch diggers, lawn men, guys who hung insulation, Pudgie Mudgie there in the background still sucking the thumb he hit with his hammer.

They all shouted a welcome, a backslapping gang of locals that liked me because I always paid them. They couldn't trust lots of contractors, but I'd been on their end for ten years, scrabbling to save money and buy land, so I couldn't cheat them and they knew it. Besides, there was enough money in a house to pay everyone, according to how much they worked on it, so why cheat anybody?

I made my way over to where Vince Catalone sat with his pinstriped elbows on the bar, a butt smoking in a tray. He was drunk, his tie yanked loose under his chin, cubes tingling in the glass when he slurped his Jack and Coke. He smiled and slid his arm around my shoulders.

"This one's on me." He burped sweetly of soda and alcohol. "What can I get you, my sunburnt friend?"

"A Genny Cream Ale and a...a 'not guilty.'" I clunked my elbows on the bar. "How's that for a chaser?"

CHAPTER 5

The Fisher Pangbourne impersonator and Metallica fan, Harvey Epstein, turned defiant as Binks grabbed his flabby arm and jerked him ahead.

"But I didn't do anything!" Binks led the kid, a bad mood rising up his throat, tightening his jaw, so he made sure the fat boy saw his fist clench. Epstein blurted, "Where are we going? I want to call a lawyer. What are you gonna do with me?"

"Is this the Crime Channel? You get a phone call when I'm done with you."

Epstein hurried to keep up with Binks. His breasts of adipose tissue shook under the devil screaming on his t-shirt, his forehead shiny with sweat, his Air Jordans pattering on the pavement. They began downstairs to a traffic circle. Binks glared at Epstein when he slapped at his sleeve, but the kid's voice was pleading. "What do you want to know? I didn't do anything illegal."

"Shut up! I'll read you your rights at Campus Security and then you can say whatever you want."

"Why? I didn't do anything! Why am I being arrested?"

Binks suddenly grabbed him, took the fat boy's breath away and slowly, clenching his teeth, pushed Epstein up against a concrete wall and looked into his eyes, the kid skewered and panting. Asian girls were sitting along the top of the wall, laughing and chatting in the sun, so Binks whispered it.

"Why are you taking his classes? What's in it for you?" Binks stared into Epstein's eyes, the black of the kid's irises contracting with fear, his hands coming up to protect himself. Binks pushed his hands aside, still bunching up a fistful of his shirt. "What's in it for you, Epstein?"

"He keeps me in..."

"In what?"

Binks could smell the milk of the kid's breakfast. Epstein whispered, "Stems."

"He's a crack dealer?"

Epstein nodded, his chin quivered, he was about to cry. "I don't sell it," he whispered, "but I need it. Please don't tell my parents."

Binks let him go, stepped back, spread open his jacket, put his hands on his hips, and looked at Epstein. The kid's dirty little secret was out and the tears were leaking down his cheeks. Binks said, "Telling your parents, that's your job. Let's go."

They followed a curving sidewalk, Epstein sniffing, gasping faintly as he tried to control himself, downstairs to the rear entrance of the administrative tower. Binks motioned Epstein through a set of sliding glass doors and herded him into Campus Security. A woman in a white shirt and name tag, Offcr. Dubinski, glanced over, as did Crandall, her boss, a fifty-something in a tweed suit who was unduly proud of having been a desk jockey in the CIA. Binks said, "Hold him until someone comes from my office."

The gray threads in Crandall's eyebrows bent as his nose went out of joint. "Thanks for letting us know you're on campus." He looked at Epstein, the kid wiping his cheeks. "What's up?"

"Uttering. False use of a social security number." Binks looked at Epstein. "But he might have to go into p.c."

Epstein sniffed and wiped his cheeks. "What's that?"

"Protective custody."

"Why? Fisher wouldn't do anything to me. He just likes to party."

"And?"

"And he's a cool guy. I really like him."

Binks repeated his favorite word. "And?"

Epstein sniffed. "And he's a crack dealer but he's...he's pretty okay. He's into Metallica."

"He still living at 168 Beethoven?"

Epstein nodded. "Can I handle this myself? Do I have to tell my parents?"

Binks glanced at Crandall and turned for the door. "Mr. Epstein, you need a lawyer and a detox."

Binks slid into the familiar hushed sanctuary of his unmarked cruiser, a dark blue Chrysler Imperial, started the engine and drove. The bad mood was turning real. He approached the Vestal Parkway entrance, athletic fields spreading out around the road. Young people kicked soccer balls across the grass as Binks pulled out onto the highway. He drove, lost in thought. Kids. Dumb and innocent victims. On-ramp. No. Not innocent, not dumb. Victims, yes, but of what? Themselves? Human flaws and frailty?

More than that. Simple pipeline from the Rotten Apple, routes 84 to 87, 88 to 17, and boom, junk hits the Triple Cities and fans out like fingers into a glove. Maybe this Fisher Pangbourne has a hand in the traffic. Gets a few knuckleheads, spreads his tentacles, and puts his dirty fingers into high schools, middle schools, even messes with the elementary kids. Little bastard. Kills kids when I can't even have any of my own.

The clock is ticking. What'll she do if...if we don't ever...?

He found himself on the other side of the river, the road arcing into a traffic circle, the first turn-off to Riverside Drive, the nice area of Binghamton; but he didn't take it. He drove the circle to the second outlet, cruised on Floral Avenue into the workingman's heart of Johnson City, and pulled out his cell phone.

Emma's voice. Endwell Substation, State Police. "Sweets, send a unit over to B.U. Campus Security to pick up a material witness. The car in the river might be a homicide, drug-related. Call Walt in forensics and expedite. The gunk on the driver's seat, I'll call in an hour and if he doesn't have the work-up ready tell him I'll be pissed."

He parked in front of 168 Beethoven, a double-decker two-family. Eleven a.m., nobody around. He knocked on the right front door, bright red and green kiddie toys on the porch. A housewife opened the screen door, her sculpted eyebrows rising. "Yes?"

"Sorry, I'm looking for Fisher Pangbourne."

Manicured fingernails, no diamond ring, a shapely arm led to light brown curls and rose-colored lipstick for lunch. Divorced. She looked at Binks with veiled interest and said, "He's my upstairs tenant. I haven't seen him in a few days."

Binks pulled out his best tool, opened the flipcase, and she glanced at his shield and ID. "Can you let me in? I'm looking for him."

"Sure...Detective Binks. David." She chuckled and they started climbing a flight of gleaming varnished stairs, her hips moving in front of him. She kept them in good shape, the stairs, no creaks. She unlocked the second floor with a skeleton key and watched him, amused as he walked into the foyer. "Should I stay and chaperone?"

"I'd prefer not. Your name is?"

"Cathy Otis. If you need anything I'll be downstairs, just let me know."

He produced a fresh yellow pencil. "Anybody else living here?"

She shrugged. "He's a healthy young guy, there's a different girl every week. Lots of friends too, he's in college, but no roommate. He's a really nice kid. Well mannered."

"School year lease?"

"Not this time." She stepped to the door, but stopped when the telephone rang. She said, "The phone rings all the time. I'll be downstairs."

She closed the door. Three rings and the phone stopped. Binks stepped into the front room, a living room flooded with sunlight from a double window overlooking the street. Expensive rack system, big screen TV, VCR, a skinny tower packed with CD jewel cases. Leather sofa and love seat, candles on a glass table, cordless phone, scattered coins and a few green dollar bills. He strolled through the dining room, a computer on a corner desk, the varnished floorboards bare below a crystal chandelier. Binks leaned into the bedroom. New gleaming maple dresser, bureau, and bed.

The telephone rang three times and went to voicemail. Fisher Pangbourne, Binks thought, you've been a busy boy.

He spent a few minutes in the kitchen, poking with the pencil here and there. No evidence. No scale, no baking soda, no zip bags, no vials, nothing. The phone rang again. Yes, a very popular guy.

Binks wandered out into the living room and sat on the couch and sighed, its fine leather cushions molding to his body. He glanced about the room, soaking it in. Silence. His mind wandered. He grew vaguely dismayed when he thought of Sheila. Unfulfilled. Yes, wants me to fill her up this weekend. It brought him back to the same place and when the phone rang he reached out on impulse, irritated, and picked it up. "Hello?"

Young man's voice. Fisher? That you? Binks sat up and said, "No, this is Dave. Who's this?" A taut hesitation. Dave who? Where's Fisher? "Not here. I'm Dave, Fisher's friend, he must've told you about me." If he's not home, what are you doing there? Fuck!

Hang up. Binks lowered the buzzing phone and looked at it. Why did I do that? He let it clunk into its cradle, got up and left.

Driving, wind strafing his hair, he pressed the cell phone to his ear. A male voice. Forensics. "Walt?" Binks? I heard you were threatening me. Binks chuckled. Walt was a father of four daughters with a hefty roll of American fat hanging over his belt, hair so black it always looked greasy, and the yellow tint of nicotine on his fingertips. Yeah, I heard you were going to get pissed if I didn't hop to it and so I thought, Piss on him. But I worked it up anyway because I'm a nice guy. "Yes, Walt, that's right, you are. How's the daughters?" Scaring the shit out of me. The guys who pick them up on Saturday night all have it tattooed on their foreheads: I'm gonna pork your daughter. You think it's funny? Wait until you get some of your own.

Binks chuckled. "So what's the stuff on the seat of the Viper?" Tar. Petroleum distillate, high viscosity. Probably two hundred sources in the Triple Cities, everybody from Sears to Agway and the local lumber yard. "Driveway sealer? That kind of thing?" Roof patch and foundation coating. Binks pushed the pedal when the Chrysler made the smooth highway. "Good enough. Let's do a barbecue some weekend." Sure, unless I'm gonna be a grand-dad. Then you'll be hauling me in for homicide. "That's what I think the Viper is, a homicide, so keep me posted. Later."

Walt's humor lifted Binks for a moment, but his spirits sank as soon as he lowered the phone. Not a good time to be by himself. He thumbed #3, Sheila's cell phone, and glanced toward the bank of trees off to the left, beyond the eastbound lanes, greenery that hid the Susquehanna River. Click. Hello? David? I'm showing a property, what is it?

His lips compressed with disappointment. "I...I'm heading up to the house. Can you meet me there?"

He couldn't say more, didn't have it in words yet.

What is it? Is something wrong?

"No, not really, but I...I just..."

She knew him well.

If it's that important. But I don't know when, exactly. Okay? Are you sure you're all right? Dave?

"Yeah, I'll be fine. I'll see you tonight. Bye."

He turned up the ramp to Endwell, gazed out the window and sighed with the irony of it. "Is this any way to spend your life? Alone in a car, talking on a damn cell phone?"

He stopped at the curb, left the driveway empty in case she showed up in her mini-van—a realtor's car, accommodating for families—climbed the stone steps to their modest house, and let himself into silence. Why? What am I doing? What good is any of it, empty like this? And if she's not happy, will she stay? Will she...? He wandered through the empty rooms, his shoes rasping in the shag carpet, looked, listened, lifeless, lowered his head, and felt his neck stiffen. What am I, an idiot? She loves me.

He looked up. An engine. Footsteps. The door opened. "David?" She walked into view, slim in her realtor's modest dress, and he felt a house of cards tumble down inside him as she walked closer. "David, what's the matter? You sounded terrible. What is it?"

He put out his arms and she took him in. Warm harbor, so known, so much a part of him now that he squeezed her and whispered, "Don't leave me."

"What?"

"We can adopt if I can't and...and I'm sorry I can't, I'm trying, it's not my fault and I love you and so I'm...I don't want you to leave."

She stroked his face.

"Oh David, don't worry. This weekend," she said. "It'll happen this weekend. And if it doesn't, well, we can try something else."

She looked at him with those green eyes glinting so that he couldn't look away if he'd wanted to. Her green eyes, sparks glistened way down in them, and the first time he realized they would always fascinate him was the first time he thought of marrying her. But he also knew the look in them, bedroom eyes, a look of tough concern.

"Sometimes," she said, "you think too much."

The stroke of her hand traced the lobe of his ear, the hook of his jaw, the pulse of his throat to his collar, his shirt, and farther down. He mumbled, "I have a new case, I...maybe I shouldn't go away."

Her period was coming and she needed it, she gripped him like a pump handle. "Don't even think about it."

He groaned and shoved her against the wall, her dress bunched up, his hands going down, nylons down, panties down, pubic hair, and a musky smell as he pushed her thighs apart. Control. A bit angry, he pulled her down and she toppled groaning in the foyer with the front door open, her thighs falling open. She gasped as he entered and pushed in deep and hard, hard and grinding himself against the warm cup of her desire that would not yield. Ever.

Her throat tightened, her words bitten off. "Hard...deep... Dave, I'll come. Dave?"

He looked up. Outside the screen door he saw a pale blue cap bob into view. It was Chester, their mailman. Their glances met. An older man with a thick mustache and thickening jowl, Chester let the corners of his mouth rise, amused, set the mail on the porch and snuck off.

CHAPTER 6

Eduard watched the man. Blake the drug man, big time, he drove hunched over the wheel, his brow crunched like that, the man not talking, and Eduard didn't like it. He shook his head, his dreadlocks scraping the headliner of the SUV. Man be too serious, he thought. Man about to do something he later regret.

Always the clown, with a huge hand Eduard grabbed one of his dreads, lifted the yard-long branch of hair over his shoulder, swung it between the front seats, and smacked Scooby in the face. Nursing on a fat joint, stoned, Scooby freaked out.

"Jeez Christ! You big ass Jamaica fuck, whattaya doing!"

Eduard chuckled, revealing the gap of a missing tooth in his otherwise perfect smile. Beside him in the back seat, Norbert snorted and sniggered, his carefully shaven chocolate brown head gleaming in the afternoon sunlight.

"He playing with your shaggy dog ass, Escobito," Norbert said.

Norbert laughed, snort-snig-snig, as he slipped a chrome-plated nine millimeter semi-automatic out of his shiny greenish-blue dinner jacket. He pointed the gun at Scooby's head. He spoke like a rapper, but Eduard noticed there was a precise grittiness to his words. Norbert said, "Me too. Time to play with your shaggy dog ass."

"Hey now," Scooby said, "that ain't cool you fuckin' Hershey Easter egg." Norbert snorted as he squeezed the trigger. Scooby shouted, "Coconut! Put it—" Click. Snig snig, Norbert pulled the trigger, click click click, and Eduard poked at him with a dreadlock. Scooby swatted at the black fur branch and shouted, "Fuckin' crazy fucks!"

"Cut the shit!" Blake's voice sliced the air. "Get rid of the bone, Scooby. Norbert, keep your gun out of sight. This is the sticks, they arrest people out here."

Route 88 had led them through green pastures, an occasional country burg sprinkled in the valley, the highway finally cresting at Belden Hill before it began a long decline into Binghamton. They reached a first suburb,

Chenango Forks. The Chenango River spread to the right, a sheet of water rippling around weedy islands, a sheer cliff to the left, the highway leading into a chute of cement walls.

Norbert wasn't religious but he wore a gold cross on a chain that stood out against his black tee-shirt, nicely framed by his greenish-blue jacket, because it looked frosty. He looked out at the river and said, "Look at that. God's country."

"We not in Kansas anymore, Scooby," Eduard said.

"Got that right, Dorothy Dreads," Scooby said. "Blake'll shoot the Wizard in the ass if he don't find his brother. He pissed, look at him."

Blake leaned over the wheel as he drove into the chute, the lanes striped between cement walls, no turning back, he hit the gas, ninety, ninety-five, three-digit speed. Norbert fastened his seatbelt, Eduard too, but Scooby chortled and held onto the door handle as the Explorer arced up a curve onto a bridge, over Route 81, down ramp, sprint—who gives a damn—Route 17 and Blake was still doing ninety when Binghamton spread below a long curve, filling the valley of the Susquehanna River.

"Where now?" Blake asked.

Scooby peered at a computer screen under the dashboard. "Take the exit for Vestal."

Norbert asked, "The essit for Vestal? What's an essit, shaggy?" Scooby looked down at the pistol butt visible below his seat. Norbert poked his arm and said, "I ask a question, you answer. That's human communication."

"You ax me a question? You chop it into pieces?"

Eduard whacked Norbert with a hair branch. "Shut up or I beat you dead."

They followed the computer map and found Beethoven Street, old houses with railings and porches wedged together, driveways laid in two strips of cement with grass between, bushes well-tended on front lawns the size of dry green door mats. Blake curbed the Explorer, hopped out, and said, "You knuckleheads stay here." He strolled across the sunlit street, the breeze sweet with the smell of mown grass. He climbed three steps to a porch like Swain's porch, but no surveillance cameras, just a scatter of kiddie toys.

He knocked lightly on a doorframe. A shadow behind the screen solidified into a sweet-looking mommy type. Yeah, Blake thought correctly, Fisher's doing her. "Yes?" Cathy Otis asked.

"Hey," Blake said and stuck his hands in his pockets. He shifted from foot to foot, shifting gears, acting like a goof. "I'm looking for Fisher. I'm his brother. Is he here?"

"He lives upstairs, but no, he isn't."

"Oh." Foot to foot, nervous grin, Blake put on the goof act, as if he wouldn't slash her face with a box cutter. "Well," he mumbled, "uh...can I go up and wait for him?"

Cathy Otis glanced over her shoulder, her toddlers playing in front of the TV. "What's your name?"

"Blake. Can you let me in? Oh, here." Blake pretended to fumble with his wallet, flopped it open, then pointed to his picture license. "Blake, see? Fish and mom call me Blakey."

She unlocked the screen door. Glancing back at her toddlers she said, "I can't leave them for long," and stepped out. He followed her upstairs, uncharmed by her lean waist and hips, and followed her in after she unlocked the door. "Lock the door when you leave and I'll let you in again," she said.

"Sure, thanks," Blake said and nodded too much.

As Cathy Otis closed the door Blake's motion changed. The cords of his forearms rippled as he clenched and unclenched his fists, his eyes narrowed, his back stiff. Her footsteps faded below the door as he walked into the living room. He glanced around, riffled the junk on the table, checked the sofa cushions, strode to the desk in the dining room—not much in the drawers, paper, pencils, shit Fisher never used except for cover—and in the kitchen Blake found pots and pans, no coke, no baking soda, no nothing. Good boy, Blake thought. All in your storage unit. He stepped into the bedroom, opened a bottom drawer, and riffled the long underwear and turtlenecks.

He froze. The knob ruckled and the door swished on the carpet, opening. A girl's voice. "Fisher?"

Blake stepped out of the bedroom and startled the cutest blonde babe he'd seen in a week. Straight hair, blue eyes, heart-shaped mouth, plenty of cleavage, and black bra lace, lacy fringes at the bottom of her shirt, white against blue jeans tighter than shrink wrap. She saw him and blinked. He said, "Close the door."

She half hid behind it. "Who are you? Where's Fisher?"

"That's what I want to know. I'm Blake, his brother." His name registered on her face. "Where is he?"

Two steps, he pushed the door shut and stood over her. She stepped back, backed up against a wall the way he used to trap coke whores before he...but instead he looked down into her beautiful blue eyes, aware of her perfume, some kind of lilac scent.

"Who are you?" he asked. "His girlfriend?"

She nodded. "Cassie. Excuse me, but you've got bad breath."

Low, cold, edgy. "Where is he?"

"I don't know, I'm worried too. I haven't seen him since yesterday morning, and he hasn't called." She saw him look down her cleavage, but she couldn't read his eyes like the looks of other guys, didn't know how to play him. She said, "He always calls me. We've been going out for three months."

Blake looked at Cassie like a Stairmaster, a chance to exercise, but thought better of it and stepped back. He said, "I'm worried about him too. Let's go look for him. I might know where he is."

"Where?"

"I'll show you." He opened the door, shifting character again, gesturing for her to go. "Fisher told me a lot about you. He said he really loves you."

Stepping down, Cassie tripped, a hand on the rail. "He said that?"

Blake opened the door for her. "Yeah, he loves you a lot." After they crossed through the warm spring breeze he opened the back door of the Explorer and said, "Eduard, move over. That's Norbert, that's Scooby. Guys, this is Cassie, Fisher's girlfriend."

Cassie hesitated, looking at Eduard, a huge Jamaican dressed in a white nylon work-out suit accented with red. Eduard moved over and flashed his perfectly imperfect smile. She climbed in as Blake went around the Explorer. The Explorer smelled of pot. She said, "I have an AmLit class in an hour. Where are we going?"

Blake drove, squeezing the wheel. "Over to his storage unit. You know where he was the last couple days? Was he making any big drops? Collecting?"

Scooby twisted in his seat, looked at Cassie, and she knew the wolf's look in his eyes. Scooby said, "Oh, so you know 'bout the business?"

"Of course. Fisher and I, we've been going out three months. If you want to go to his storage unit take a right here." She directed them to the Oakdale Storage Mall, on a back street across from the Oakdale people mall. When they pulled up to the gate Blake waved a bar-coded card in front of a reader and the gate fence trundled aside. "I didn't know there was a third key card," she said.

Blake watched her in the mirror. "Where was he going yesterday? Cassie?"

She inclined her head. "He didn't tell me everything."

They all bailed out on a throughway lined with corrugated steel doors, garages with padlocks. Blake twisted a key, popped a lock, and Scooby bent to haul up the corrugated steel. Eduard bumped him with his hip and laughed.

Scooby struggled for the handle. "Is mine, hula girl!"

"Shaggy dog, sit." Eduard barked at Scooby and bumped him aside.

"Hey bozos." Blake stood to the side, unamused. "You done?"

Scooby yanked Eduard's hair branch, Cassie laughed, and Eduard chased him across the street.

When the steel door hung on silent tracks overhead Blake stepped into the storage unit. Bare cement floor except for a single box, one-by-two feet. He yanked open the flaps. Tiny ziplock bags, pinky size, thousands of them, each with a pebble of white crystal sealed inside. Blake gave it a light kick and said, "It wasn't a drop. A week's worth of product right there."

"A few day's worth," Cassie said. "Paul was selling—"

Blake wheeled on her. "Smart bitch! Paul who?"

Cassie backed up until she bumped into Norbert, a sharp hardness. She glanced back and down and saw the chrome pistol under his greenish blue jacket.

She looked angrily at Blake. "Real volume, six thousand rocks a week, that's what Fish and I were selling," she said. "He met people through me, tons, that's why it took off. I don't know why you're mad at me, I helped you, helped Fisher connect at B.U., in Endwell, Johnson City, Endicott, all over the place. He'll tell you himself, so don't yell at me."

Blake looked at Cassie. Scooby lit a cigarette, smoke clouding them. Eduard watched. He saw Norbert part his jacket to reveal his gun. Norbert looked at her ass and said, "She a mouthy little piece. I like that."

Blake kicked the box, sixty thousand in crack, sniffed and walked toward the entrance. "Come on. We're going to Endwell."

In the Explorer, Blake gunned the engine. Eduard watched the precision of his rage as he yanked the stick back, stabbed the cigarette lighter and yanked it out, the element glowing hot as he lit a butt. "Paul who?" Blake asked. "Cassie?"

"Paul Jones, a friend of my little sister's." In the back seat, Cassie felt the beefy hulk of Eduard on one side, Norbert's spring-loaded watchfulness on the other. She didn't dare look at him, crossed her arms, and gave directions past a golf course, then up Country Club Road. Cassie said, "I hooked them up and now Paul's selling fifteen hundred rocks a week by himself."

"Where can we find him?"

"Four o'clock, he's out of school. Drive by his house. Take a right here. But aren't you looking for Fisher?"

Blake turned with that low edgy voice. "This Paul guy might've been the last one to see him."

Blake's tone said something Cassie couldn't touch. The last one to see him alive? No, the last one to hang out with him. But where? Fish, where are you? I don't like your brother. Can't even jump out if I...

They drove up Verna Drive, a long street of anonymous little houses, the kind she never wanted to live in again. Never. She pulled her feet up onto the seat, hugged her knees, and said, "Up there on the right, with the green shutters."

They pulled to the curb. One house further ahead a dark blue Chrysler Imperial pulled away, Mr. and Mrs. Binks leaving for a baby making weekend, Sheila's coiled blonde hair catching Scooby's eye. But they all looked over as the garage door of the Jones house rumbled open and a skinny high school guy started humping a garbage can toward them, fat bags of garbage bulging out. The kid had messy hair in front of his eyes, but when he looked up they went scared and he halted.

Blake said, "Call him over."

Scooby opened the passenger window as Cassie called, "Paul? It's me, Cassie. Come here a sec, wouldja?" Cassie leaned into view, and the kid shuffled closer, hitching the garbage can ahead until he set it down by the curb. He looked into the SUV, a mean-looking version of Fisher sitting behind the wheel. Paul's eyes, even scared he couldn't help it, went to Cassie's cleavage, those two soft warm-blooded and beautiful breasts, those nipples he...

"Paul?"

He looked up. Fear. He wasn't breathing, but he was still thinking, so Paul looked down at his jeans, at the square lump of a remote control in his pocket. He slapped it and the garage door rumbled down behind him. Can't get into the house now. He let go of the garbage can, checking out the two men in the back with Cassie, one huge dark guy and a brown baldie with a greenish-blue jacket. A Spanish guy in the front seat, those three definitely not from Endwell, no way.

Scooby reached out and snagged him by the shirt. "Gotcha, punkass!"

Blake jumped out and circled the Explorer, grabbed Paul and shook him. "Where is he?! Fisher, where?"

"I don't know!"

"Bullshit! You little—"

Paul whipped his sneaker up between Blake's legs and broke away. Blake bent over gasping, holding his crotch as Paul ran, darted between houses, through a hole in the bushes, and didn't look back.

Doors swung open on the Explorer as Blake shouted, "Fuck! Little bastard!" Blake staggered to the back bumper and yanked out his pistol. Norbert had his chrome piece in hand and was about to fire at a twitching twig on a bush with long branches of little yellow flower things.

"No." Eduard grabbed him from behind. Norbert whipped his piece around and stuck it up under Eduard's jaw. Eduard let go of Norbert's jacket and said, "Man don't fire no guns here. You crazy?"

"Get in." Blake straightened, teeth clenched. "He's right. Norbert, get in!"

Norbert lowered his gun, glaring at Eduard. They climbed into the Explorer, Blake behind the wheel, clenching his teeth, an ache in his groin. He pulled out, screeching the tires.

"He knows. That kid knows exactly what happened to Fisher, where he's at, everything." He glared into the mirror at Cassie. "You haven't told us everything either."

Cassie blinked. "I have too. What—"

"Lying bitch. Monday night Fisher sent Swain an e-mail telling him that Paul Jones, that little shit, was trying to rip him off for five hundred rocks, saying somebody from Binghamton set him up."

Cassie's mouth opened. "No, he wouldn't, he...I didn't know that but, but I don't believe it. Paul's just a stupid kid."

"Shut the hell up! Where do we get some beer? Where's the god damn woods?" He glanced savagely at her. "No time to find Fisher right now, we're heading for Buffalo...but first I wanna see some country. Where is it?"

They stopped at a Great American grocery store. Scooby went in for six-packs of porterhouse ale, good stuff, and Blake drove with a hand on his crotch. Norbert and Eduard said nothing, they could sense it, the coming of a purge. Blake drove, sucked a butt so hard the smoke seared his throat, pain he wanted, drove the way Cassie directed him, out Rural Route 38B, and his anger fell behind as the houses appeared fewer and far between.

He glanced at the rearview mirror, into the back seat. "So, Norbert," he asked, "are you Baptist?"

"What the hell?" Norbert had spotted a goat in a wire pen. "Say what?"

"Are you deaf? You're wearing a plain cross. Catholics wear crosses with Jesus on them. That's too simple, so are you a Baptist?"

Norbert smoothed down the lapels of his greenish-blue jacket, the gold cross standing out against his black tee-shirt. "You kidding. I'm atheist, don't believe in fairy tales. Cross looks frosty, that's all. Throws off the heat."

Cassie said, "That way."

Blake felt distaste harden in his stomach. He turned the SUV onto Dutchtown Road, and Eduard pointed into a barbwire corral. "Beefalo!"

They gazed out at hulking smooth-skinned beasts, dark brown, horned, matted hair, tons on the hoof. Scooby shook his head. "Like I say, Dorothy Dreads, we not in Kansas any more."

The SUV climbed a steep hill where the road fell apart into potholes and gravel. Cassie directed them onto a dirt road. They rode through an evergreen and hardwood forest on dirt ruts, dry or muddy, a splash through a creek. Cool menthol darkness. A clearing, a fire burn, and Blake drove out into a field that opened onto the womb of the night. He parked where a line of pines hung dense green branches over the grass, wild and crackly.

Blake got out of the car, feeling better. "Scooby, fire up a joint. Gimme a beer." Birds chirped. Scooby opened bottles with his teeth and graciously offered the second to Cassie. Blake felt his anger surge, but let it wait. Clouds of smoke drifted over the meadow. Stars glistened, Eduard played Broken Spear. When Norbert put in a disc of rap music Blake yanked it out of the player, "Tribal shit!" and threw it like a frisbee into the dark.

"You brain-fucked, that was ma man, Dre."

Norbert stumbled in the crackling grass, his movements no longer precise. Cassie giggled and put her hand on a flank of the Explorer. "Buffalo?" Stoned, beer-buzzed, she saw swirling halos around them. "You're going to Buffalo? To get married?"

Scooby laughed with her. "Whathefuck?"

"At Niagara Falls. It's..." She burped. "...a tradition."

"We have to get rid of a rat." Blake wasn't laughing. "But first...well...it's important to appreciate nature, yes it is...but we came out here for a purpose."

Scooby, Norbert, and Eduard looked at Cassie. "For what?" She blinked. "Purpose? What's that?"

"You haven't been telling us the whole story." Blake's eyes glistened out of dark sockets. Low and dangerous. "And you've been smoking product."

"No," she said. "Not me, no I haven't, no way."

"With Fisher."

"No way, we didn't..."

"And now—" Norbert gave her a little push. "You seen us. Bitch."

"What?" The dark, the men, Cassie's whole body tightened. She dropped her bottle of ale. Eduard stepped in behind her. "I helped you, I..."

Blake turned his back. "First one has to shoot her in the head."

Norbert looked at Eduard. "I'll flip you for it."

"Please...no." Cassie backed away from Norbert, bumped into Eduard. "No!"

Eduard muffled her screams as they dragged her kicking under the evergreens. Blake called, "Stuff her mouth. Don't feel like hearing it!"

He looked out over the field. A man who noticed patterns and went against them, gaining an advantage, he observed how the meadow grass sloped away, rippling in the night breeze like seaweed on an ocean floor. A swell of darkness, the ridge across the valley rose black against the lighter darkness of the sky. Cassie screeched. No stars glistened. He lit a joint and passed it to Scooby, smoke drifting lazily.

"Man." Scooby glanced over and shrugged. "She way hot, but nada, I can't do a woman like that. Too Catholic."

Blake looked at Scooby through a haze of dope smoke and ale. "Me too."

Scooby laughed. "No kiddin'? You go through catechism an' all that, body of Christ, no sex before marriage, all that crap? You too?"

He chuckled. "My dad was way into it. Cross of St. Michael's." Blake drew down his tee-shirt to show off the tiny golden Jesus that had hung crucified for the last seventeen years below the hollow of his throat. He said, "I had such a hard-on for Sister Alexis."

Scooby laughed. "Sister Madelina, me too!"

Blake passed Scooby the joint. "I was an altar boy."

"Aw man! Madelina make me so hard, I know she need it too, so every Sunday after mass I go into the alley and make it shoot. It drib down the brick wall and I say, 'That for you, Madelina.'" Scooby chuckled. "One day Julio catch me, he hot for her too, so he yank off right next to me!"

Scooby laughed, the locks of black hair quivering against his copper-colored forehead. He reminded Blake of Fisher, easy laugh, same fun-loving troublemaker grin, and Blake wanted to reach out and pinch his cheek. He really wanted to, his hand moved, his wrist rolled, started to rise, Blake chuckling.

A pistol shot. Scooby flinched. A troubled look in his eyes, he cleared his throat, passed the joint back and looked out over the field of black rippling grass. Blake watched him, his hand still at his side, and he knew he wouldn't reach out and pinch his cheek, not in a million years, even if they all suddenly grew as quiet as that country field sinking into dry midnight, the death of a day.

CHAPTER 7

I still had three plastic poker chips scraping together in my pocket, free drinks the guys gave me at the Pine Inn, when I pulled into Carla's driveway and threw the stick into park. She lived on Rath Avenue in Endicott, an old grey stucco two-family her ex-husband foisted on her in divorce court, which she couldn't sell for ten bucks anymore, since IBM poisoned the aquifer.

Before I even shut off the headlights the right front door flew open and Carla ran out. "It's Paul," she said, "he called twice, something's wrong."

I yelled, "Follow me!" and pulled out. Suddenly tighter than a tie wrap, I cranked the Codger out of the driveway and made her wail up the hill. The lights of Carla's Pontiac lit up behind me as I groaned uphill into Endwell and ran a red light. Sweating, tasting salt, I was glad I didn't have to answer her questions, scared, tense, squeezing the wheel and praying, God please, he's my kid, my only son, please I...

The Codger barreled down Country Club Road. I had a thought. Take money out of the safe and buy a new truck. The old girl was ready for a merciful bullet by the time she tilted into our driveway and died lurching with a cough. I jumped out, ran up the steps, Carla pulling to the curb. "Paul! Paul!" Not in the living room. I ran down the bedroom hallway. "Paul!"

"What?" He was in his bedroom, sitting at his desk, a lamp glowing over an open book. He must've finished off a few more bags of potato chips, the oily smell stronger as I stumbled into his room and slammed on the brakes. He looked at me like I was crazy. "What?"

"Are you all right? What's wrong?"

"Now? Nothing. Where've you been?"

"Talking over the job with a couple subcontractors."

He saw through me and snorted. "How's Charlie? Leave him a nice tip?"

Charlie was the bartender at the Pine Inn. I realized it: it was a battle of wits. I couldn't ask why he called Carla so I said, "Are you feeling all right?"

"Yeah, why?"

"You're doing homework. Are you sick?"

Carla walked up the hallway and stepped in, slipping against me. "Are you all right?" He looked down at the algebra book on his desk. "Paul?"

His finger traced an equation and he said it without looking up. "I thought the guys who hassled me might've found you."

"What guys?" I felt the distance, the wall Paul put up when Carla was around. He leaned over and dragged an open bag of potato chips out from under his bed. "What guys hassled you?"

"Cassie and four guys in an SUV. One guy was Fisher's brother." He held up the bag to me. "Chip?"

I grabbed the chips and threw them on the desk. "Why don't you listen? I told you to stay in the house!"

"What do you care!" He flared into belligerence. "As long as you have a few beers and go to your girlfriend's house, what do you care?"

I threw up my hands. "Are you nuts? Why—"

"Darryl." Carla's hands were on my shoulders. "Calm down. Okay? Please?"

She was already pulling me out of there when the doorbell rang. I strode out and down the hall, my face hot, teeth clenched, and yanked open the front door. Mrs. Kavidge, a heavy-bodied woman with big gray sausage curls on her head, stood holding Patty's hand until my little sweetie, her hair tied in blonde pigtails, jerked free. "Carla!" She ran past me and threw herself into Carla's arms, the two of them hugging, already tight as lovebirds.

What am I, chopped liver? Not that I was in any mood for hugs as I turned to look at Mrs. Kavidge. I took a deep breath to calm myself and said, "Mrs. Kavidge, hi, how are you?"

"Fine, yah, and you?" She smelled vaguely of boiled cabbage and cigars. Her husband smoked big stogies, which Patty hated, but the old woman, like her accent, was as reliable as Poland. She handed over Patty's backpack full of schoolbooks and said, "She gets her homework done, I make sure of that, but she won't eat the food I make so you don't pay for no dinner."

I pulled out my wallet. "I appreciate it, Mrs. Kavidge, really. How much do I owe you?"

"Twelve hours, seventy-two dollars, plus three dinners I make for her that she likes enough to eat." She nodded, her waddle of double chins shaking. "Eighty-four dollars is enough, yah."

I handed over the cash. "By any chance, can you pick her up at school? I'll pay extra."

She shrugged. "Mr. Kavidge has a car, sure, every night you want me to?"

"Can you?"

"Patty is a good girl." She tucked away her money. "Okay, I pick her up at the school, start Monday. Okay, goodnight."

I closed the door on Mrs. Kavidge and turned around. Down on one knee, whispering with Patty, Carla was chuckling. She said, "Tell your daddy."

Patty turned to me, swept a blonde pigtail back over her shoulder and said, "Mrs. Kavidge plopped this big thing on my plate and I said, what's that? She said 'brautwurst.' It sure smelled like the worst."

"You told her that?"

She looked at me like I was dumb. "No. I said, 'Brautwurst? What brought it?' That made Mr. Kavidge laugh."

I smiled and hugged my sweetie against my hip, feeling her skinny bones, and she wrapped her arms around my leg. You never love your kids more than when they're children. After that it gets complicated and sometimes you want to kill them, or you're terrified they're going to kill themselves, or you wonder how they can be so embarrassing. Patty wasn't there yet. I hugged her and knew she didn't hold it against me that her mother went to California with Mr. Spinach and, yes, she was still Daddy's little girl even though he killed somebody just the night before.

Paul appeared in the hallway behind Carla, looking resentful, as if the battle lines were drawn and Patty and I had already fallen to the invader. My face must've changed because Carla glanced over her shoulder. Paul turned and disappeared into the hallway. We didn't see him again that night as we tucked Patty into her sheets and pillows with her teddy bear, Squeebles, kissed her good night, took off our shoes, and padded in our socks into the kitchen. I poured a glass of homemade strawberry wine for Carla, she sipped it, and I took her by the hand to lead her to bed.

I stopped. She said, "What's the matter?"

The door out the back of the kitchen, to the basement, made me feel guilty. I exhaled slowly. "I can't yet. I'm behind."

"Darryl." The edge in her voice was a warning. I looked at her. She saw I wouldn't be satisfied unless I did—went down and worked some on the books—so she let her hand slip off my chest, groaned quietly, and sighed as I opened the door.

I trooped downstairs to my office. She called down from the kitchen. "I'll be in the bedroom. With a magazine."

"I'll only be an hour."

Yeah, right. I booted up the computer, slow as molasses, sat down, accidentally kicked my safe, "Ow," opened up Quicken, and ripped open envelopes, scanned bills, wrote checks—I still use a checkbook for that, I'm superstitious—then I was having such a rollicking good time I entered dollar figures in the on-screen general ledger, accounts payable, accounts receivable (none), and wrote addresses on letterhead because I couldn't get my printer to print them right.

Start a business and it enslaves you. I thought about Carla, upstairs in bed, and purposely kicked the old steel safe under the desk. That's where I stashed all the cash for our new house, and sometimes it was a handy little reminder of what I was working for, my family secure in a good home. I stuck checks into envelopes, wrote Thanks! on overdue bills, licked and sealed, stacked the letters, and took them upstairs to the mailbox on the front porch.

I hustled for the bedroom where she was waiting.

Oh yes, she was waiting. She was asleep.

I took a shower and slipped beneath the sheets. She'd woken up, but when I reached for her she said, "My turn," and slipped out.

There is no feeling quite as nice, in a quiet way, as watching the woman you love primp before she hops in the sack with you. I caught a glimpse of her in the bathroom doorway before she shut off the light, black lacy panties below a New York Giants tee-shirt, and it sure made little Darryl stand up and take notice.

But taking a woman to bed is a bit of a ticklish operation when your kid is in the next room. Can they hear us? How do they feel about somebody staying over? They know it means something. A man's gotta worry about that when his kids have gone through a break up, which must feel like a house falling in on their heads. Then again, he's gotta have a life too.

I also had the feeling Carla wasn't going to let me start the festivities without some pleasant conversation. I raised the sheet and she slipped into my tent and my arms. Her ribs were warm to my fingertips.

"So?" she asked, "you want Frank to go with you?"

Oh boy, here it comes. "Frank, your boss? No thanks. But Monday morning, go ahead, call a big shot lawyer, I'll go then. Then I'll turn myself in...maybe."

I kissed her, or tried to, but her mouth was moving. "Paul's scared. He wasn't showing it, but he is. Darryl, get your head out of your butt. This is serious."

"Really?" I looked at her, her hair spread wetly on the pillow, and squeezed her arm. "It might trash everything I ever worked for, and everything I want with you and the kids, and the business, but no, it's not serious. It's a joke. I might go to prison, or worse, but it's all pretty funny and it's all my fault."

Not a good start. "Darryl, nobody said—"

"Nobody said so, but it is. He's sixteen, he's my kid, he's smoking it, so it's my fault a coke dealer showed up at the house, our house, a new life for us, and it's my fault I killed him. Is that what you want me to tell a jury? They'll strap me down and turn on the juice. Sounds like a joke to me, sure does, and it's all my fault."

"The electric chair? How dramatic." She lifted her hand to my cheek and traced my jaw with her fingertips. She whispered, "I can get you in to see Kelly Singer Monday afternoon. He's the best defense attorney in the area. Please let me call him." She pulled me close and kissed me. "I love you, I want to help. Paul needs it. Please?" She kissed me with soft lips. "Please? I love you and the kids and it scares me to...to think something might happen to us. Please let me call him."

Of course I said yes. I didn't want to think about it. I wanted to get mindless, so I kissed her, the thin sweetness of strawberry wine on the tip of her tongue, and I kissed her until I could smell the musky change in her mood. She was ready, and we got it together without a thought in our heads, mindless at the same time.

We made a lot of noise, but with dawn turning the curtains pale and the birds chirping, it was a hazy memory. The kids didn't see her because Carla kissed me and slipped out of bed. I woke up, tangled in sheets, but I was almost asleep again by the time she was out the door.

That was one reason I loved her, she knew the right thing to do. But we both thought we had more time. The weekend would pass without any problems, but it was just the calm before the Monday storm.

Monday, the tenth of September. The worst day of my life.

CHAPTER 8

Friday was party night and Albert Borque wanted it. A helluva good buzz.

He guzzled the dregs of his microbrew and laughed. On his mega TV a blue schnauzer in a cartoon lit a match and stuck it into the green fur of a sheepdog that ran away barking with its ass on fire. Borque cackled and said, "I told you they blow off everybody. Man, they're classic."

Exhaling a cloud of smoke, Tony held out a joint pinched in a roach clip made of four red dice, his bicep swollen from pumping the dumbbell that was now under the coffee table. He waved the joint and said, "Take it, boner, I gotta piss. You check on them downstairs?"

"You do it, loser, I'm watching this."

Tony stood up off the sofa and started upstairs. "Lazy pork."

"Muscle head." Borque laughed and took a long hissing toke. Ashes dropped onto the screaming Metallica skull on his shirt. He slapped at the ashes, his gut shaking under the screaming skull. He glanced over at Eric and pointed at his chest. "Aw man, that was the best show, the Garden in '09. You see that on YouTube?" He held out the joint to Eric. "Take it, homer."

Eric's head looked like the eraser of a large pencil, his temples shaved smooth, his afro rising four inches to a flat top; but his eyes glistened with a hesitant intelligence. He waved a hand with two spots of white on his brown knuckles. "Lacrosse," he mumbled, "I gotta chill."

"You feeling all right?" Borque stood up, glassy-eyed and grinning, and waved the smoking joint. "I know. You're taking Psych. 101 now and you can't hack it while you're also taking, holy shit, basket weaving and gym class."

"Up yours, brainiac." That thought, that premonition, intruded into Eric's head again. Leave. Get out of here. Weird. It made him look troubled. Borque saw that he wasn't amused, turned, and plodded into the kitchen. Eric planted his hands in the ratty cushions, hearing that voice again, leave, and he was about to get up when Tony came downstairs.

Tony, a twenty-year-old with curly blonde hair and a gold stud in his lower lip, sank onto the broken cushions of the sofa. "How many rocks we got left? Any word from Fish?"

Eric shook his head. "Fifty, that's it." Leave now, leave. Eric shifted on the sofa as Tony grabbed the iron dumbbell off the floor. Eric said, "He better come or we won't have enough for Saturday morning."

"You should've seen this hottie at the field house today." Tony curled the dumbbell slowly. "A-list external organs, I got a woodie just looking at her." He glanced toward the dark kitchen. "Fat ass checking on them downstairs?"

Eric nodded. "Finished his beer, that's what got his big ass off the sofa. He's still freaked about getting picked up by the Staties."

"No doubt. Human garbage cans aren't known for their bravery." Tony laughed as the dark kitchen lit up with refrigerator light. "Where'd he come up with a name like Harvey Epstein?"

"Unknown, but he was already passing himself off as Fisher Pangbourne."

"And a sentient life form, which he isn't."

Tony laughed. Looking nervously toward the kitchen, Eric didn't.

In the dark kitchen, Borque reached into the refrigerator, grabbed another bottle of ale, spotted the two egg rolls in a wax paper bag. Oh yeah, one of those too, then he shut the fridge and opened the door to the basement, right next to it. Lights, smoke, music, a girl's giggle. His feet thumped on the wooden steps, the smell of burning crack cocaine in the air. He leaned over and looked under the ceiling, toward a ratty sofa where a frat boy and two hottie blondes were nestled together.

Frat Boy had a butane lighter firing up a glass stem filled with white smoke going into a girl's glossy black lips, black lipstick smearing the end of the glass pipe, and she looked cross-eyed as she watched the flame incinerate the small white rock in the bowl. The other girl watched hungrily, wearing only panties and a tank top, and the Frat Boy's pants were unbuttoned.

Crack whores, you gotta love 'em. Not that Borque had ever porked one.

He felt a flash of envy, bit off half the egg roll, chewed, and watched the girl in panties, her brown nipples moving beneath her tank top. Frat Boy was all messed up, his eyes red and glassy, his head jerky on his pencil neck. Imitating a home boy, he said, "Whaddup?"

"You guy's cool?" Borque waved the egg roll. "Don't light the sofa on fire."

"Fug no," Frat Boy said. "We're just gettin' fried, smokin' cock, eatin' pussy, and fuggin' like frogs."

"Frogs?" The left girl giggled. "Frogs have oral sex?"

Girl in the panties. "No, but they fuck, right? Gimme a hit."

Frat Boy flicked a finger at Borque dismissively. "Sayonara, Jerry Lewis," and the babes laughed.

Borque looked up. Knocking? He said, "You need more, we got it," turned and climbed the stairs.

Borque stepped up into the kitchen, stubbing his toe on the top step, "Ow!" Bunk bunk bunk, somebody knocking. The cops? No, they'd come to the front door. All the back windows and the door had shades drawn. Borque turned on the kitchen light and drew back the shade on the door windows. A guy outside, didn't know him. Bunk bunk bunk, the guy motioned, and Borgue was about to call out to Tony when the guy said something about Fisher. Borque opened the door a crack, the chain still strung. "What did you say?"

The guy was lean with black curly hair, mid-twenties, tough looking. He said, "Fisher sent me."

"Fish? Where is he?" Borque unstrung the chain and opened the door. "Who are you?"

The man stepped into the light of the kitchen and said, "I'm his brother, Blake."

Borque stepped back, his mouth opening. "But..."

Blake snapped, "But what?"

A pang of fear shot through Borque as a huge Jamaican appeared out of the dark and stepped in, a little Hispanic dude hustled through the doorway, followed by an evil-looking black guy, shaved head, with a greenish-blue jacket. Borque backed up, Blake looking down at him. "But what? You little fat pig, Borque, where is he?"

"Fish? I don't know. How'd you know my name?"

Tony's voice came from the living room. "Porky, who is it?"

Blake pushed Borque into the dining room and the laugh died on Tony's lips. Eric saw them and in one bodily spasm of fear rose off the sofa, leaped the coffee table, and bolted for the front door. A rustle of cloth, a click, and the shining chrome pistol was in Norbert's hand, a four-inch silencer long on the barrel.

"Sit down," Norbert said, low and deadly. "Jungle boy."

Eric stumbled against the doorframe, the knob in his hand. He gagged, couldn't breathe, shoved his shoulder against the jamb, feebly tried to hide, looked back, saw the cyclops pistol staring at him. Beyond it Norbert's two black eyes and hateful face watched him. They were all watching him.

Blake sniffed. "Going somewhere, Eric?"

Norbert shouted it. "Nigger! On the sofa!"

Eric retreated to the sofa. He stumbled over the dumbbell, Tony still on his feet, staring at Norbert's gun.

"You know us?" Borque asked.

"Know you? The three stooges?" Blake slapped Borque on the back and squeezed the fat on the back of his neck so hard the boy cringed. "We know where you're from, your class schedules, sex lives—none—and how to get through the hole in the fence and onto your back porch without being seen."

Blake jerked Borque toward the stairs to the second floor. "Norbert, watch the crackheads down below. No, on second thought, you watch Grace Jones here and the gym rat. Eduard, you go downstairs and cover the smokers."

"Aye boss," Eduard said, his branches of hair swaying behind his back as he lumbered into the kitchen.

Blake herded Borque upstairs to the second floor. Three rooms with messy beds, cheap desks, shelved textbooks. "Yours?"

Borque's hand flinched toward a doorway. "Why? What are we doing?"

"I just want to ask you a few questions. Sit."

He motioned to the bed. Borque settled onto the rumpled and unwashed sheets. "Questions about what?"

"What you meant downstairs."

"When?"

"In the kitchen. When I walked in. I told you I was Fisher's brother and you said 'but.' But what?"

"But nothing." The intensity of Blake's eyes scared him. Borque shrugged. "I just, you know, you just caught me off guard, that's all."

Blake looked down at Borque and shifted gears. He exhaled slowly. Quietly, in a soothing whisper, he said, "Lie down." Borque licked his lips and looked at the yellowed sheets that stank of his body. Blake murmured, "Go ahead, I'm not going to hurt you. As they used to say, it's your bed, so lie in it."

Borque lay back. Blake swirled his finger in the air and Borque rolled over to face a poster from yet another heavy metal rock band, a skull staring at him, blood dripping down the sides. Blake settled quietly onto the bed, behind Borque's back, and leaned over the fat boy. He pulled a pillow out from under Borque's arm, lay it on top of his flabby hip and leaned lightly against him. He said, "I'm going to ask you again. But? But what?"

"But that's it, Blake, that's all I know. I don't know where Fisher is, I swear it." Borque looked over his shoulder, scared, his face flushed. "I know that's why you're here, he's missing. We haven't seen him either."

Blake drew a small black pistol out from the small of his back. He whispered, "That's not what I asked you. But what do you know about it? Where could little Fisher be?"

"He went to get his money from Paul Jones, in Endwell. He's a high school twerp, but he was trying to take Fisher for five biggies. Fisher fronted him, like, a huge bag of rocks, and then he said some guys from Binghamton ripped him off."

Blake's thumb edged back to a little button, pushed it until the safety was off, the gun would fire. He murmured, "You believe him?"

"I don't know, it could've happened, but he'd still owe Fisher the money for it," Borque said. "I always pay for what I sell, no shit Blake, I'm committed, I'm reliable, I move product faster than anybody. But the high school twerp didn't have the money so he was going to take Fisher and go ask his father for it."

"His father?"

"Yeah, no shit, I couldn't believe it either. Jones said that his dad had sixty thousand dollars in his office, in a safe, so he could pay off Fisher. I told him it was so stupid to go to some kid's dad, but you know Fisher, he thinks he's mister likable."

Blake sat with the pistol resting in his lap. His voice was low and calming. "That's what Fisher is. Mister likable."

"But not that likable. I told him not to go, but he didn't listen, and what happens? They find his car..."

Albert Borque knew he said too much. He fell tensely silent. Blake leaned over and breathed on Borque's neck. "How did you know about his car?"

"I...I heard it on the news."

"Liar!" Blake swung the pistol, whack! Borque screeched, blood welling up out of his hair, and Blake said, "But what! You fat piece of shit. Why? Why were you so surprised to see me, you damn fat turd? What'd he say about me?" Whack! Borque squealed and Blake shouted, "What did he say?!"

"Nothing!"

Whack! "Liar!"

"Please, I didn't do anything!" Blake raised the gun to swing it again and Borque cried, "You're dead! He said you're dead!"

Blake flinched, the gun poised, a red smear of Borque's blood on the barrel. Blake closed his mouth and sat back. He said, "That's what I told him to say."

"Please, Blake, I helped him, he trusted me. You gotta believe me. Blake? Blake? I do his homework for him. I haven't seen him so...I don't think...I don't think he's...around."

The fat boy let out a blubber. Not around? Not alive? Blake felt his face heat up, something raw, mean, and painful making his jaw clench. He shook his head, staring down at the fat boy whimpering on the bed. He whispered, "And I got him into this business? Where he has to deal with scumbags like you?"

"Blake?" Borque glanced over his shoulder. Blake's face was flushed, his teeth clenched, he was staring at Borque. Their eyes met. For an instant they both knew what had to happen. Borque lurched up, "No! Blake I..."

Blake jumped on him, pinned him, clamped the pillow over Borque's head, the gun beneath it, and shot him. WhumPANG! Muffled, noise escaped the pillow and echoed off the wall, buzzed off the ceiling, and Blake heard the boy scream, he was kicking, so Blake shot him again. Borgue went limp. His arms fell to the sheets and smoke curled out from beneath the pillow with the stench of burnt cloth, brimstone, and blood.

Blake climbed off Borque's twitching body as a chain reaction went off downstairs. Coming loud out of the basement, Eduard's .357 magnum sounded its distinctive cracking, which drowned out the spitting of Norbert's semi-automatic, muzzled by the silencer. It didn't silence Tony and Eric, who cried out as Norbert shot them.

Silence. Those alive watched the newly dead. Six dead, no movement. Blood ran in streaks and began to drip.

Blake turned his back on Borque's body and sank onto the edge of the bed. His ears vaguely rang from the sound of his shots. His elbows on his knees, he let his head hang.

Silence.

"Fish?" Blake whispered it. "Fish, where are you?"

Shoes pounded up the stairs and Norbert appeared in the doorway.

"Yo, we gotta ghost out of here, now." Blake, gazing down between his knees, tapped the bloody barrel of the black pistol against his forehead, marking his skin with a tiny red crescent. Norbert pulled him to his feet and said, "Out. Move!"

Blake stumbled into the hall and went slowly down the narrow stairs.

The living room. Eric lay on the floor in a pool of blood, Tony sprawled on the couch, a bullet hole leaking blood that dribbled down between his staring blue eyes. Blake gave them a glance, shuffled through the dining room, irritated when Norbert shouldered him from behind. The kitchen, a light, he hated it. Eduard saw and swung his magnum and the light exploded.

Darkness.

"Blake," Scooby asked, "wassa matter? Wake up!"

They crept into the night, a dog barking two houses away. The darkness hung heavy as they dodged across the back yard and ducked through a hole shattered low in the corner of a stockade fence, shards of glass glittering on the tar on the other side. Blake's SUV sat parked against the back wall of a laundromat. Scooby said, "Keys?"

Blake fumbled them out of his pocket. Scooby snatched them, popped the locks, and they climbed in. "Stay up!" Scooby gunned the engine and screeched the tires. They lurched out of the parking lot, rocked onto Main Street, and he drove hard for a hundred yards before he said, "Okay, get down."

Blake didn't, so four in the car looked like two as Scooby drove slowly through the heart of Johnson City, two run-down blocks of desperate shops, a box car diner, and a church with a For Rent sign. Six murders and nobody spoke. They made a highway. After a minute Eduard sat up. Norbert sat up and said, "Anybody feelin' hot in this chariot?"

"I'm with you, bro. We gotta get 'nother." Scooby looked over at Blake, shadows passing over his face. "You all right? Blakey?"

Blake lit a butt and sucked it hard, the smoke searing his throat. He said, "My family calls me Blakey. You call me that again and I'll kill you."

Norbert popped the clip out of his Browning, bullet nubs lined up, but he palmed in a full clip anyway. Gonna need it, he thought.

Eduard watched him, watched Scooby drive, watched the back of Blake's head, and kept his mouth shut, his teeth biting a crinkle of flesh at the back of his lips.

They crossed the Susquehanna River, black in the dark, and came to an exit for Endicott. Blake said, "Get off here. That way," he said, pointing. Scooby drove up out of the river valley and turned onto a back road when Blake said, "Down there, slowly."

They cruised at ten miles an hour, Blake peering at the houses. "Eduard, what kind of car you want?"

"Fo' what?"

"For Monday morning. You're going on a special mission. What kind of car do you want?"

Six months in America, Eduard didn't know luxury cars. He said, "Don't matter, long as it's big enough fo' me."

Blake reached out to touch Scooby's arm. Scooby stopped the SUV. Blake gazed across the road to where red metal fenders shimmered in the starlight. "How about a Mercedes Benz convertible? Looks showroom."

Eduard looked over and didn't answer.

"We come back here?" Scooby said. "After doin' six kids? Whyn't we go up to Buffalo, just do that thing and head home?"

Blake lit another cigarette and sucked it until the end burned the hot orange color of hell. He said, "I have to find my brother. That's all we have to do."

Norbert, his arm hanging out the window, slapped the side of the SUV. "What jive ass shit is this? Big Johnson say I'm going for Buffalo, the snuff job up there, not find your god damn brother down here."

The SUV felt too warm for Eduard, he rolled down his window. The shootings, senseless, and Blake, giving off that sick vibe, gave him a bad feeling.

Blake spoke over his shoulder. "Ed, this place, 124 Kinsey Road, remember it for Sunday night. And you, Norbert, you flake out on me and Big Johnson will be out of crack in three days. He's out of crack, you're out of luck."

His chrome piece shimmered in the darkness before Norbert slipped it beneath his jacket. He fit it snugly into its holster. Blake didn't know he was Big Johnson's brother-in-law. He picked lint off the lapel of his satin jacket. When he looked up he met Scooby's glance in the mirror, watching him.

Scooby said, "This is loco. Blake, we just kill six people."

Blake motioned for him to drive. "So?"

CHAPTER 9

The worst day of my life began well enough.

Monday morning. I shuffled into the kitchen in my boxers and made coffee. Behind her bedroom door, Patty's feet thumped when she jumped off her bed and ran around getting dressed. I leaned in and said, "Morning, sweetie."

"Which ones, the pink or the blue?" she asked, flapping two pairs of stirrup pants.

Not this again. I asked, "Which ones do you like?"

"The pink ones. You bought them for me. Would you put my hair in pigtails? Daddy, please?"

"I can try."

This, I thought, will be a new one. I divided her hair in half, bunched it up and grabbed a stretchy loop off her dresser, slipped it onto the ponytail, let go, and the whole thing hung there.

Pigtails, not my strong point. "Um..."

"Here, like this." My little sweetie double-looped the elastic band, reached back, tugged and folded her blonde hair through it and had a nice little tail. "Like that."

"I see." I did it on the other side, Patty scrunching up her face when I pulled her hair too hard, but then I made a nice little pigtail. "Choconuts for breakfast?"

I rousted Paul, sullen as usual, and we trooped out into an overcast day. I scowled up at the clouds, puffy like bruises, as if the sky got its lights punched out, but there were no dirt balls in the driveway that could link me to a murder, so I unlocked the door of the truck and the kids hopped in. I climbed in behind the wheel, turned the key, got the Codger to cough, she farted blue smoke and came awake.

Beyond the dirt patches in my yard and the lush green grass of the Binks' lawn, the front door of their house opened and the trooper himself stepped out. He looked over the grass and started toward us.

Uh-oh. Couldn't tell, but it looked like he was just waiting for us to come out of the house, it was no coincidence. I stiffened as Binks reached our patchy lawn, flagging his hand for me to wait, a glimpse of his sidearm appearing beneath his suit jacket.

I didn't roll down my window until he was right beside me, looking through the glass, his dark hair perfectly cut, his cheeks smoothly shaved, his throat too, right down to his tie, perfectly knotted with a little dimple in the middle of a half Windsor.

"Morning, Darryl." He nodded to them. "Hey kids."

They just looked at him. I said, "What's up? I gotta get them to school."

He stuck his hands in his pockets, jingled his change. He said, "Oh, just wondering how's business. Sheila saw the cans of tar there and thought you might have another house going. Any possibility she could list it?"

What boloney, he didn't care. "No, it's for us. I started a house out in the country, toward the airport, for when I get married next summer."

"I heard you got engaged." A sniff of his thin nose, a jingle of pocket change, and he glanced at the tar cans lined up along the edge of the driveway. "I know this sounds odd," he said, "but Sheila's sensitive. About how the neighborhood looks."

I sighed, slid out the door, snagged two empty cans of foundation coating, and walked toward the tailgate. When I reached the back bumper I glanced back and I swear Binks was staring at my butt. What the...? I tossed the cans over the tailgate so they clanged in the bed, made the other two cans clang, and walked back around past the rusted rear fender. That's when I caught Binks looking into my truck. He was staring down past the steering wheel at my seat.

His interest scared me, which irritated me, so I snapped at him as I circled back toward the driver's door. "That's why I'm moving out to the country."

"Now why is that?" he asked.

"Because out there I won't have to worry about my neighbors getting hyper about diddly." I opened the door. "A couple cans in the driveway? Be serious."

Binks leveled his glance at me and it stopped me, the door open. He looked fearless. My bluster had zero effect on him, so I slid in behind the wheel and blustered some more. "Tell Sheila I said, 'Have a nice day.' You too, Dave."

He spread his jacket open, put his hands on his hips, and watched us back out of the driveway, the cans rattling behind us in the bed. I glanced over at Paul, Patty humming a tune between us. He looked back at me and I could see it, he was scared, it was finally sinking in that we were in really deep shit and it involved guys like Binks, with guns and badges.

I stopped on the Pruyne Street hill and Paul let Patty jump out. "Sweetie? Wait for Mrs. Kavidge to pick you up."

"Okay, Daddy. Bye, Paul!"

She scampered to the door where a monitor mommy stood waiting. We coasted down Pruyne Street toward Hooper Road, the Binghamton Savings Bank on the right. Everything looked different, more valuable somehow, maybe because it was at risk. But seeing the bank made me remember my question.

"So tell me—" I glanced at him. "Why did that coke dealer think I could hand over five grand in cash?"

He looked out the window. "Because I told him."

"Told him what?"

"That you had it." He scraped the floor with his sneaker. "In your safe."

"In my office? Why'd you tell him that?"

His eyes turned away. "Because you do."

"Petty cash, yeah, but not five grand."

His head swung around, his eyes angry. "Don't lie to me. My bedroom is right over your office and I can hear every word you say on the phone."

"Oh yeah? How much is in there?"

"Sixty thousand dollars!" Oh shit, he knew. He snapped, "You got it by doing side jobs and getting paid in cash. By not paying taxes. By cheating the government!" He yanked his backpack off the seat and onto his lap. "You think I'm brain dead? I hear you talking on the phone to Vince, telling him what you have in there, how you stashed it all tax free. I know you cheat on your taxes every chance you get."

"You don't understand."

"What? That you cheat and lie every chance you get?!"

"Cheat who? Lovely Uncle Sam? He'd eat us alive if I didn't do something about it."

"Yeah, right."

"Right! There's a self-employment tax, extra taxes for the little guy, but it's big money. Do they tack it on because we make more? No. They take more because they figure we're all cheating on our taxes anyway."

We were already climbing the hill toward the high school. He said, "They had you figured right."

"But it means if you're not cheating you pay too much, so you gotta do it. You gotta cheat." Buses and a thousand kids looked like turmoil, the high school driveway plugged up, so I spun the wheel and swerved left into the drive of Northminster Presbyterian Church, across the street from the high school.

"Dammit!" I gunned the Codger in and stopped her with a screech of tires. "Yeah, okay, I cheat on my taxes. I cheat my ass off. I cheat for me, for you, for Patty, and I cheated for your mother, so we'd all have a nice warm house to live in and a weekend trip every few years."

He started to say something, but I cut him off.

"And another thing: you think I like building houses? I like houses when they're finished, but everything before that is a royal pain in my ass. I do it for you, for me, for all of us." It was his turn to look like he took a punch, but I kept going. "You don't understand. I'm afraid all the time I'll run short and not be able to pay the mortgage or put sneakers on your feet. Then your mother up and takes off with that damn Mr. Spinach—"

"Spinaker."

"Whatever. And that drains my bank account back down to nothing and I have to start all over again."

"Yeah, right."

"Damn right! So I scrimp and save and get us back on solid ground again, and what happens? This comes up, and it just might flush everything down the toilet anyway, everything, the house, the business, your college money, Carla and me, all of it. Down the god damn toilet!"

"But that's why I—"

"You want to know the truth?" I never let myself talk to him that way, but I was on a roll. "I'd put a gun to somebody's head and blow their brains out if that's what it takes to keep you out of harm's way. But that's how it looks, how it'll look to a jury. You two show up, you owe him five grand, and he ends up dead. It looks like murder and like I did it!" I squeezed the wheel so hard my hands hurt. "But you act as if I'm a thug, somebody for you to hate. Is that fair? To me? Is it?"

"Were you fair to mom?"

"What the hell does that have to do with anything?"

Beet red, he was furious, and he had been for a long time. "I heard you and Vince scheming, figuring out the cheapest way to get rid of her."

"She left us!"

"But if you were fair with her I...I wouldn't..."

"Wouldn't what?" He didn't want to tell me. I sensed it, so maybe that's why I subsided a bit and asked, "You what? Paul?"

"I wouldn't have to send her money."

"What money?"

"Profits. I could've paid off Fisher and none of this would've happened." I was so angry I was sweating, but suddenly I didn't know what to say, to think. He snapped, "I sent her thousands. Thousands!"

"For what?"

"To pay her mortgage! She bought a condo."

"I know that. But I paid her ten years of mortgage payments, up front. Why would she need money from you?"

"She's broke. Spinnaker took off with a bunch of her money."

"My god, are you kidding?" He wasn't. I felt stunned, like when a scar gets ripped open and you see raw flesh underneath. Lynn, how could you be so stupid? I stared out through the filthy windshield. Take money from your son? Where do you think he got it?

Suddenly I wasn't the least mad at Paul, my fire was out, I just...it was just too much to handle. But all that old anger was coming up and Paul was still raging. He shouted, "You schemed so you wouldn't have to give her much to start with!"

I looked over at him. I shook my head and spoke quietly.

"She wanted a lump sum. I paid her a hundred and fifty thousand dollars. Vince had to lend me thirty thousand, I didn't have it. No joke, she dumped us, you and Patty too. Just like she didn't know us anymore."

Then I felt like a thug and shoved my arm out the window because I could tell by Paul's face that he was about to break down. His voice came out husky. "She said you didn't love her anymore."

"It ripped me apart. You saw me, I was a basket case for a year after she left. She just painted me out to be the villain."

Tears glistened in his eyes. "She never saw you anymore."

"Well...no, she didn't, not much." It felt like he was on the other side of a chasm a mile wide. "She was going to school," I said, "and I was working. That's what happens when you're in business for yourself, you work all the time. Christ almighty, if I could do it over again I'd get a job and we'd be renters." I felt so lonely and defeated and pointless. Bleak. I sighed. "That's what I always thought, that everybody wants their own house, their own piece of the dream. Is that cheap? Is life cheap? Not in America."

I rubbed my face and looked in the rearview mirror, back at the church we went to on Sundays, a habit that fell apart along with the family. I glanced over at my son, my handsome half-grown boy, flushed and trying to keep it together, his backpack on his lap. His shoulders shook once, he made no sound but he was flushed, suffering, and then he sobbed just once. He mumbled, "I'm sorry."

"Ah hell, we all make mistakes. I made some and your mother too. Don't send her more money, she's gotta pay for her mistakes just like the rest of us. But right now, the bottom line is that we want to stay out of jail, and if we don't cover for each other they'll put us away. Catch my drift? I cover your backside and you cover mine. Otherwise we won't make it. We'll go to jail, you'll never go to film school, and I'll grow old in a cell someplace with hair growing out of my ears."

My sorry attempt at humor didn't touch him. He'd been thinking and worrying all weekend and he was in a black pit, scared, red-eyed, beat up inside. I sighed and my hand flipped off the wheel in some pathetic attempt at body language.

"All we have to do," I said, "is keep our mouths shut. Don't tell anybody where that body is. Don't tell the cops, your friends, your mother, nobody. Don't tell anybody, not ever, not even Carla; it wouldn't be good for her to know either. If they don't have a body they can't file murder charges against us, that's what she told me. That's what we're talking about, murder charges. Understand?"

He nodded. I reached over, squeezed his shoulder, and said, "We both screwed up, but we don't deserve to go to jail. Right?" He nodded, kind of, sniffed, and sleeved his cheeks. I said, "Lighten up. Listen to me. We'll get through this if we're careful. Okay? Just stay away from Cassie and don't talk to anybody you don't know. Okay?"

He nodded and looked a bit better. He slid out, but before he slammed the door he said, "I'm sorry, Dad. I am, I'm really sorry."

"Yeah, I'm sorry too, for everything. Now hurry up, you don't want to be late for homeroom."

I watched him jog toward the school. Brave kid. When he suffered I suffered, and I was suffering. And you certainly don't have to support your mother.

I put the Codger in gear and drove, even though I felt like somebody beat me with a two-by-four and it was only half past seven in the morning. On auto-pilot, thinking black thoughts, I drove to work. Uphill. Turn. Drive down. Up there. I steered the Codger up the street Darryl built, past all those shrines to the work ethic, IBMers pulling out of driveways and waving to me as they headed toward their own shrines to the god of work, and none of it made me feel the least bit better.

Then again, I knew it: if I wasn't cracking the whip on this slave ship I'd be in the traces somewhere else. I'd go crazy if I didn't have a place to traipse off to every morning, I knew it, so my spirits lurched a bit upward as I stopped the Codger in front of my latest shrine, Mudgie standing in the doorway with a cup of coffee smoking in his hand.

Thank god some people don't change.

I killed the engine, rolled out, and walked back to the bed and hoisted out my toolbox. As I carried it inside the house Mudgie slurped his java and said, "When's the last time you bought some new shitkickers? The steel toes are showing through."

"So shoot me. No, just gimme a hand." We hoisted the generator out of the truck and carried it downstairs, into the basement, so it didn't deafen us, then snaked the hose up to the roof for the air nailer. I liked roofing except it made my knees ache. But the sun fell warm on my back, I tied a bandanna around my head, and Mudgie's jowls shook and he dripped sweat on the black tar paper as we nailed down the shingles, bap!bap!bap! The gun drove nails through shingles, into plywood, and a crow flew cawing overhead.

About eleven o'clock I paused to look at Mudgie. I said, "I had a big fight this morning with Paul."

"The pot dealer? I hope you spanked him."

I didn't feel like fighting so I didn't say anything. A truck from the p.o. trundled by on the street below, a mailman stuffed news of the world into boxes. I glanced in the other direction. Wind rippled the grass of the abandoned golf course, riffled the water of the pond, and all I thought about was getting the job done. Then the back half of the roof was shingled and I looked up at the molten sun and said, "The gun needs oiling. Lunch time."

I settled my bones in a bedroom, my back to the bare studs of a wall, opened my lunchbox, and stretched my legs out over the plywood floor. Peanut butter and jelly sandwich, yum. I scarfed that down in four sticky bites, then started spraying WD-40 on the nail gun between bites of an apple, holding the McIntosh between my teeth like I was a pig on a platter.

Car tires chirped against the curb out front. Mudgie looked at me. "You expecting somebody?"

I took the apple out of my teeth. "Not me."

I hooked the air hose to the gun and jammed another plate of nails into the magazine. Outside, the car engine shut off. Mudgie and I sat as still as mice and looked at each other. Footsteps crunched in the dirt. Clunk clunk, somebody stepped inside, down below. A man's voice, deep like it came out of a barrel, rolled up the stairs. "Somebody in here?"

Clunk...clunk...clunk, footsteps up the stairs. Thick brown tentacles. Hair? It was a man's huge brown head with long branches of hair sticking out from it, then his glance met mine when his eyes rose above the floor.

He yowled like a wild man, a laugh that ripped through the house as he leaped upstairs. He was dressed in a white jogging suit with red slashes, and beyond the stud frame of the walls for the bedroom he looked like he was behind bars. Not for long. His big white hi-tech sneakers rasped on the plywood floor as he charged around the corner of the hallway. He laughed wildly as he jumped through the doorway of the bedroom, and he was so damn big that when he landed the whole house shook.

Clowning around, he wore a huge smile, one missing tooth making a clean gap. He shouted, "I found the man! Man can't hide from me!"

Sitting on the floor, Mudgie and I just stared up at him. What the hell planet did this one come from? His branches of hair scraped the ceiling, he was six foot ten if an inch, with arms as thick as my legs and thighs like my waist.

He chuckled. "Man be scared? I'm scare the man?" The jogging suit couldn't hide the rocky muscles underneath it. He shook his brown furry tentacles. "Man, don't be scared. I'm jus' here lookin' for somebody."

Mudgie asked, "Are you a Rasta? For real? One of them crazy Jamaican fellas?"

"Man, I'm the real t'ing." His accent thickened, as if he was indulging in an act. "And you be da man here, Darryl Jones?"

"Who's asking?"

I said it, he looked at me.

"You be the father of that boy, Paul? Yah man?" He looked down at me, the joking humor in his eyes changing as he sized me up. The odds were in his favor. He shook his head, his branches swaying. "Don' answer, that be okay, I know. I got a friend, he lookin' for his brother. Your boy, he know where that brother be. Don't he."

"Nope." My lunch box sat open on my left, a box of raisins in it. The air nailer sat to my right, the hose snaking into the hall. I reached out for my lunch box, lifted it over my lap, set it down to my right and picked up the nail gun in one smooth motion. I said, "He doesn't know a thing."

"Man, he do. He do because he in business with m'friend's brother."

"No, you're wrong." I looked the giant Rasta man in the eye. "He doesn't know anything about anybody. And if you ever bother him again I'll settle your hash. For good."

Stillness.

His teeth clenched, the muscles by his ear playing under his brown skin, but my glance dropped as he slid his hand inside the jacket of his jogging suit, across his stomach. I figured he was going for a pistol. I lifted the business end of the nailer. His hand stopped, he looked at the nailer. He looked at me. Looked at the nailer. Looked at me.

He shoved his hand back and grabbed his pistol before I pulled the trigger. Bap!bap!bap!bap! Four nails hit him in the face as he yanked out the pistol and covered his eyes.

I never saw Mudgie move so fast. He grabbed a scrap of two-by-four, a three-footer, and slammed the big man's arm. The gun fired, stunning thunder, a slug splintered the plywood floor near my boot and the pistol rattled across it. I grabbed it, swung it up, but I didn't need to fire.

Mudgie swung the two-by-four, wham! The Rasta giant stumbled to the wall, growled, and swung a fist at Mudgie, who hit him again, wham! "No! Not gonna!" Mudgie slammed him, wham! wham! The Rasta fell, the house shook, and Mudgie bent over him, "Fucker! Fucker!" and hit him the hardest, a blow to the back of his head that made a sound like a melon cracking.

The Jamaican giant slumped onto the floor, eyes open, but he wasn't seeing a thing.

Mudgie dropped the two-by-four and stepped back, panting loud. Blood spilled onto the plywood floor below the Rasta man's broken head. The bright red drip became a blotch, a big blot, and Mudgie backed away.

"Darryl? Holy shit, I...I killed him. I killed him!" Red pooling blood. On my feet, I dropped the pistol. Mudgie cried, "What are we gonna do?!" I threw up my hands and stumbled, I couldn't think, hands in my hair until Mudgie grabbed me. "What are we gonna do? Jesus Christ! What the fuck? What about Marge? What the fuck am I gonna do!"

Mudgie's face was so red he was about to burst. I stopped, looking at him. Mudgie had a spatter of blood on his shirt, below the pocket, and for some reason that put me in a crystal clear place and I knew what to do. "A tarp," I said, "in my truck, go get it."

"For what?"

"We gotta get him out of here!"

A car outside. Mudgie froze. I ran into the front bedroom, to the window hole. It totally blew my cool. "Oh fuck!"

"Who is it?"

"My neighbor, Binks."

The cop. I ran into the back bedroom where the dead Rasta giant was still bleeding. Mudgie was about to cry. I don't know why I do things sometimes, gut-level, but I grabbed Mudgie by the shirt, swung hard and smacked him good, jerked his head, and put shock on his face.

"Lunch! Grab your lunch!"

I snagged my lunch box with the raisins in it and headed for the stairs. When I got to the first floor, Binks walking toward the house, I stopped. A sound behind me. Spat...spat...spat. I stepped into the kitchen area, two-by-four walls and bare floor. Bare floor spotted with red. The Jamaican's blood was dripping through a crack in the ceiling.

Spat...spat...spat.

CHAPTER 10

Binks slid behind the wheel of his unmarked unit and watched the Jones family truck grow smaller and smaller in his side view mirror. He knew where they were going, to drop Patty off at Homer Brink School, so he put the sedan in gear and cruised slowly around the corner and down Lyndale Drive. Well kept, a good neighborhood, the houses became more modest the closer he got to the main road until he reached the odd three-way intersection at Lyndale, Pheasant, and Hooper. He stopped there to wait by the curb, early morning traffic droning by on Hooper.

He felt good. The weekend was a pleasure. Swimming in Lake George, hiking the Tongue Mountain Range, enjoying the views, shopping for knickknacks in the village, and having sex. Sex from the front, the back, the side. Sex in the woods, in the bed, the tub, the chair, and on the rug. He kept it up, gave as good as he could.

Sunday afternoon it took a long time for them to come, and they came together. She climaxed hard, and as she came she said it over and over again, that she loved him. He started to say it too, coming so hot and shooting so hard it scalded him, buried inside her. They were locked together, mindless for a whole minute afterward, and seared speechless. Damn, that was a good one. Then she whispered that she loved him and that she would never leave him. Never.

What more could he need?

Binks woke out of his reverie as Darryl Jones' rusty pickup truck rolled past, Paul and Darryl in the cab, the empty tar cans rattling around in the back when it hit a bump. Binks let a few cars go by and pulled out. The truck climbed the hill rising to the high school on the right, but the Jones truck lurched and pulled into the left, the church parking lot across the street.

Interesting. Binks cruised slowly past the high school as Jones stopped the truck in the church parking lot, yelling at Paul, a brown-haired kid that Binks never paid much attention to. Until now. He pulled into the faculty lot of the high school, stopped the sedan, and watched Jones and his son a hundred yards away. The kid didn't look happy and Jones was shouting. Arguments, a sign of trouble. Binks said, "Uh-huh."

He squinted. The father reached out to his son, shook him gently by the shoulder—reassurance—then the son hopped out, said something, shut the door, and trotted toward the high school. Binks pulled behind a row of cars as Jones drove past in his truck, heading out of town. Binks didn't follow him, sat and thought. Lots of reasons for a father and son to argue. Murder probably wasn't one of them.

But then again...

He put the car in gear and pulled ahead until he could look down into the lower parking lot where basketball hoops were bent like drooping lips and the garage doors of the wood shop stood closed. The high school was a long low building of blonde brick, surrounded by parking lots, a lawn out front, and a stadium out back. A sign on the building said, SMOKING AREA. Three Goths in black leather and chains, a few girls and guys in ratty pants and jean jackets, sucked on cigarettes and exhaled blue smoke. Binks shook his head. Those were the future felons of America, not the kid living next door to him.

Binks drove to the station. Clouds overhead as he crossed the parking lot. He walked in and said, "Hey sweets."

Emma's mouth, dull red lipstick on her wrinkled lips, didn't lift into a smile, she knew he'd be mad. She held out a pink slip of paper and said, "Message from Binghamton U. The Epstein boy got away."

"Those idiots." Binks glanced at the note. "Four o'clock Friday? Cummings, you take this call?"

Cummings came out of the break room, a pot of coffee in hand. Dressed in his pressed grays, stripes down the outside of his legs, Cummings said, "They called about four o'clock."

"And why didn't you call me?"

"I did. Your cell phone must've been turned off. And I just called over there and you know what? Epstein isn't his real name either. It's Albert Borque and he lives in Johnson City."

Binks didn't like being upstaged. He felt his mouth kink irritably.

Cummings sipped coffee and said, "You think it took this time?"

"What took?"

Emma chuckled. "Did she sleep with a hot water bottle on her stomach?"

"That's enough, you two." Binks crumpled the note and walked into his office, sat down, and saw the calendar with little x's by the day numbers. He sniffed. Had enough of that too. If it didn't happen this weekend, he thought, they'd do it in a Petri dish. With a buzz of ripping perforations he tore off the September sheet and stuffed it crackling into the garbage can.

Cummings appeared in the frame of the doorway, across the room. The look on his face said it: tearing off the page for September on the tenth of the month? What's wrong with you? Cummings walked out of sight when Binks shot him a look and picked up the phone. He checked the phone book and dialed. A woman's voice. Town of Union. May I direct your call? "Permits."

A male voice gruff from smoking too many cigars. Permits. "Harry, hi, it's David Binks. I'm a detective at the Endwell Substation." Oh, okay, what's up? "Just a couple questions. You know Darryl Jones?" Why? He make the ten most wanted? Binks couldn't even force a chuckle. "How many permits has he taken out this year?" For houses? Just three. Two are finished and he's got one going in his subdivision, for a client. "How about in the Town of Maine?" Yeah, a house for when he gets married. You know Frank Paganetti, the lawyer? His fiance´ works for him, and she's quite the hot number. If I sold heavy equipment I'd say she's a front loader.

Binks picked up a pen and rolled his eyes. "You know where the house is, in Maine?" On Donnelly Road, off of Wyack, along the creek there. Darryl said he's got the foundation poured, half in the woods. Shouldn't be hard to find, it's not a long road. "Thanks. And don't bother telling anyone I asked. All right?" Sure. But the last guy who called, not twenty minutes ago, he didn't say that. Didn't give his name, just wanted to know about Darryl's permits. "You told him?" Yeah, it's public information. "What did he sound like?" Slick, pleasant, a salesman type. "Uh-huh. Thanks."

Binks hung up, frowned, stood up, walked out. "Cummings?" Cummings leaned out of the supplies room, raising his eyebrows. Binks asked, "Can you do me a favor? Go over to Johnson City, to this Albert Borque's house, and pick him up. Flight, uttering, and p.c."

"P.c.?" Cummings perked up. "Something going on?"

"Drug related. I've got a lead, probable cause, but it's my next door neighbor so it might just be cop overload. You know. Can you do that for me?"

Cummings grinned. "If you take care of my dog when I go fishing next week."

"The flea bag? God forbid."

Outside, as he strode the parking lot he squinted up. Clouds moved thick and slow in the sky, the breeze heavy and warm. He climbed in and gunned the sedan, drove, traveled up through Endwell, the three intersections of the town, Hooper Road houses on plot after plot, the curve up to the high school, the hill past the middle school, and Farm to Market Road toward the airport.

He passed a long driveway littered with a tricycle and toys, picked up his cell phone and pressed a button. Voice mail. "Hello, honey? I'll be there, 10:30. I love you. Bye."

He turned onto Wyack Road, the tar broken into jigsaws. The sedan's tires whumped in potholes and he braked on a hill declining into a valley, rolled over a stream, stones dropping through the old metal grate of the bridge and plunking in the water. Death Valley Road, stony ruts, a furry pancake of road kill, and he turned at an arrow, drove until he reached a sign with a bullet hole in it. DONNELLY ROAD. Binks thought how Darryl liked to be hard to find. And hard to stomach.

He found Darryl's lot. A narrow opening had been cut into the trees, the trunks half hiding an area cleared of stumps. Binks shut off the V8 and got out. He glanced about, ambled into the hush that hung over an oval of raw dirt. A bulldozer sat in front of a backfilled foundation, the ground running level to the foundation before sloping away in the back. Tall thick-limbed spruce and hemlock trees stood guard around the clearing, the clean-sided square hole of the basement in the middle, the trees whispering and sighing with a breeze.

The evergreens swallowed his voice. "You picked a good one, Darryl."

He walked to the basement, kicked dirt chunks. The top two feet of the foundation rose above the dirt, pink foam sheathing stuck to the outside of the walls with tar foundation coating. Binks thought, That's when he got the tar on his jeans. Then he got it on the seat of his truck.

And the seat of Pangbourne's Viper?

Bulldozer tracks and crusty dirt balls surrounded the rectangle gap in the ground, but the backfill looked haphazard, half finished, or done quickly. Wouldn't Darryl do a careful job on his own house? Then again, he wouldn't be putting in the lawn until next spring. Binks walked over to the bulldozer, the blade resting on the ground, strafed to gleaming white metal by the earth it carved.

Binks stepped up onto the foundation and glanced around. An absence of tracks. "He did it and got out," he said. A single pair of boot tracks led from the bulldozer back to the road. Other than that, the prints were of Binks' wingtips from when he walked in. No tire tracks. He parked the truck on the road during the backfill. Binks stepped down off the foundation wall and thought how Jones would see his tracks and wonder who'd been there.

He stopped, looking at the ground. He bent down, scooped up a handful of dirt, loose, and let it sift between his fingers. Freshly backfilled. Hm. He brushed his hand off and didn't like it.

Binks got in the sedan and drove. Dirt roads, Farm to Market, civilization. Endwell. He looked at his watch. 10:15 a.m. He made the turns for home. Her mini-van sat in the driveway. He climbed the stone steps to the front door and stepped in.

A quiet hissing. He strolled down the hall. Showering? He stepped into their bedroom. The sheets were still tucked in on the bed. Wisps of steam escaped the bathroom, white tendrils around the door until he opened it and stepped into the moist hot air. She was showering, water splashing and sizzling off her lean white limbs and body, distorted by the pebbled glass doors.

His glance dropped to the familiar dark meeting place of her thighs, then followed the rising arc of her spine, a smooth curve, her hair like a yellow fin as she bent over bathing a long thigh, her breast quivering, the pink nipple hidden by her arm until she straightened.

She turned her head out of the streaming water and saw him through the glass. She blinked. Their glances met, her face wet, her cheeks glowing as she slid open the door. "How long have you been there?"

Water dribbled off her jaw and over her breast, the nipple erect. "A few seconds."

She beckoned. "You always come fast in the shower."

"After this weekend you want to do it this morning?"

Her fingertips traced up her wet thigh. She said, "I want it now because of this weekend." Her chin lifted, the cords tensed in her throat, and she exhaled as she hid the dark of her pubic hair with her hand. She began to touch herself, moving a finger. She smiled at him playfully and, of course, Binks pulled his tie loose.

Coming wet out of the shower, panting and spent in his loins, Binks stepped on his tie and had to find another. As he dressed by the closet, twisting a half Windsor knot below his chin, Sheila came and held him, her body wrapped in a towel and smelling of flowers. "David," she whispered.

He snugged the tie up to his collar. "What?"

"We can always adopt. Can't we?"

He smoothed down his tie. "If necessary. But it's still fun trying." He gave her a quick kiss on the lips and said, "I love you," before he opened the door and left.

As he walked down the steps and out to his car, Mrs. Kavidge across the street, a heavy-bodied grandmother type, straightened up from her rose bushes. He waved to her. Surprised, she hadn't waved back by the time he slid into the sedan. He drove. No more time to fool around. On Hooper, instead of turning off toward the high school he drove straight. Hooper Road ended at Taft Avenue that climbed to the high top of a ridge and dropped down the other side to where it became Twist Run Road. Twist Run Road led to where Green Meadow Way opened on the other side of the crossroads.

Binks remembered when a nine-hole golf course lay on the land Darryl bought, a smooth fairway inclining to a hilltop. The club went broke and the land grew weeds for twenty years. Not the best of locations for a housing development, steep roads in three directions, so Binks knew Darryl bought the land cheap and was making a ton of money off it. He drove past houses all twice the size of his own, well appointed, skillfully built. Yes, he had to admit it. Darryl was a grumpy jerk, but he'd built some very fine houses.

At the top of the street he spotted Darryl's pickup, a newer full-size truck, and a showroom Mercedes Benz convertible shimmering along its fenders. He stopped behind the ragtop, opened the door of the sedan, and climbed out. The smell of oil from the newly tarred road hung in the air. Banging in the half-finished house, shuffling sounds, he strolled across the dirt of the front yard, glancing around. The house, plywood and foam sheeting on the shell, had the roof on, no windows in, no front door, and the porch was a shelf of dirt and gravel inside a concrete footer.

A drip inside the house, spat...spat...spat.

Darryl appeared in the doorway, jumped down to the gravel porch, and opened the lunch box in his hand. "Binks," he asked, "are you following me?"

Darryl took a crackling bite of an apple. Binks gave him the deadpan look. "This is business, Darryl, so don't give me a hard time."

Boots thumped downstairs from the second floor. A man with a tee-shirt stretched over a big round gut sat down suddenly in the doorway, blocking the entrance, a metal coffee jug in his hand. Flushed, sweaty, he threw a quick glance at Binks and jerked the cup off the jug.

"Mudgie," Darryl blurted, "this is Binks, my next door neighbor. The state trooper."

Mudgie glanced at Binks, nodded, and quickly looked down to unscrew the cap off his jug. Binks tilted his head and looked at them. Darryl asked, "So what's up, Binks, old buddy?"

Binks looked at them, half closing one eye, a look that unnerved people. The jowly carpenter slurped coffee, glanced at him and down, crossed his arm over the top of his gut, but not before Binks saw his shirt. Against the shadow of sweat, flecked with bits of sawdust, a line of red spots crossed the crest of his belly. Blood? Binks narrowed his eyes. The man's hand had the fine tremor of adrenalin.

Darryl said, "Cat got your tongue, Dave?"

Binks watched his reaction. "I'm investigating the disappearance of a crack dealer from New York, a kid by the name of Fisher Pangbourne. You know anything about it?"

Darryl snorted. "Sure, I buy crack all the time. Don't I look like a crack head? Mudgie?"

Mudgie chuckled a bit too hard. "You're cracked in the head, if that's what you mean."

Darryl bit his McIntosh. Binks squinted. The skin of the apple had sawdust stuck to it, but Darryl was chewing away like nothing was wrong.

Something was wrong, Binks could feel it. He glanced out at the street. "Who owns the convertible?"

Darryl shrugged. "A neighbor maybe, I don't keep track. Why would I know anything about a crack dealer?"

The cell phone rang on Binks' belt and he raised it to his ear. "Binks here." Dave? Emma's voice, the tone of it. "Cummings found him?" At home. Shot to death. A long tightening silence. Binks glanced away from the house, from Darryl. "When?" Sometime early in the weekend. Binks' mind lurched. He wanted Darryl to hear it so he said, "Rigor mortis?" Advanced. That's not all. The kid had housemates. And customers. "How many?" Six. Six in all.

Binks felt himself go still. "Six?" Looking at Darryl, Binks said, "Call Albany. I'm on my way."

He cut off the call and started for the sedan; but half way across the front yard he stopped and turned. Darryl and Mudgie were looking at him, the fear plain on their faces.

"If nobody's told you, Darryl," Binks said, "you're a wise ass son-of-a-bitch. But these people are lethal. Don't be a fool. If you know anything, tell me."

Darryl recovered his cocky front. "Sure, Dave. Thanks for the compliment."

CHAPTER 11

Binks did a U-turn in his big blue copmobile and took off like a bat out of hell. As he went Mudgie and I turned and scrambled inside and upstairs to the second floor bedroom where that dead Rasta giant lay like a fallen tree with branches all bloody and dripping.

Holy Hannah. We just looked at him. A big blotch of blood surrounded his head. The bloody two-by-four Mudgie used to beat him to death lay there, red-tipped nails that I shot into his face scattered around, a slug hole splintered in the floor, and the revolver on it.

Mudgie whispered, "Stinks like hell in here."

It stank with the fire and brimstone of hell and burnt gunpowder. I said, "Go get that tarp in my truck. A couple pair of gloves too, we gotta wrap him up, get him out of here." My hands shook, I scratched my forehead, and Mudgie looked down at the Rasta giant staring into his own blood that was soaking into the plywood floor.

I picked up the revolver, popped out the spinning part of it, and looked at the shells. Big loads, .357 magnums. Holding that gun, Mudgie staring at the bloody two-by-four and looking upset, it hit me how close I'd been to buying the farm. I mumbled, "Thanks."

Pudgie Mudgie looked at me holding the gun. "He would've shot us, but we're still going straight to hell."

"What? I kill a crack dealer last Friday and you tell me to forget about it. Today we kill his hit man and we're going to hell? Sweet Jesus, get the damn tarp!"

I pushed him out the door. He clumped downstairs and left me alone with that Rasta, huge, tree-like, dead, bloody. I didn't want to touch him. Had to. I slapped the dead man's pockets but didn't feel any car keys. Must be in the ignition. I hefted the revolver. What the hell do I do with it? The same as Fisher's, I stuck it in my lunchbox, next to the raisins.

I stumbled up. Crack dealer? Binks said Fisher was a crack dealer. Paul? Oh my god, you're not... I closed my mouth, couldn't swallow, the fear rising into my craw.

"Mudgie, hurry up!"

Mudgie came back with a blue plastic tarp, some old rope, and two pair of canvas work gloves. Clumsy in the gloves, we rolled the Rasta tree onto the tarp, wrapped it around him, folded over the ends and with the rope, tied it all into a neat package.

"Come on." Mudgie looked like he was about to sit down and give up, so I snapped at him, "Don't flake out on me! Let's get him down to the dining room, then you can drive the car out back and we'll put him in the trunk."

"What car?"

"The Mercedes. We can't leave it parked there, they'll figure out it was his and know something's up." We grabbed the dead man's legs, wrapped up neat and clean, and dragged him downstairs, his head thumping on every tread. Gallows humor. I said, "I can't believe you. You beat his head in and then got scared about what your wife would think."

We dropped his legs, a seven-foot blue package bound in rope. Out beyond the raw dirt of the back yard stood the stump, the pond beyond, and the overgrown golf course. Mudgie said, "If you worried more about what your wife was thinking you might still be married."

"Shut the hell up! Why'd you say that?"

He stopped in the doorway. "I just killed somebody and your kid was selling his crack. The first commandment, thou shalt not kill, well god damn I never thought I'd break that one!"

"The car, okay, just go get it." I pointed toward the front. "Go!"

He drove the Mercedes ragtop, metal shipping bands jangling off the muffler, around to the rear of the house, and backed it up to the doorway. The trunk lid popped up as I tried to haul out the dead Rasta tree by myself— oomph, no way, too heavy—but with the both of us heaving on the heavy end we got the big blue package out the door and thump, half into the trunk.

Clunk. The shocks on the Mercedes bottomed out, half of the package draped off the chrome bumper. Mudgie bent the legs, stuffed the feet in, I shoved and pushed on the folded Rasta tree, but he wouldn't fit, so I lost it. I kicked him, gave him a couple hard stomps, and something broke, crack! He was all in there, I slammed the trunk and looked at Mudgie.

"There you go. Nice and neat."

Mudgie bent over and threw up, barf splashing his new boots. Then he straightened up, scowling and wiping his mouth. He looked at the trunk and shivered. "Where to?"

"First we gotta cut that flooring out and get rid of the bloodstains. No way I'm leaving that for Binks to find."

I got my circular saw and cut out a three-foot square of the floor. Mudgie zipped a patch off a scrap piece of decking, and with a few bangs we nailed it in place. It didn't look too odd, so we did the same thing on the first floor where the blood dripped into the kitchen. I gave Mudgie the keys to the Codger and opened the driver's door of the Mercedes.

Door? It was so small it was more like a lid. About to get in, I stopped. Mudgie hadn't moved. I said, "What?"

"Why should I drive your junker?"

"Because."

"Because why?"

"Don't be a doofus. What's it matter?"

"I may not get another chance to drive a convertible," he snapped, "before I go to jail!"

I waited out back until I heard the Codger, out front, fart blue smoke, cough, and ready herself to roll. I fit myself into the coup, my boots too big for the foot pedals, and slipped it into gear. It must've been a tight fit for the Rasta tree too. I figured he stole it, so I deduced that we didn't kill one of the good guys and that made me feel better. Didn't matter. I drove out to the street, jumpy and biting a fingernail, Mudgie looking pissed behind the wheel of the Codge. I let him take the lead.

Green Meadow Way, as usual during the afternoon, was empty, all the resident yuppies gone to more exciting pastures. If they only knew. We coasted down the unblemished blacktop to the stop sign at Twist Run Road, the road to the right twisting down between the rocky walls of an old river gorge, the road rising steeply to the left. Mudgie turned left and I followed the Codger as she chugged up Sally Piper Road.

The Mercedes shifted like butter even though I was wearing canvas work gloves. We kept to the back roads, down into the dip past Endwell Greens golf club, and up the other side. For a minute on Robinson Hill Road, the whole valley, the floodplain of the Susquehanna River, spread below us. I glanced out over the quiet lives of a hundred thousand people. The blight had arrived, I thought, and all those folks didn't even know it.

We took a right at the bottom of the hill, a hard left at the Hess Gas Station, and turned in at the mall. Acre after acre of striped parking spaces spread all around the giant building. Sears, Victoria's Secret, the Cheesecake Factory, the Oakdale Mall had all you could ever ask for. I parked the Mercedes in the middle of hundreds of other cars, stuffed a note in under the windshield, BE BACK SOON, and opened my lunchbox. I dumped the Rasta man's blue pistol out onto the passenger seat and slid out.

Looking in, I hesitated. Yeah, take it. I reached in, grabbed the revolver, stuck it back in with the little box of raisins, and shut the top of my lunchbox. I slammed the tiny door of the sports coupe and locked it. Looking around, Mudgie got out from behind the wheel and hurried around to the passenger door. I was so tense my neck hurt. Looking around, relieved to see not a soul in sight, I hustled my butt onto the busted cushions of my trusty truck and pulled out, the engine groaning.

I glanced over at Mudgie and tried to lighten up a little. "I feel bad leaving him at the mall for eternity."

"They'll find him when the white sales are over."

I nursed the truck out of the mall exit, past the gas station, and made her rumble and grind up Robinson Hill Road, back the way we came past the racquet club. Mudgie didn't say anything. I knew he was thinking something, which bothered me, so I had to crack him open.

"Mudgie, listen to me."

"Where is it?"

"What? Where's what?"

"The Rasta man's gun?"

I shrugged. "Why?"

He grabbed my lunchbox and yanked it open. "Are you crazy!"

"We might need it."

"We? What's this 'we' shit? I'm not part of your family. I'm just an employee!"

Ah, the old pet peeve. I wanted to punch the wheel but just squeezed it and said, "Just listen to me, okay."

"No, don't tell me. It's your gang, you'll get half the loot and the rest of us will split the other half. Hey, that's a great deal for Pudgie Mudgie and his fat wife, Marge the Barge. I know what you say about us."

"You know what I say? I don't know what I'd do without you. No kidding, ask Vince." It was old stuff, so it pissed me off. "But do I have to remind you of how we met? You were flat on your ass drunk. I got you to dry out and that's when we decided to go into business together. But you turned into a beer fish again and that's when I had to start it by myself. Remember? Do you?"

He remembered. He looked out the window and chewed a fingernail. He went dry for about five years after that, then started drinking again, and I would've let that sleeping dog lie except he gave it a kick. He said, "As if you don't lift a few."

I shut the lunchbox and drove.

"Not like you. We go to the Pine Inn, I stay for an hour and have a couple beers. You stay two hours and have six, then three more at home so you can pass out. Me, I go home and do two or three hours on Quicken—the computer, get it, the accounting program?—pay bills, order prints, estimate jobs."

He glared out the window. "I'm not drunk every night. I go fishing."

"But according to you, if I worried more about what Lynn was thinking she'd still be around. Did I have time to ask her how she's feeling? And now Paul's been smoking crack for three months and I never knew it. I'm always down in my damn office!"

He started to say something, but I cut him off.

"Your drinking, it's bad again and it bothers me. Like I said, I don't know what I'd do without you. I don't want to see anything happen to you. You're my best friend. I love you, Mudgie, I need you, and I'm scared shitless. Don't you know that? Can't you see that?"

He chewed his thumb. The Codger groaned beneath us. He looked out the window at the passing homesteads. He said, "I am the best thing that ever happened to you."

I snorted, he was half right, and he laughed because he was half joking.

"One of the best," I said. "But seriously, Mudgie, you're one of the two pillars I lean on. The other one was Lynn, and then she took off. I would've fallen apart if it weren't for you and Vince. And now this with the crack dealer? I hate it, that you're mixed up in it, and that Paul and Carla are covering for me. I killed that kid and it didn't have to happen. It was just my temper, I just lost it."

Mudgie finally looked over at me. "He had a gun. He threatened you with it."

"He was a dumb kid, it was all bluff. But now..." I coasted down the steep tilt of Twist Run Road, toward where my street opened. I felt overwhelmed and all but defeated. I said, "And now we killed that Rasta man. What the hell, I feel..."

"That was self-defense. We've got a bullet hole in the floor to prove it. But, Darryl..." Mudgie had to clear his throat before he said it. "When I grabbed that board and, and killed him, all I knew was...you know...I couldn't let him hurt you."

I turned the Codger onto the smooth blacktop of Green Meadow Way, the street that Darryl and Mudgie built, and pushed the gas pedal. What Mudgie said sank in for about five seconds. I felt it, how big it was—who else would kill someone for me?—and it was a very quiet moment I will never forget.

I won't forget it because it lasted five seconds and then I saw them parked at the top of the street, behind Mudgie's truck. A white SUV with three men in it.

I spun the wheel. "It's them!"

"Who?"

"The crack dealers!"

I wheeled into a U-turn. Mudgie shouted, "They see us!"

I backed out, empty cans clanged in the bed, and I thought the Codger was going to choke when I stomped the gas pedal. She lurched, papers flying off the dash, and in my mirror I saw the SUV pull out and grow big.

"They're on us!"

"I know!"

We stood no chance going uphill so I turned down Twist Run Road, the Codge creaking and clattering, tools crashing in the back, Mudgie hugging the door. The SUV was on our bumper in seconds. We roared down between the rocky walls of Twist Run Road, the road living up to its name, guardrails swerving along a whitewater brook, a face full of wrath in my side view mirror. Pangbourne? I could see them all, a white guy driving, a small guy on the passenger side, a black guy in the back seat.

Mudgie shouted, "What're we gonna do?"

"I don't know!"

We were swerving at sixty miles an hour. The SUV roared up beside us. I swerved, bang! The Codger got another crunch, the SUV skidded, tires screeching, and I could see Pangbourne cursing in my mirror.

Mudgie shouted, "Head for the Inn!"

"I am!"

We barreled down toward the end of Twist Run Road. Stop sign. I slammed on the brakes. The Codger slid twenty feet, rubber screaming, and Mudgie slammed against the dashboard.

"Christ, Darryl!"

"I had to!"

The SUV slid up beside us. I looked over at the Spanish guy in the passenger seat. He jerked a pistol out of his coat and pointed it at me. I spun the Codger as I heard a crack! A white-rimmed bullet hole appeared in the windshield.

"Holy shit!" Crack! Another hole. Mudgie yanked open my lunchbox. God bless him, he grabbed the blue revolver, twisted around, and fired, boooooooom! I couldn't hear anything, the cab filled with thin smoke.

"Out the window!"

Mudgie's shot speckled my back window with gunpowder, bullet holes pocked the glass, then the cracking came fast behind us and a slug shattered my rear view mirror. Mudgie hunched with a curse and dove to the floor. "Faster!"

"It's all she's got!"

"No, faster!"

We barreled over the bridge over Nanticoke Creek and hit Route 26. Heavy traffic. Shit! I didn't stop, cranked the wheel, the Codger slid, horns blared, squealing tires, the truck sliding, a shout, a crunch of metal, and we rolled toward Endicott.

A quarter mile to the Pine Inn. Oh god help us. Help us!

"Are they still coming?" Gunshots, Mudgie ducked to the floor.

Neon beer signs in the window, a little sign over the road, I swerved into the gravel parking lot of the inn, slammed on the brakes, and threw open the door before we even stopped. I ran to the entrance, looked back, thumps and clunks in the truck. What the hell? I ran back and yanked open the passenger door. Mudgie was stuck between the dash and the seat, the crack of his ass showing above his jeans. I grabbed his belt and dragged him out, he fell in the gravel, jumped up, and we staggered for the inn.

The SUV skidded outside as I threw open the door and charged inside. As I expected, Vince was on his usual bar stool. I shouted, "They're right behind us!"

"Who?"

"Crack dealers! Trying to kill us! Can we—"

"Go!" Vince threw me his car keys. As we ran for a door on the other side, Vince, wearing a dress shirt, striped tie and Dockers, grabbed a pool cue. Charlie the bartender leaped over the bar in his pizza-stained apron. Two guys in jeans and crusty work boots, day laborers, one hefting a beer pitcher and the other gripping a cue stick, stood jumpy on the other side of the door.

Yeah, some guys love to fight. Not me. Mudgie's boots clunking behind me, I ran straight for the far exit. As I hauled open that door the crack dealers from New York barged in on the other side.

A pistol went off, a slug hit the door, it shivered in my hand. A yell. The pistol blasted, shouts, a scream ripped the air, then we were out and the door slammed. Muffled curses. Vince's Cadillac, a big-bodied cruiser, dark green, sat right there so I popped the locks and we jumped in.

Mudgie shouted, "Get moving!"

I twisted the key, "Shit shit shit!" I couldn't tell the engine was running until I gunned it.

"Haul ass!"

I yanked the shift into reverse and backed out, stomped the pedal, tires threw gravel and we hit the blacktop with rubber screeching, a cloud of dust behind us. I took advantage of the Caddy's muscle. Trees blurred, houses whipped past. Mudgie twisted around to look.

"See anyone?"

"Nobody. Holy Toledo, that was...damn crazy."

Nobody showed in the mirrors. I slowed the Caddie. "Lemme borrow your cell phone."

He handed it over. I thumbed Frank Paganetti's buttons. After four rings his wife Zelda croaked into the phone. Hello, Frank's office. "Carla there?" She's in back. Is this Darryl? "Yeah, hurry up."

"What are you doing?" Mudgie asked.

Carla's voice. Hello? Darryl? All tensed, I sagged. What's wrong?

"We gotta see a lawyer. Did you make that appointment?"

No, they're booked solid. Why?

"Dammit. Those New York guys, maniacs, we gotta go to the police. Call 'em."

What happened?

"I'll tell you later."

Tell me now!

"I can't, really, I'm sorry. I love you, bye."

I cut off the call and dropped the cell phone. "How come you can spring for that?"

"For what?"

"The phone. I can't."

Mudgie rubbed his mouth, he needed a drink. "No kids. You're going to the cops?"

"Damn straight. We keep you out of it, totally, you don't know squat, not a thing. All right?" Mudgie nodded and chewed his thumb, the one he hit with a hammer, his jowl shaking under his chin, his eyes troubled. I said, "You all right?"

"Yeah. You?"

"Worried. They might go looking for Paul."

"What are we doing now?"

"Circling back. I'll drop you off at your truck—I don't think they'll go back to the subdivision today—then I'll drop this beast at the Pine Inn and get the Codger back. Take the kids, go see a lawyer, call the police, drop out of sight. That's what I should've done first thing. Damn, this is nut-job crazy."

"Got that right."

By the time I dropped Mudgie at his truck on Green Meadow Way, looking around all the time, a few BMWs were already parked neatly in the driveways along my street. I looked out the door at him. I said, "Watch your backside."

He saluted as I cruised out. The canyon of Twist Run Road looked different, it scared me to think we took it at 60 miles an hour; but the real scare came at the Pine Inn. Police cars, ambulances, flashers, staties, county sheriffs. Not the right time to face them, I kept going. Vince could get his Caddy back later. I drove through Endicott, up into Endwell, and home.

4:00 p.m. I parked the Caddy two houses up the street, beyond Binks' house, but nothing moved up and down Verna Drive, no unusual cars, nothing suspicious. I got out and walked up our front steps to the door. I stood on the porch, looked up and down the street, opened the door and stepped in. I stood just inside the threshold, listening.

The crackle of a potato chip bag. "Paul?"

"Dad?" He appeared from the bedroom hallway, tossled hair, knee-length shorts, purple tee-shirt, a bag of potato chips in hand. He saw me and his eyes went serious. "What's up? You look like crap."

"Helluva day. Where's your sister?"

"At the Kavidge's. What happened?"

"We're going to the lawyers. Those people are maniacs, they tried to kill me and Mudgie today." I stepped to the door and looked up and down the street. All clear. I said, "Stay inside," stepped out, skipped down the front steps and started across Verna Drive.

A blue mini-van rose out of Lyndale Drive. It was Sheila Binks. She waved to me as she pulled into her driveway but I wasn't in the mood to wave back. I walked past Mrs. Kavidge's rose bushes, all the flowers snipped off, and at the Kavidge's front door I pressed the doorbell. No answer, I pressed it again. Bing bong inside but no one came.

I opened the screen door and stepped in. The house stood dim, the curtains dulling the sunlight coming in the windows. It was a small house, the living room beyond a waist high divider with plants along the top, the kitchen opening to the right. No one in the kitchen, but Mr. Kavidge was sitting in his Barcalounger in the living room.

The smell of his cigar always reminded me of my grandfather. "Mr. Kavidge?"

No reply. He was sleeping, the curve of his bald head shining, his chin to his chest, a newspaper clutched in his hand. I sniffed. Odd stink. I squinted. That was odd too. His pants were smoking.

"Patty!" It was his cigar, still lit. It was charring the cloth of his pants. "Patty!"

Mr. Kavidge was dead, a bullet hole between his eyes, blood leaking down the bridge of his nose. I ran upstairs to the bedrooms. "Patty!"

I jumped downstairs to the first floor, spun around the railing, leaped downstairs to the basement, and ran into a laundry room. "Oh god, holy Christ!" Mrs. Kavidge lay on the floor in a pool of blood. I rolled her over. She'd been shot once in the chest and once in the forehead. "Oh my...my god. Patty!"

No answer. I stumbled against the washing machine, holding my head. No. God dammit, no!

Yes, they took her.

CHAPTER 12

Binks walked toward 124 Kinsey Road, green-and-white squad cars of the Vestal P.D. parked all around the bungalow, yellow perimeter tape fluttering across the front. He knew the suit who came to greet him, Carl "Bumpy" McCaffrey, wide at the hips, curly red hair cresting at two inches over five feet, three fatty tumors the size of dimes marring his brow and an attitude to match.

Binks wasn't in the mood. McCaffrey blurted, "Binks, yeah, I heard about the six in J.C. Now we got two here. You call the Feds?"

"What do you think?" They strode up the driveway, Binks eyeing four tire ghosts on the blacktop. He asked, "Make and model?"

"A Mercedes convertible. The car's worth as much as the house." McCaffrey nodded to a 10-year-old sedan, a rusty four-door. "Left the wife's car, and the kid too."

"A kid where? Here?"

McCaffrey rubbed his bumps and motioned. Cops milled around the driveway and back porch, the same as at Albert Borque's house. Bodies there too, all three floors, dead kids, crack cocaine, and it was all linked, Binks knew it.

Who was the missing key and where was he?

As McCaffrey led him up the back steps a uniformed cop moved aside. They shuffled into a country kitchen, glowing maple cabinets, linoleum patterned with yellow and blue flowers. Eight of those flowers were covered with rust, a dead man's blood dried beneath him.

"Three shots," McCaffrey said, "one before he had the door open." He pointed to a bullet hole in the door glass. "Stumbled back, took two more and fell."

McCaffrey stepped past the dead husband, toward the dead wife. Face up, she'd been in her early thirties, curly auburn hair, flimsy bathrobe, panties. and a tee-shirt.

"Looks like she heard the shot," McCaffrey said, "came downstairs, turned the corner, and took one through the forehead."

"Stumbled back and hit the floor dead."

McCaffrey nodded. "The one's in J.C. any different?"

"Some, but definitely professional. You mentioned a kid?"

McCaffrey motioned and they took the stairs, their shoes husky in the shag. The Irishman turned his wide hips and stepped through a doorway, past a plainclothes cop Binks didn't know. A child's bedroom, Winnie the Pooh wallpaper, Tigger too, and the bed looked like a little choo-choo train.

A female cop sat with a thirty-pound girl in her lap, a child modeled on her mother, curly auburn hair, teary cheeks.

The cop glanced up, regret cramping her lips. Her nameplate read Offcr. Tate. Tate said, "A man came up the stairs and pointed a gun at her, but couldn't shoot her."

McCaffrey said, "Couldn't?"

"Couldn't." Tate looked at the little girl and wiped the tears off her cheeks. "Right, honey?"

The girl nodded and sniffed. Tate stroked the girl's cheek with long feminine fingers, the nails clipped short. She said, "Chelsea? What did the man look like?" Chelsea cried a little, looked up at Binks and McCaffrey. Tate said, "Was his hair like mommy's or daddy's?"

"Daddy's. Where is daddy?"

Binks' cell phone chortled at his belt, startled Chelsea, and the two Vestal cops looked at him. Binks walked out into the hallway and opened the phone. "Binks here." Dave? Sheila's voice. "What? I'm in the middle of—" Get over here, I'm home. Darryl's here. Mr. and Mrs. Kavidge are dead and his daughter's been kidnapped.

That stunned him into silence. It stretched, snapped, and he clipped his words. "On my way. Twenty minutes." He cut off the call and leaned into the bedroom. McCaffrey looked up, rubbing his bumps. "I'll keep you posted."

He skipped downstairs, skirted the wife, skipped past the husband, out the back door and along the drive. The Kavidges? "God dammit!" The uniforms parted. He jumped into his blue unmarked and burnt tread. Drove. Called Forensics. Walt here. "Any prints on the Viper?" Negative. That you, Binks?

He cut off Walt and called his office. "The Feds call?" Serial homicide's on the way. Dave? "What now?" We got a call an hour ago from Binghamton P.D., a missing persons for a Cassandra Williams, a sorority girl. He rolled his eyes. "Put it on the list. There's two more cases and a possible abduction."

My god, this is crazy. You heard about the Pine Inn? "Yes, but this one's my neighbors."

He hit excess speed climbing the steep pitch of Pruyne Street, the car screeching on a tilt as he turned onto Verna Drive, where he made the sedan hurtle the last half mile and skid to the curb.

He jumped out and ran across to the Kavidge's. Stopped. Listened for a moment. Silence. Gingerly he opened the screen door by the rim of the knob. He stepped into the dim house and saw Mr. Kavidge dead in the Barcalounger. Sheila appeared outside, a shape moving beyond the screen.

"Stay out."

"Darryl said she's downstairs."

The stairs creaked as he descended into the basement. Old sofa, throw rug, and a 16-inch TV. Across the room a door with glass let in light from the garage. The light fell on Mrs. Kavidge, staring up from a halo of her own blood. He knelt over her. Deceased, her face recorded the terror of her last moments.

Nice old Polish lady, that's all she was.

The stairs were harder to climb than to come down. When he reached the top he looked over at Mr. Kavidge and said, "Where's Darryl?"

Sheila beyond the screen door. "Home. He's in bad shape."

Binks stepped over to Mr. Kavidge, who looked asleep except for the bullet hole in his forehead. Binks carefully lifted the burning cigar off Mr. Kavidge's pants and lay it in an ashtray with a ceramic bulldog leaning over the lip. He said, "Darryl say anything?"

Sheila said, "They want a ransom."

"What's he doing?"

"Calling his bank."

"Oh great." Binks couldn't think, pushed open the screen door, sighed, and waved back at the house of the dead, the third that morning, and hardly noticed when Sheila touched his sleeve. He shook his head, scowling, and said, "There's too many, I'm losing track. Where's Darryl?"

"I told you, in his house."

Binks motioned for Sheila to go home, and as he climbed the steps to Darryl's porch he felt his teeth clench. People like Darryl, too stupid to know they're stupid, bothered him.

"Hello?"

Silence. He opened the screen door and stepped in. The living room, nobody. Sniffling sounds, he walked through a doorway into the kitchen.

Paul, the kid, sat at the table, his head in his hands, flushed, his cheeks streaked with tears, eyes glistening as he looked up at Binks.

"Where's your father?"

A noise beyond a door. Binks opened it and looked down a stairwell of worn treads, a light at the bottom, in the basement. Darryl barged out of the doorway of his office and started up the stairs.

"Binks! They took her, Patty, my seven-year-old." He barged into the kitchen, papers in hand, deeds, legal documents. "I need your help, dammit, but you can't tell anybody."

"What are you doing? Darryl? You can't do business with kidnappers."

"The hell I can't." Darryl grabbed the phone. "They want $160,000. I'll fork it over, get her back, and kill every damn one of them."

"You and whose army? Is it Blake Pangbourne?"

"How should I know? Hello?" Darryl turned around and around, pacing, his hands shaking as he spoke into the phone. "Yeah, Vincent Donadio please."

"What are you doing?"

"Mortgaging my land. Hello, Vince?"

"With a loan shark? No!"

Binks slapped the cradle, cutting off the call. Darryl threw the handset, grabbed Binks and shoved him back, a chair tipping over, a skillet clattering on the stove as they slammed against it. Instantaneous. The cop gripped his hand and squeezed. "Ah...Binks!" Darryl dropped to his knees, gasping, fell over kicking in pain as Binks squeezed his thumb against its joint. "Stop! Binks I—"

"Will you listen?"

"All right! Let go!" Binks let him loose. Darryl curled up on the linoleum, Paul looking terrified as Darryl held his hand. "Damn, Binks, you lousy fuck! You damn near..."

Darryl pushed himself up and sat with his back against the cupboards under the sink. Binks shoved the table back against the refrigerator to give himself a clear view of Darryl, down on the floor.

"First off," he said, "you don't deal with kidnappers. Besides, Blake Pangbourne doesn't care about money, he's got plenty. So? Why did he take Patty? Spill it."

Paul blurted, "It's my fault."

Darryl kicked the table leg. "Shut up!"

"Why? Was it crack?"

"Shut up!"

Paul nodded and wiped his cheeks. "I was smoking it and I got behind."

Darryl let his head hang, groaned, and squeezed his eyes shut. Binks asked, "And?"

"I took him...um, Fisher...up to meet Dad and they—"

"We got in an argument." Darryl shook his injured hand. "Fisher wanted five thousand dollars, I said no, so he got in his car and drove away. That's all we know."

Binks looked at Paul, the kid puffy-eyed, his lower lip quivering. "Is that true? Is that what happened?"

Paul's hands were shaking and he looked sick. He nodded. "I don't feel so good."

"No doubt," Darryl snapped, "all the garbage you been smoking. Crack too? And you, Binks, you know it all now, so will you help us?"

"Where is he? Where'd he take her?"

"He's gonna call back. If I don't bring him $160,000 and tell him where his brother is, he's gonna kill Patty. He said if I call the police he'll kill her."

"Then why did you run over to my house?"

"He wouldn't know you're a cop, just my neighbor. He said someone's watching us. That's why you can't tell anyone, dammit. Binks, I need your help. Please?" Darryl's face flushed, crumpled, he was about to crack, but he pulled himself together. "Please? Binks, please?"

Binks watched Paul duck out the door, hunching.

"Darryl," he said, "did you hear me? You don't do business with kidnappers, ever. These are the same people who shot your buddies at the Pine Inn, so we're—"

"Who?" Darryl struggled to his feet. "Shot who? At the inn?"

"The bartender and an older man, Vince something." Darryl rolled against the counter, turned away, leaned over the sink. He blinked, and for the first time he wanted to cry. Binks said, "A friend? Not anymore. But the black guy with the shaved head, he's dead too. Apparently someone hit him with a blunt object. Many times."

The telephone rang. They looked at it. Binks grabbed it.

"Hello?" Darryl watched from the counter, deflated. Binks blinked. He said, "I live next door, I'm a friend, I'm coming with him." Darryl swallowed an ache in his throat. Binks said, "No, I'm coming. We have to take my car, you shot his truck full of holes."

Binks gestured, scribbling in the air, and Darryl snatched paper and pencil for him. Binks wrote and said, "Just don't hurt her. How do we...?" He looked at Darryl and said, "My cell number is 607-755-2424. I..."

Buzzing handset, Binks hung it up. "We're heading for New York City."

Darryl leaned over the sink, thinking of Vince. Dead? Vince? Absently he whispered, "We?"

"I don't have a choice now, do I? And you're right, you need help, a lot of it."

Darryl shook his hand, almost back to normal, and felt the fear surge through him. He scooped papers off the table and headed for the door. "And a lotta money."

"The money isn't the point!"

Darryl burst outside and the clump of his boots faded. Binks rubbed his brow, Blake Pangbourne's last words still resonating in his thoughts. If he doesn't know where Fisher is, the girl is dead. Dead! But why repeat that to Darryl? What would it accomplish?

He raised his head as Darryl's boots clumped back up the steps and he yanked open the door. "What the hell?" Binks heard it too. Vomiting. Noticing the play of Darryl's shoulder muscles through his tee-shirt, he followed him into the bedroom hallway.

First bedroom, Darryl ducked in. Clothes all about, messy desk, the air sour with the smell of stomach bile, Paul on the bed and vomiting his guts out into the crack between the mattress and the wall.

"Paul, what?" Darryl bent over him. "What is it?"

The kid looked terrified. Binks said, "Withdrawals."

"From coke? Crack? You been smoking—"

"No!" A spasm wracked the kid. "I didn't, not crack, I..."

Binks stepped in from the doorway and twisted Paul's arm, looked at it. Nothing.

"The hell are you doing?"

Binks grabbed Paul's foot, jerked off the kid's sneaker, shucked off his sock and there they were, tiny scabs between his toes. Needle marks. The dots of dried blood climbed the top of his foot, ghostly purple bruises over the veins. Darryl's mouth fell open.

Binks said, "Heroin."

"Jesus Christ!" Darryl turned around, throwing up his hands, air hissing through his clenched teeth. He grabbed the chair at the desk and swung it up, bang! It hit the ceiling, he brought it down, wood crackling as the legs shattered off the floor, then he flung it crackling in the corner.

Darryl slapped his son's leg. "He was a nice guy? He was cool?"

CHAPTER 13

Scooby looked over at Blake, driving with his hands clenched on the wheel, a cigarette between his knuckles, his jaw set, smoke jetting out of his nose like some crazy bull. Yeah, he a loco bull all right, Scooby thought.

He glanced into the back seat, the little girl letting out squeaky whines under the blanket. It all felt bad, all crazy ever since Norbert and Eduard killed that blonde, out in the woods. Now here was another one, little one, more of a know nothin' thing to do. She gonna die too? Didn't seem like a thing anybody should do.

Blake said, "Speak up or shut up. You're mumbling."

A nervous drag on a butt and Scooby tasted menthol.

"Blake, man, this crazy," Scooby said. "Kidnappin' her, smokin' the babysitter, them college boys, and the rednecks in that bar. How many people you take out when you get the ragtop? Now Eduard and Norbert dead too and their people gonna be pissed. Over-the-top, Blake, you crazy."

The first thing after they charged into the bar was Norbert shooting a redneck in his red throat, after which another redneck broke Norbert's hand with a beer pitcher. Norbert dropped his gun, Scooby grabbed it, but when he stood up something exploded on the back of his neck. The bartender's pool cue. Blake's gun blasted and the barkeep's apron turned bloody as he fell. Norbert fell, guys beating on him, more deafening shots, shattering glass, shards tingling down on them as Blake dragged Scooby back out the door, still clutching Norbert's gun.

So now the chrome-plated pistol lay on the seat between them. Scooby shook his head and said, "What happen back at the fat boy's place? You gone loco, man."

Suddenly the gun wasn't on the seat, it was in Blake's hand, its dark eye looking at Scooby, who froze with smoke going down his throat.

"Call me crazy again, you greasy P.R., and I'll rip your eyes out."

"Okay, be cool. Be cool! Come on, I dint mean nothin'!" Tense silence, Scooby coughed out the smoke. He said, "Blake, come on."

Blake sniffed and lowered the gun to his lap. Scooby felt his insides go slack. But he had to know some things, it was time to ask.

"Swain," he asked, "you tell him what happen? And why we go to Buffalo and smoke that guy, shoot his car full of holes? Fisher another thing, right?"

Blake tapped the steering wheel with the pistol.

"The guy in Buffalo was a rat, a mole," he said. "It was a favor to that branch, a public favor, a 'demonstration.' I told you: we have stakeholders. He flipped on one of them, went to the Feds, so…"

A Trans Am, black and low-slung, caught them and came abreast on the left, a young woman behind the wheel, her big curly blonde hair turning as she looked over at them. Her face froze as Blake raised Norbert's chrome pistol and scratched his forehead with the muzzle. Blake looked over at her, she looked away, and Scooby kept his mouth shut.

"No," Blake said, "I didn't tell Swain, but Norbert and Ed's people…well…they'll go ballistic, but not at me. At Jones."

He unclipped his cell phone, flipped it open, thumbed two numbers, and listened. A tribal grunt of a greeting. He said, "Get Big Johnson. It's me, Blake."

Blake hit the gas, the stripes on the highway blurred, the tires sang higher, they gained on the blonde in the Trans Am, her curly hair bigger than her headrest. They were eastbound. Below and left was the westbound highway, the valley of green fields and hill farms looking perfect as a jigsaw puzzle, little black cube-like barns here and there, bridge over a sparkling stream, hawks floating like ashes over a fireplace.

Blake hit the gas, hypercharge, and the tires went soprano. The red splint of the speedometer edged past eighty. Scooby watched the blonde's head tilt as she checked the mirror, the Trans Am picked up speed and kept ahead. Blake pressed the phone to his cheek and pushed the pedal, 83, 84, 85.

A tinny voice on the phone. Blake said, "Big Johnson?" He nodded, 86, 87, 88, the blonde's car keeping ahead. He said, "Bad news. Norbert's dead." Blake held the phone away, spiky tin sounds coming out of it as he glanced at Scooby. He shook his head and let the car slow, 83, 81, 79.

They blasted past a state trooper hiding in a stand of evergreens. Roof lights went on behind them, flashing red, and the cruiser pulled out rocking onto the blacktop behind them. Scooby slid down in his seat. Blake watched the cop in the rearview mirror and raised the phone to his ear.

"Some people here, upstate," he said, "took out Norbert. Beat him to death. Ugly way to go, Big J., I'm sorry. But the guy who set him up is coming down to our turf now. Tomorrow."

Blake nodded and watched the mirror, the cop's flashers coming up behind them.

"You know some place we can meet this guy? Where we can get the drop on him?" He listened and nodded, watching the cop in his mirror. "That sounds ideal. Nice if we could bury him there too. A little before dawn?"

The state trooper in his grey-and-blue cruiser blew past them, Blake nodding. He said, "Later," and cut off the call. They passed the trooper as he pulled over the blonde. Blake glanced over at Scooby. "That's at least half a dozen bad-asses on our side, so I don't care if the cops do come. And Jones? He's dead meat."

Blake glanced back at the trooper and the blonde in her Trans Am, then pressed more buttons on the phone. He held it up, listened to it ring. A different voice answered, and even Scooby could hear the accent in it.

"It's Blake." The flashing lights dissolved behind them. "Put Raphael on."

Scooby opened his window, the cigarette haze in the car clearing out. The little girl cried under the blanket. Going from bad to worse, Scooby thought. She never forget today. Saw the old folks get shot, both of them. He bit his thumbnail and glanced over at Blake. She never forget that.

"Raphael?" Blake said. He shook his head. "Not so good. Bad news. Eduard didn't make it."

Blake scowled and held the phone away from his ear, sharper tin spikes coming out. Blake rolled his eyes and waited until the voice dropped off.

"I know who killed him," he said. "A guy named Darryl Jones. But now it's our turn. I'm setting him up. He'll be down here, in New York, tomorrow morning. You want a piece of him?" Blake cleared his throat. "South Bronx, somewhere near Yankee Stadium, just before dawn. I'll stop over and firm things up. Later."

Blake snapped the phone shut, glanced over the seat, back at the little girl under the blanket. "Shut up! You shut up!" Blake glanced over at Scooby. "Jones knows where Fisher is and he's going to tell me, or else."

"You gonna kill his little girl?"

"He won't feel bad for long. He won't live for long." A sound in his throat like a snarl and he flipped open his cell phone. "Hold the wheel."

Scooby leaned over and held the wheel, steering as Blake pulled a slip of paper out of his shirt pocket. His eyes fastened on Scooby's bicep, the barb wire tattoo circling his muscles. Blake pushed buttons, lowered the phone, and Scooby sat back as he took the wheel. "Jones? Who is this?" Blake looked at the phone, Scooby steering. "I don't care. I'll shoot the fucking kid!"

Blake looked over at Scooby and gestured as if to shoot the man on the other end of the call. He snorted. "All right, you're in for a joy ride. Head toward New York. You have a cell phone? What's the number?"

He gestured, writing in the air, and Scooby grabbed a map and a pen. Blake repeated, "607...755...2424. And I'll repeat what I told Jones: $160,000 in small bills and he tells me where Fisher is. If he doesn't tell me his daughter is dead!"

Blake cut off the call. He looked at Scooby. "You help me with this and all the money is yours, one-sixty large. All right? I just want to know where Fisher is."

Fisher, the bad boy everybody loved. Yeah, right. "You know he prob'ly dead, right?" Before Blake turned his face away Scooby glimpsed a tightening fear in his eyes. And suddenly he knew why. Why it was so important to find Fisher's body. "And you want to bury him right, consecrated ground, all that mierda. So he don't..."

"Fucking piece of shit!" Blake's eyes had hardened into rage, a glint, a knife point, his nostrils flaring, lips pulled back from his perfect white teeth. "I'm going to cut this guy's throat. And his daughter's too." He looked over the seat at the blanket. "While he's watching!"

CHAPTER 14

I stopped Vince's Caddy at the curb, jumped out and hurried toward Donadio's front door. The first time there and I didn't stop to admire the loan shark's house, a grey fieldstone front blending with wood siding painted dark blue, a wide bow window full of red and gold flowers. Hedges lined the walk that led to the front door, the entrance hidden behind a curving turret of brick, plants in hanging baskets, and a trellis covered with honeysuckle buzzing with bees.

Looks rich. No wonder, at thirty percent interest.

I pressed the doorbell, bing bong, and a young South American woman with bronze skin opened the door, an apron covering a dynamite figure. I said, "Mr. Donadio? I called."

She nodded, swept a lock of black hair behind her ear and smiled shyly. "This way."

She gestured, still showing her perfect pearly teeth, and led me into the house, past stairs to the upper floors, six-panel oak doors, a floor-to-ceiling mirror with beveled glass, and a gleaming gold frame. In the mirror I didn't look ready to bargain. I looked terrified and desperate. She knocked on a heavy door, heard something I didn't, opened it, and stepped in. I followed and sank into the deepest shag rug I'd ever seen.

It was a man's room, football trophies on the mantel of a fireplace with a brown marble apron. A buck's head with a 12-point rack hung on the wall, a lunker largemouth bass flipping its tail off a plaque, a big desk with a glowing top in the corner. Donadio stood up from behind the desk, a short bowling ball of a man in a pink polo shirt with a cue ball for a head, a few silver hairs growing around each ear and wrapping around the back. He held out a pudgie hand and I shook it.

"Mr. Jones," he said, "good to meet you. Esmeralda?" He nodded to the South American maid. I looked over my shoulder as she put her hands on me. Donadio said, "Just checking."

Esmeralda's small firm hands rubbed down my back, patted around my ribs and traveled down to my hips, down to my package and delved deep, around my jewels.

"Uh," I said, "can I borrow...the money? A hundred?"

Donadio sighed. "Afraid not. Sit down."

Esmeralda was still squeezing the inside of my thighs, but I shook her off and followed him over to two chairs by the fireplace. "Afraid not? Why? That's what I came for."

He sat in a thick chair, broken in like an old shoe, and motioned to the other. "Sit."

I sat. "I brought my deed and abstract for my land, the title to my tractor. I need that money."

"I know you do. But I'm not going to give it to you."

"Why not?"

"Because the word's out. The FBI is looking for you."

I blinked. "It is?"

"They are. They know you were mixed up in the shooting this afternoon at the Pine Inn; and I'm not pleased about that, not at all. Vince was a good associate. It's your fault he's dead." I swallowed—he was right—and it didn't make me happy either. "I'm disappointed and I'm not lending you the money. You'd never pay it back and then I'd have to do what's necessary."

"You know I'm good for it. When I borrowed thirty to pay off my wife, remember, I paid it back early."

"With Vince guaranteeing the loan."

"But I'm wanted? How do you know? I called you forty minutes ago."

"I pay for information. That's one way you can make money, supply me with information." Donadio's huge stomach bowled out between his legs as he leaned over and patted my hand, the papers shivering in my fingers. "Darryl, you are a highly respected businessman. You have an excellent reputation as a craftsman and a manager. I would lend you the money in a heartbeat if I thought you'd pay it back. But I don't think so, not right now, so I can't."

The papers shook in my hand, the room seemed to roll, I couldn't stop, I snapped. "They took her, god dammit!" I grabbed him by the shirt. "My little girl! I need it! Please!" He pulled back, his shirt bunching in my hands, and my knees hit the shag. "Please! You gotta give it to me!"

"Let go!" He was old and weak and I started shaking him. "Darryl!"

"You gotta! You gotta, please, you gotta!"

Something cracked inside me and I let go of his shirt and slumped back out of his lap—for someone so fat he had bony knees and hard skinny legs—

but when he shoved me off I fell like a rag doll against the other chair. My eyes burned, my face hurt, clenched so hard it felt swollen shut, and then I sobbed. Once.

Not a high point of my life, bawling at the feet of a loan shark.

Donadio nudged me with his shoe. "You son-of-a-bitch, calm down. Darryl?"

Two hooks latched into my armpits from behind, I rose off the carpet and landed gently in the empty chair. I looked up through my blubbering and saw a man who looked like Jack Lord in Hawaii 5-0, hard-jawed, big, with a pompadour of black hair. Donadio's muscle. Big Jack Lord looked at me sternly, but the loan shark motioned to him and he stepped back.

Donadio let me recover my dignity somewhat, then leaned over and turned red in the face as he collected my papers off the carpet. He lay them on my lap, put my hand on top of them, patted my knee and asked, "Who is it? Darryl, calm down. Who took your daughter?"

"Drug dealers from New York. Crack, heroin. They took my little girl so you gotta help me." I rubbed my face so hard I squeezed the last tears out of my eyes and got my hands wet. "I...I need it, the money. Get my little girl back. Gotta."

Donadio looked at Jack Lord, dressed in chinos and a button down shirt, who turned and walked out. The fat aging man looked at me and shook his head.

"Drug dealers are the scum of the earth. No morals. Call the FBI or you'll never see her again." Jack Lord walked in with a slip of paper. Donadio handed me the note with a telephone number on it. He said, "Call them, they'll find you anyway. I've got another appointment in a few minutes. Good to see you again, Darryl. Good luck."

We stood, and he squeezed my shoulder sympathetically as I turned away.

The door shut quietly behind me. Bees still buzzed around the honeysuckle, but I felt wrung out, burnt, stressed, witless. The steel toes of my boots swished in the grass and then I shut myself in the silence of the Cadillac. What now? I needed to feel something concrete so I leaned over and bumped my head against the steering wheel. What do I do? The banks are closed. But...maybe if Carla and Mudgie can...lend me some and...and...

And what? Give it to Pangbourne? Who kidnapped Patty? Who wants to know how I killed his little brother? His little brother who got Paul hooked on crack? On heroin? Carla and Mudgie are supposed to give their money to them? I'm supposed to give my money to them? Bankrupt myself? Give away my business? My future? My future marriage? My family? My house?

"God dammit!"

I punched the steering wheel, whunk! Whunk!whunk!whunk!whunk! It felt better, the rage, the heat, the power, the pounding and—

Bunk bunk bunk. I looked at Jack Lord, knocking on my window, his eyes serious below his big black pompadour. I touched the button and the electric window hummed down.

Jack Lord said, "Mr. Donadio wants you to leave the neighborhood."

Breathing hard, I started the Caddy and gunned the engine. Jack Lord stepped away.

"Hey!" Disgruntled, looking down at me, he put a stick of Juicy Fruit in his mouth and started chewing. I said, "Your boss, does he have any guns for sale?"

Jack Lord rolled his eyes, so I wanted to belt him. I clamped my mouth shut, put the Caddy in gear, and drove.

I knew where I could find a gun. My lunch box.

I drove up Taft Avenue, a long road rising up the side of a ridge, and on the way up I felt myself change. Some part of me snapped in Donadio's office and maybe I felt the shards of the old me crumble away. The old me was civilized. The old me got horrified when I killed Fisher Pangbourne. The new me clenched his teeth and growled in anticipation. The new me couldn't wait to kill a Pangbourne.

Blake was lucky. If he'd been there I would've choked him to death. As it was, my knuckles went white on the steering wheel. I wanted to see his head snap off his body, blood spurting, and I thought of ripping out his throat.

Blake Pangbourne. From that moment he was Blake, that's how I knew him, we were on a first name basis. I knew him well because I became him, in a sense. Nothing I wouldn't do. One thing left. The goal. Murder. One thought. Kill him.

I knew it: he wouldn't stop until I did. Kill him.

All the rage, fear, and anxiety melted down into a blade inside me. I could feel it, a knife cutting a cramp, a hot crease of pain over my stomach. It made me know I could do it. I could cut Blake open without a thought. Yep. Stab that fucker fifty times.

Slowing down, I glanced up and down Twist Run Road and up my street. Nobody odd, no unusual cars, no police cruisers. I crawled the Caddy up past all those beautiful houses I'd built, came to the shell of the house under construction, plywood faces and empty window holes, but I didn't feel the same about that one.

A man died in there. We killed him.

I got out of the Caddy and walked through the crumbly dirt to the front door opening. I glanced in. Creepy silence. The walls stood skeletal, two-by-four bones rising floor-to-ceiling, sawdust, wood blocks, the hose for the hydraulic nailer snaking up the stairs, and I knew my tools were inside, there for the stealing. I didn't go in to collect them.

I trudged out back, through the dirt, threshed into the weeds around the pond, and looked around as I hunkered down behind the stump. The surface of the water rippled a few feet away, a light breeze sifting through the long grass, and it was all beautiful and peaceful as I lifted away a chunk of sod, scraped away cool dirt, and slipped my fingers into the handle of my favorite lunch box.

I lifted it out of the ground, flipped the latch and checked on a dead boy's pistol. Fisher's pistol.

Like the Rasta man, Fisher had carried a revolver. I opened the spinning part and looked at the bullets. It was a .32, a pop gun compared to the Rasta man's .357 magnum. Didn't matter. I stuck the sod back in place, put the gun in my lunchbox, and trudged back toward the shell of a house.

No doubt about it, I was armed and dangerous, at least to people named Blake. Now all I had to do was find a hundred thousand dollars before I left town, or borrow it long enough to get my kid back.

I stood a chance if that damn Binks didn't screw it up. But I had a feeling things were too calm as I parked the Caddy in front of my house and Sheila Binks came out of theirs.

Sheila is a hot number, blonde, slim, leggy. She said, "Dave's inside, packing. You have to leave immediately. He got another call."

"Where's Paul?"

"They took him to Lourdes Hospital, he'll be okay." We climbed the steps in front of my house. "Are you okay? You look...different."

"Didn't get the money."

Got a gun instead and I didn't want her to see it, see me, the new me, so I let the screen door bang shut between us. Odd silence in my house. No TV, no cooking sounds, clattering dishes, children's songs, phone chat, no crackle of junk food bags, no nothing. I strode through the bedroom hallway.

Don't think, just do it. I stepped into Paul's room, the air sour with vomit smell, grabbed his backpack, and dumped out the bubble gum wrappers, CDs, pens, half a sandwich in a baggy, a Japanese cartoon novel, and silence.

I sighed. I moved to the window. Damn weird. No cops and the poor Kavidge's dead in their house across the street. Something wasn't right, I could feel it, but I set my jaw and went out.

In my own bedroom I stuffed in a shirt, socks, toothbrush, and the .32 wrapped in a pair of sweatpants. I hustled through the kitchen and down the creaky stairs to the basement. My office smelled of printer ink and boot dirt, the silence heavier below ground, so I hunkered down quick by my desk, an old door laid across two filing cabinets, and spun the dial of the safe.

The thick steel door swung open and there they were, neat stacks of money, packets of twenties, fifties, and hundreds. I dragged out all that cabbage and let it spill onto the concrete floor like the guts of my business. I looked at it with an angry grunt. Sixty thousand dollars. A new house for Carla and me, that's what it was, but it still wasn't enough for Blake, that pig. That kidnapping son-of-a-bitch who...

Wait a minute. Can't you...can't it look like enough?

Why not? I mumbled numbers. Fifty bills in a packet of hundreds and that's $5,000. Doctor the twenties with C-notes, one on each side. You only have to fool him long enough to get the drop on him. Thirty-two packets of hundreds and that would be enough.

I slipped big bills onto the fronts and backs of packets of twenties and I had my $160,000. The element of surprise, get the drop on him...then what? Who knows, play it by ear. I stuffed all the doctored money into Paul's backpack and looked at the rest of it, a dozen packets of tens and twenties, about $10,000.

Take it, I thought. You might need it.

With Paul's backpack heavier and another ten grand in hand I climbed the kitchen stairs. Hallway, bedroom, closet, I yanked a jean jacket off a hangar, pockets on the inside, a place to stash. I wedged packets of cash inside the jacket, pulled it on, I was ready.

Ready, sure. Weapons, cash, rage, and not a clue what to do.

"Darryl?" I walked out, feeling packets of money flat against my ribs. Binks stood at the front door. He looked me up and down. "I got a call," he said. "We have to meet them tomorrow."

"Where?"

"The South Bronx. At dawn." He gestured, eyeing me. I got an odd feeling. He said, "Let's go."

I locked my front door. A stake body truck coasted to a stop at the curb of Binks' house, a sign for B&R Landscaping bolted to the boards around the flatbed. His blue copmobile sat beyond.

"We're taking the Cadillac."

"No," he said, "my car."

"Hell no, it looks like a cop car."

"Won't make any difference."

"How do you know?"

"Because I know!"

"Yeah?" I pointed at the stake body truck, a teenager unloading a lawn mower. "You know as much about dealing with kidnappers as you know about mowing your lawn."

"Who owns the Cadillac, Darryl? Did you steal it?"

"Up yours."

"Who?"

"A friend. Friendship, you know? An idea foreign to you."

He snorted. "Belongs to someone else. Get in."

You pick your battles. I got in the copmobile.

We pulled away just in time. Red lights lit the far end of Verna Drive, sirens, squad cars, an ambulance, but our neighborhood fell behind. We made George F. Johnson Highway and Endwell fell behind. I sat there stiffly, afraid to move, afraid I'd kick the scanner or slip up and babble about my two murders.

Binks let me stew, glanced at me, turned off the scanner, and called his wife. He said, "I love you too. Bye." He pocketed the cell phone. "She'll watch your house."

"Can I use it? That?" Binks handed over his cell phone but didn't tell me how to use it. It took me half a mile to figure out that after you punch in the numbers, and they appear in the window, you had to press the talk button. She said, Hello?

"It's me."

Thank god, I've been worried sick. Where are you? I called and called the house and no one—

"I know, I'm sorry. I'm headed for New York City with Binks, my next door neighbor. You won't believe what happened. Paul went to the hospital with heroin withdrawal and Patty's been kidnapped."

Silence. That's not funny.

"Some guys from New York took her and we're meeting them down there, in New York City, tomorrow morning. I'll tell you about it later."

Darryl...seriously. Are you all right? I didn't answer. Raw fear in her voice. I love you.

"I love you too. Very much." Then I said, "Bye," my voice a bit strangled, and handed the phone to Binks.

He shut the phone. "Does she know?"

"Know what?"

"That you killed a drug dealer?"

I opened my eyes. "Excuse me?"

"Why else did Blake Pangbourne take Patty? Where's Fisher buried? That's what his brother wants to know."

Gonna be a long slow ride. "Are you calling me a murderer? That's really rude, even for you."

"I didn't. But did you? Kill him? What happened that night? Did you run him over with your truck?"

"Don't bring my truck into this."

"Funny." A malicious smirk on his mouth. "Did Paul drive Fisher's car into the river? No, that's got your forensics all over it. It does, the car, it has your prints all over it."

"Yeah, uh-huh."

"But you're the one that drove it down to the river, right? And Paul drove the truck down?"

"You going to keep this up all the way to New York?"

He looked at me like a goldfish in a teacup. "How did you kill him? Pound on him with a hammer?"

"Of course." Two could play that game. I imitated a TV handyman. I said, "The proper tool makes the job so much easier."

CHAPTER 15

Patty woke to the sound of scratching. Darkness. She blinked, scratch scratch scratch. It was the scratch of her eyelashes against the blanket on top of her, heavy, hot, and she moved to get it off. Uh-oh, hurts inside. She lay still, hoping it would go away. It didn't. She thought, Gotta go pee.

Gotta go bad. "Daddy?" The seat hummed pleasantly under her cheek but her head hurt from crying. The worst was the hurting down there, inside, the pee pain getting sharp, don't wanna go on the seat, uh-uh, but...those men and...and...she went still. Those men. Two men, guns, explosions, screams, her screams, and Patty stopped her breathing.

She tugged the blanket down to uncover her eyes. Back of a seat, two heads, those men. Man driving, smoking a cigarette, stinky smoke, it was him, he...he...

Patty curled up, pulled her legs in, but that sharpened the ache inside her. She held in a groan and stuck out her legs...better but...but she couldn't put it off, pushed herself up and felt the blanket fall away. Cool air strayed across her cheeks, good feeling, she was hot, her head hurt. Where are we? Ucky, that smoke. That other man, greasy, he looked scared too.

Patty was right, Scooby was scared and he felt bad, it all felt bad, worse and worse the closer they got to Swain's place. He didn't say anything as he glanced over at Blake. Blake kept his stare aimed over the wheel into the flashing lights of heavy traffic, driving like a fired bullet. Scooby had to say it, but had to light a cigarette first. He exhaled and said, "You gonna kill her?"

The little girl, eyes puffy from crying and her blonde hair messy, sat in the back seat looking at them. Blake licked his lips, looked in the rear view mirror, saw the girl looking at him. He glanced at Scooby.

"If you gonna," Scooby said, "not me. I want nothin' to do with it."

Scooby saw the crazy gleam in Blake's eyes, but there was a crack in them too.

"I'll kill her myself, candy ass." Blake stopped the car behind flaring red taillights, lights ahead, headlights glowing behind them. He swung his arm over the seat and stuck his finger at the little girl. "What's your name?"

She drew back. "Patty."

"Well, Patty, you heard me. If you don't behave yourself I'm going to kill you. But you know what else I'll do? If you don't do exactly what I tell you to, I'm going to kill your daddy. You hear me?"

Patty pulled the blanket up to her chin. "I have to go pee."

"We'll be there soon, you hold it. And you, Scooby," Blake snapped, "when we get to Swain's house, back me up no matter what I say. Understand? For your own good, back me up. We have to tell the same story or Swain will tear us up."

Scooby blew smoke out the window. He looked out at headlights of cars and trucks, the glowing bulbs of a fruit stand, pools of white light below street lamps, people hurrying through the pooling light and into the dark. Always dark, Scooby thought. Dark as hell.

The SUV groaned ahead with the rest. He glanced out of the window, up into the sky, the night, the darkness bearing down on them. Gotta get out of here, he thought.

As they left the main thoroughfare for a side street the darkness deepened. They turned onto a street of old single-family houses, the neighborhood where he met Swain three days before. If I could take it all back, he thought. His brows closed down on his eyes as he thought of Keeshon, the black crack dealer he shot in the back, twice. At his mama's feet. In cold blood.

He glanced over as Blake curbed the SUV. Small neat house with a swing on the front porch, the trellis thick with roses, the door half in shadow. Swain's lab used to be his grandma's house. No lights, all dark, like the man's heart. Scooby said, "Nobody home."

"Don't sound so hopeful. Stay here."

Blake slammed the door and leaped up the steps in the dark, into the porch shadows. Car silence. Scooby sucked a last hot drag off the cigarette, rolled down his window, and snapped the glowing butt onto the sidewalk across the street.

"Where's my daddy?" Patty asked.

"Back home. He lied, he can't kill your daddy. Be quiet, he comin'."

Blake slid in behind the wheel and jerked the cell phone off his belt. He pushed a button, Scooby heard the number ring, a click, a recording.

"Swain," Blake said, "we're back. Where are you? We have to get together, something came up. Call me."

He shut the clamshell, clipped it to his belt, did a screeching U-turn, and drove out.

"When you need the guy you can't fucking find him." He glanced in the mirror, Patty half buried in the shadowy back seat. "You have to go?"

She nodded. "Number one."

"Then piss on the floor."

"She can't do that," Scooby snapped.

"Why not? We're about to ditch this shitbox."

"She get her clothes all pee." Scooby waved at her. "She gotta eat, she hungry. I'm starvin' too."

Blake growled with anger, wheeled the SUV to the curb, and they climbed out. A shoe shop, dollar store, and braiding salon stood dark along the street, a Korean deli lit with fluorescent tubes. Two black teens strolled past, one talking fast about girls, chucking his bro on the shoulder as they passed bins of plantains, mango, jicamas, and starfruit.

Blake hurried around and opened the door for Patty, who struggled out, still wearing her blue stirrup pants and striped sneakers. Scooby asked, "What food you like?"

"The salad bar here," Blake said, "you can find anything."

Patty crinkled her nose. "Salad? Uck."

A deadpan Korean man, arms like sticks, his throat stringy in his open collar, looked away as they straggled in through the bright doorway. Shelves floor-to-ceiling stood jammed with candy, cigars, bread, hot sauces, chewing gum, rolls of scratch tickets, racks of potato chips and nachos.

They strolled past the salad bar in the middle of the store, dozens of tubs of salad greens, shredded carrots, dressings, gooped up macaroni curls, green Jello cubes, diced meats. A cooler stood against the back wall. Blake lifted out a six-pack of Magic Hat and nodded to a passage, a filthy door. "In there. Hurry up."

Patty trotted past a rickety chair, opened a door with WOMAN crayoned across it and pulled it shut behind her. Blake turned to survey the salad bar. He glanced at Scooby, imitated Patty and said, "Uck." Scooby didn't chuckle. Blake glanced toward a door with MAN scrawled across it. He said, "Hold this," and handed Scooby the six-pack.

Blake stepped into the men's bathroom. Scooby looked toward the dark street, the Korean stick man watching as he skipped to the door, glanced out, trotted back to the passageway, looked at the doors. Blake's urine dug into the toilet in the men's room.

Scooby grabbed the rickety chair and carefully, silently wedged it under the door knob of the men's room, stepped to the women's room and yanked open the door, Patty still tinkling. She snapped, "Get out!"

"Scooby?" The men's room door rattled, the chair creaked. In the men's room, Blake shouted, "Scooby!"

Scooby yanked Patty out of the women's room, her panties at her ankles. "Ow! Stop it!"

"Shuddup!"

He dragged her toward the front door. The joints of the rickety chair crackled as Blake slammed himself against the men's room door. "Scooby!"

Scooby dragged Patty out into the dark, looked east, west, back toward Blake, yanked her around the corner onto a side street. Sidewalk, buildings, cars, curbs, fences, a school. He bolted up the walk. Patty tripped, hit her knees and let out a screech. Scooby yanked her panties up, scooped her up in his arms.

"Silencio!"

He ran with her in his arms, dodged between bumpers, ducked behind cars, ran low on the dim walkway. A hundred yards back, Blake appeared.

"Scooby!" Scooby glanced back. *Christo, help us!* Scooby staggered, panting, Patty clinging to his neck. A moment later Blake reappeared, a black silhouette with a shimmer in his hand. Norbert's gun. "Scooby!"

Scooby rounded a corner and shucked Patty down onto her feet. He waved at a dark alley, trash cans, a fire escape. "Hide."

She scurried in. Scooby ran up the street, zigzagged between cars, staggered at the corner of the next crossway. Glancing back, he saw Blake reach the alley. He staggered onto the crossway, panting as he ran.

Blake sprinted around the corner fifty yards behind him. "Scooby!" He raised Norbert's pistol, the silencer long on the barrel. A quiet pfft, a ping as the bullet skipped off a car. Scooby dodged into the street. Blake stopped and fired. Pfft.

Lightning ripped into Scooby and he cried out, his mouth open as he hit the ground. Moaning, blinded by the lightning pain, he reached out. His blood smeared the street as he kicked his feet and pulled himself ahead with one arm, the other useless. He dragged himself between cars, gleaming bumpers above him, footsteps beating closer. *Oh god...oh god no.*

He raised his head. Who...es tu? Jesu? Curb, sidewalk, a man standing by a hedge. Christo? Man with a beard watching calmly, someone he knew, and Scooby let his cheek settle onto the tar. Too late. Too late.

Blake appeared above him. "You fuck! Trying to take off on me?"

"Christo. Oh Christo."

Blake shot him in the back of the head. Scooby's foot kicked. Blake dragged a sleeve across his mouth, his chest heaving, something worse than rage hard in his face. Scooby's fingers twitched. Blake shot him again, between the shoulder blades, twice, the body jerking. Then Blake let out an animal sound in the presence of a naked spirit.

Blake jammed the gun into his pants and ran back toward the corner. He slowed to a walk and tilted his head. Listened. Stopped and bent over, scanning low. Beneath each car lay thicker darkness. No hidden souls. A few yards farther, the mouth of an alley, he inhaled slowly and gazed in.

Gloom. From above came the laughter of a sitcom, light sifting from apartment windows. He stepped in. Fire escapes diced the light into bars and grids of pale grey, broken glass glistening on the tar. Blake kicked bags of garbage, a broken tricycle, a toppled garbage can, a dozen cans standing along a brick wall. The audience laughed. "Patty?"

He heard her breathing. Maybe he just sensed it. He heaved a ratty mattress up and over, whump, and found Patty huddled beneath it. He grabbed her by the shirt and yanked her off the ground. "I'll teach you to run away!"

She squealed, struggled in his arms until he flipped her upside down and spanked her bottom four times. She screeched and kicked until he smacked her bottom hard, then she went limp and hung like a bawling rag doll.

At the SUV he pulled open the driver's door and tossed her in past the steering wheel. She tumbled on the passenger seat and sat up, clung to the door handle, and wailed. He tossed in the pistol, gunned the big V-8 to a roar, and drove with his teeth clenched. Tears dripped down her cheeks.

"You brat, what did you get into? You stink!"

"I hate you!"

"Good! But the big bitch won't even like you now, you stink so bad. Shut up until we get there."

Patty cried with her face to the door. Blake drove. He drove beneath the Cross-Bronx Expressway, kept to the avenues, headlights filling the car, the pathetic little girl bawling. He zigzagged through Harlem, past murals covered with graffiti, sooty brick fronts, sidewalks, people, crowds, windows stacked like peepholes looking in on so many incubators for the city.

That's how he thought of it, a breeding ground for human feed, the Manhattan maw of sharp teeth standing to the south. A platform at the end of the #4 line, and Blake drove a long curve past the cemetery, into Woodlawn where trees stood black and shivering against the city sky.

Familiar terrain in the glow of street lamps. Cars lined up along the curb, cracked walks, hedges, stubby driveways laid against old houses, blue TV light casting a deathly pall onto dry lawns. 238th Street. He pulled the car to the curb in front of a house like a block of wood, square, shudderless, blunt.

There it is, he thought. The boyhood dump.

He leaned toward the blonde girl. "That house? That's my mother's house." He jabbed his finger at her. "You're going to keep your mouth shut. You breathe one word about where you're from, or who you are, and I'll kill your daddy."

"Scooby said you couldn't."

"Scooby lied. Open your mouth and I'll kill him. Understand?"

"I hate you."

He reached for her, she shied away. Rolling his eyes, Blake opened his door, slid out and gestured. "You want me to throw you in the river?"

Patty climbed across the seat, past the steering wheel, and jumped down to the grass by a fire hydrant. Blake shut the door and took her hand.

He stopped. Beyond the top of the car, across the street, the Fitz's house looked the same even though Ricky Fitz was three years dead from an overdose. Blake's gaze found a gleaming angle in the dark, the downspout near the back of the Fitz's garage. He blinked. That's where they played in the dirt, digging with toy trucks, him and Fisher and Ricky, and where Fisher talked Carlita Evans into showing them her panties when they were nine.

Patty wiped her eyes. Blake woke out of his reverie and led her toward the front door. He stopped again. Missing? In the dark it took a moment for memory to fill the gap. The hooded statue of the Virgin Mary, space in the bushes, an oval of black dirt where it stood, and the grass hadn't grown. Getting bleached out, yes, but it was Dad's and so Blake turned irritable as he lead Patty to the front door.

A corner lamp lit the front room, the same vile smells assailing him, chlorine pine cleaner and the cloying breath of cheap rugs, varnish, and gossip rags. Nothing new except the feel of more years dead and gone.

A muffled clang below the floor, the closing of a machine, he knew she was washing clothes. Toenails clicked on linoleum. A reddish brown dachshund appeared in the kitchen doorway.

"Freddy the mute hotdog. Here Freddy." Blake knelt and beckoned. He said to Patty, "He's mute, she beat the bark out of him. Here boy."

A door opened, Freddy clicking out of sight. Mrs. Pangbourne appeared in the kitchen, swaying on shapeless slippers, her ankles wrinkled, veins climbing her calves to the shivering hem of a faded apron. Thick chapped hands, brown dress, big bosom.

Dorothy Pangbourne's jowl shook. "You find him?"

Blake stood, a defensive anger rising inside him. "Anyone call?"

She glanced at Patty. "You talk to the police? Go to his school?"

"Couldn't say, they don't know. This is Patty, she needs something to eat."

Mrs. Pangbourne lumbered toward them. "What did you get into, sweetie? Is it on your shoes?"

"What happened to Dad's Virgin Mary? Out front?"

"Threw it in the trash." Patty looked at the floor. Mrs. Pangbourne smiled at her and got down on her knees to untie Patty's sneakers. "What beautiful blonde pigtails. Blake? Nobody knows anything? "

"No, they don't."

Blake stepped past his mother, down on her knees, but she grabbed his leg. "Take your god damn shoes off! I want rugs that stink with your shit?"

"All right!" He wrenched his leg free. "Christ on a damn bicycle!"

Blake kicked off his shoes, Patty's sneakers left untied as Mrs. Pangbourne struggled up and followed. Blake opened the refrigerator. The dachshund ran under the kitchen table as she scooped up a gossip rag, the fat of her arms shaking as she twisted the paper, rolled it tight. Blake grabbed boloney out of a drawer.

"So?" she asked, "why didn't you call me? Didn't you talk to his friends?"

"Where's the mustard? They don't know where he is either. Nobody does."

Blake tossed out cold cuts and bread, found the mustard and plunked the jar on the counter. Mrs. Pangbourne twisted the paper. "You talked to Cassie, his girlfriend?"

"Let me eat, okay?" He knew the sound of paper being twisted, slopped mustard on bread, and ripped open the boloney package. "It's obvious why he liked her. Only way to get her clothes off is with an apple peeler."

He lifted the fat sandwich. She shouted, "It's Fisher, damn you!"

She hit him with the rolled paper, whack! Blake almost dropped his meal. "Don't start!"

Whack! "You don't care how I feel!" Whack!

"God dammit!" The sandwich flapped open as he turned on his mother and cocked his arm, his fist clenched. "Cut it out!"

"I needed to know! You and your father. But you don't care how I feel and you never did!"

"Aw shut up." He lowered his fist self-consciously. "I didn't know anything so why should I call? But there's one more lead, one more guy to talk to. Then maybe..."

Mrs. Pangbourne sagged against the stove, gripped the edge of the counter. Blake went to bite the sandwich but couldn't. The rolled newspaper slipped out of her fingers and fell to the floor.

She already looked broken, but Blake only felt rage.

"That's why I never come over. You always hit me with some damn thing or another. And the worst of it is, you never hit Fisher, ever. So what's that make me? Another god damn house dog?"

Mrs. Pangbourne moaned. Blake threw up his free hand. "The hell with it, I'm gone. I'm out of this fucking dump."

He strode out to Patty, who backed up to a wall. "Give her something to eat. Please? I'll be back in a couple of hours." He bent to pull on his sneakers and looked at Patty. "And you remember what I told you."

Stepping out into the dark, he slammed the door and strode toward the car, sharked into the sandwich, feeling savage, the way he always felt leaving her house.

"Mama's boy, Fisher, that's what you were." He yanked it down into drive and pulled away. "Never gave a shit about me, not that bitch. So yeah, big bitch," he said out the window, "I hate your fuckin' guts too."

Blake bit the sandwich, bolted it down, feeding on bread, mustard, boloney and very old rage.

CHAPTER 16

They rolled through a toll booth, hurtled down a ramp onto Route 87, headlights pointed southeast, Binks driving with one hand, waiting, watching Darryl grow bleery-eyed with fatigue.

"Sheila's got her heart set on it." The detective half shrugged. "But if we have a kid now I'll be sixty before it graduates high school."

"Kids." Darryl rubbed his eyes. "One big adventure."

His head ached. Hours of anxiety, intense, relentless, had sapped him, he couldn't focus, couldn't think. Binks glanced at him. "You all right?"

Darryl shrugged. "I keep seeing Patty. If it's not her it's Paul, over and over, throwing up. He looked..."

Darryl shook his head. Painful thought. Binks pursed his lips. He'd seen enough fear in perps to know when they'd spill the beans, and Darryl wasn't quite there yet. He looked like hell, his hair wild, sweaty forehead, bloodshot eyes, his hand spasming as he spoke, anxiety twitching in a worn machine. No, wasn't ready yet, but he would be.

Just a little more.

Darryl looked at his hands. Dry palms, calloused, the skin cracked and raw in his finger joints. The patterns of lines on the tips of his fingers were scratched, dried to white whorls, and he counted eleven tiny scars on one hand, two scabs, a splintered fingernail. Job damage.

He mumbled, "Makes me wonder."

Binks drove with one hand on the wheel. "Wonder what?"

"When I lost track."

"Of what?"

"Them. My wife and kids. Lynn gave me warnings, tried to get me to pay attention, take off weekends with her and the kids. She knew what was going on, but I lost track of her and then...well...she let me wander off until it was too late." Darryl stared down at his rough paw. "Lost track of Paul too. Kid's been shooting heroin and I never knew it."

"I've met one parent who knew her daughter was shooting heroin. One." Binks sniffed. "Because they were sharing a needle."

The memory made Binks' shoulder jerk. He reached to his throat and pulled his tie loose and unbuttoned his collar. Maybe Darryl would take the hint and loosen up. He asked, "Any idea when it started? You losing track of them?"

"Sure," Darryl said. He looked at the window, his reflection, the world dark beyond the glass. "It started the day I incorporated. Until then I worked for myself, busted my hump to buy a new Sawzall, no big deal. But suddenly there was this other thing, the corporation, and it wasn't working for me, I was working for it. Whole different feeling."

Binks heard the story before, but he let Darryl talk.

"You'd think it wouldn't drive me, it's just something on paper," Darryl said. "But it does exist. It's the numbers, the IRS, the filings, payroll, bills, overhead, ads, signs, truck payments, land payments, all of it. You see it, hear it, it's out there separate from you and it's not human. It doesn't care whether I spend time with my family. It just wants to stay fat." Darryl shook his head. "Crazy, I know, but that's what it was. Pressure. Build build build."

Binks glanced over at Darryl, the red lights and headlights of other cars drifting with them like birds in a flock. Everybody has their excuse. But the scruffy guy surprised him when he said, "The money. It's all about money."

He didn't want Darryl to feel judged, so Binks manipulated the subject.

"It's not you," he said, "it's the culture. I'd love to nail these sons-of-bitches. If I can't have kids myself at least I can save someone else's."

Headlights flashed in the oncoming traffic. "You can't have kids?"

Binks glanced at Darryl, sagging in his seat. He waited as if it embarrassed him, though it didn't. "Low sperm count, but we've been trying. You look like hell. What—"

"Say what?" Darryl looked over bleery-eyed, but the detective just shrugged. Darryl shook his head. "I just...don't know what I...did to..."

"What did you do? Darryl? Just you and me, what did you do?" Binks glanced over. Darryl sagged against the door, his head settled back on the seat, his eyes closed, his lips moving. "Darryl?"

Binks' cell phone chortled on his belt. Darryl didn't stir, his lips going still. Binks flipped open his phone. "Binks here." A voice raspy from too many cigarettes. The nice guy neighbor? Still with us? "Right, what is it? Where do we meet you?" It's an abandoned building in the South Bronx, 189th Street and Clements Place. Sun up, 5:45 a.m. Does he have the

114

money? "He has it. Where's Patty?" None of your business. He'll get her back if he tells me where Fisher is.

Binks glanced at Darryl, half sagged against the door and sleeping. "Why do you think he knows?" He killed him. Jones and his kid were both dealing crack and my brother was supplying them. They owed him money, so they killed him. Now I just want to know where his body is so I can bury him. "Okay, what's the address again? Where we meet you?" Clements Place and 189th Street in the South Bronx. Be there.

The phone went dead. Binks snapped it shut and drove. He didn't want to think, he was tired, his eyes dry, irritated. He yawned, glanced over at Darryl, and heard the air sift in through his own nose sharply.

You're tired too, he thought, but stay on him. Darryl's no chump. But was he? Dealing? Certainly whined about working too hard. Started and couldn't stop. Always happens. Him too, probably.

They crossed the Tappan Zee Bridge, the Hudson River spreading wide and smooth in the dark. High broken cliffs stood around the tollbooths at the eastern end of the bridge. The highways through Westchester County ran like cattle chutes. Buildings encroached on the highway, loomed over high concrete walls covered with sprayed graffiti, the tires gabbled over crumbled pavement, billboards, signs, lampposts, the lights of superstores feeble against the moral darkness.

The car hit a pothole and Darryl raised his head. "What, uh...where are we?"

"New York. Pangbourne called." Darryl pushed himself up. "We're meeting him in the South Bronx, tomorrow morning."

"Is she all right?"

Binks nodded. "I'd bet on it. He didn't even mention the money. He wants to know where Fisher's body is."

Darryl snorted and looked out at the smoke-stained buildings. Windows glowed white, tenements checkered with anonymous lives, the buildings mired in darkness, then grocery store neon bled toward the heavens. Too little sleep, confusion, fuzzy thoughts, and Darryl rubbed his eyes. "Are we going...where?"

"To meet some people."

Darryl raised his head. "Oh Jesus, Binks, you didn't."

"RICO—Racketeering and Corrupt Organizations. The Feds, the FBI."

"Damn you!" Darryl punched the door. "You get her killed and I'll kill you!"

"Darryl?"

"I'll kick the hell out of you! Damn cop! Why'd I ever trust you?"

"Darryl, it—"

"Dammit all to hell! Christ, Binks!"

"It wasn't up to me."

"Who called them? What, are you getting a finder's fee?"

"Shut your face!" Binks stabbed a finger at him. "I don't have to take this. I don't have to do a thing for you."

"She's not yours!" Darryl clenched his fists, his face flushing. "What do you lose if he finds out? Nothing. I lose my daughter!"

"Are you brainless? Don't you wonder why you're not in lock-up? Why we were 'allowed' to come down here? Allowed to?" That put a hitch in Darryl's fuming. "You'll find out soon enough. In the meantime, quit whining. Shut up, I've had enough of you."

Binks rolled his eyes. He glanced at a pocket notebook, an address, Darryl whispering to himself, his face turned away, then he moaned and covered his head with his arms. Binks took an off-ramp, crossed an old iron span over the East River, the 125th Street Bridge, the wide avenue choked with vehicles, Harlem split all the way to the West Side Highway.

Binks drove north, the cars flanking them filled with black faces, sullen cabbies, back seat children wide-eyed, front seat couples fascinated with each other. 167th Street. Binks turned past a brick building, unremarkable, turned in at a gate, pressed a button on a box.

A metallic squawk. "Detective Binks, State Police." He held his badge up to an electronic eye. The gate trundled aside. Binks drove in and parked.

"Darryl?" Darryl lowered his arms, pushed out his legs, rubbed an eye with a dry knuckle. Binks said, "We're here."

Darryl glanced out at a glass door in a recessed entrance. "What's this place?"

"FBI Harlem." Darryl looked at the backpack. Binks followed his glance and said, "It'll be safe."

Darryl stared down at Paul's backpack as if seeing it for the first time. Rock band logos and a doodle. I ♥ Cassie. He thought of the gun swaddled in sweatpants. Abruptly he rolled out of the sedan, stood up empty-handed, and slammed the door. Cool air, his head cleared, good to move again, he trotted and caught up with Binks at the door.

A metal detector stood beyond the glass. The door buzzed. Binks pulled it open. They stepped into a small room, a short hall beyond the gate of the detector. Binks beckoned. When they walked through the machine a cone began to flash red light. A man appeared from a door, a wand in hand. He passed the wand over Binks, checked his sidearm, waved him on.

He swept Darryl. The red light went off when the wand reached his boots. The man waved him on.

As Darryl stepped past the metal detector a tall, painfully thin man, pale, the skin of his face loose off his cheekbones, an adams apple like a trigger, stepped out of a second door. He grinned friendly-like and doled out a Georgia accent. "Binks, hey y'all!"

"Postelthwaite, you're fatter than ever."

Postelthwaite's bony wrist stuck out of his sleeve as he shook hands with Binks. "Any trouble finding us?"

Darryl made no move to shake hands. Binks said, "Darryl, this is Special Agent Fred Postelthwaite. He'll get Patty back if anyone will."

"Swear on a stack of bibles, things'll work out."

Darryl felt the weight of packets of money tucked inside his jean jacket. "You're a special agent?" he asked. "Special at what? Kidnapping?"

Postelthwaite glanced at Binks and gestured toward the hall, a doorway at the end.

"Mr. Jones," he said, "we'll get your daughter back. But no, I don't have a specialty. 'Special' just means, as my grammy used to say, that I been around the kitchen long enough to get moldy."

Binks chuckled. "How're the girls? You have two, right?"

Postelthwaite pushed buttons, the door buzzed.

"The oldest started at Brown two weeks ago and the youngest has her first boyfriend." He led them past offices with small windows, sealed with blinds. He glanced back at Binks and chuckled. "He was the first kid I couldn't scare off. And Sheila?"

"IBM poisoned the aquifer in Endicott, so real estate's pretty slow."

"I heard about that. After you." He motioned. Binks and Darryl stepped into an office with a small table. Postelthwaite left the door open, motioned to chairs, and they sat down as he tapped the buttons of a phone on a desk. "Send down Garber, Caroline, would you please." The tall skinny man sat on the edge of his messy desk, papers, folders, scattered paper clips. He said to Binks, "Now to business. What does he know?"

"Not much."

Darryl asked, "About what?"

Postelthwaite glanced at Binks and crossed his long bony arms. He said, "What's behind all this here dust up."

"Behind it?"

"First," Postelthwaite said, "let's be clear about what we all know. We know you're gon' meet with Blake Pangbourne to exchange your daughter for a bag full of legal tender and news about Fisher, his younger brother. He wants to know where Fisher's buried. That's assuming he is, in fact, dead. But it seems that, like a fox in a chicken coop, you got feathers stuck in your teeth."

"Yeah, right." Darryl glanced defiantly at Binks, sitting next to him. "What else? My good pal here said we were 'allowed' to come down here. Why? What's in it for you?"

Postelthwaite raised one hand thoughtfully to his chin. "It'll all come out in the wash, Darryl, and you'll be in Sing-Sing."

"The hell are you talking about?"

Postelthwaite glanced at Binks. Binks said, "Stand up."

"Why?"

"I want to show you. Stand up."

Warily Darryl stood, his fists half-clenched. Binks stepped behind him.

"Here," Binks said, "right here, is proof that links you to the murder of Fisher Pangbourne."

"What? Where?"

"Here." Almost playfully, Binks pulled on the belt loops of Darryl's jeans. "The person who drove Fisher's car into the Susquehanna River left tar on the seat. Foundation coating. It was right here." Binks slapped the back of Darryl's jeans. "When we search your closet we'll find those pants."

"Bullshit. You—"

"I saw it myself!"

"So what!"

"Jones, you killed him!" Postelthwaite leaned over his desk. "Sit down and shut up! Now! Siddown or I'll sit you in the electric chair and fry you like a catfish!"

"I didn't!" Darryl stumbled against Binks, who stiffened. "I didn't kill him! I swear it!"

A black man appeared in the doorway, short and hard as a fire hydrant. He said, "Play along, catfish. I just as well burn you in a barrel myself."

"Play along," Binks murmured. "It's the only way."

Darryl looked at Binks, then at the man in the doorway whose tongue slurred his words behind a baffle of bad teeth. "Nothin' to lose."

Postelthwaite said to Binks, "Lieutenant Garber, Manhattan RICO." Garber nodded, hands clasped behind his back, folds of skin clasping his mouth, starting at his wide nose, mashed flat, his ears mis-shapen. He looked down at Darryl, whose guts tightened. Garber said, "Okay, bottom feeder—thass what a catfish is—this the deal. You shot somebody, you owed 'em drug money."

"Didn't."

"Did too, but this your lucky day. We'll cut you a deal cause we got bigger fish to fry."

"A deal? For what?"

Postelthwaite stood straight, looked down at Darryl, and stroked his chin.

"Fisher Pangbourne," Postlethwaite said, "now presumed dead, was on the third or fourth tier of a rather large drug distribution network. His older brother, Blake, is in the inner circle."

Garber's slur. "But isn't juss drug dealers."

Postelthwaite shot Garber an irritated look. He said, "In the tri-state area they've got a wide network of dealers, Asians, spics, Jamaicans, frat boys, black folk, white gents in suits, all dealing heroin, crack, coke, candy canes, and mary jane."

Darryl looked from Postelthwaite to Binks, over his shoulder at Garber, stiff and immovable, back to Postlethwaite, who stretched his throat arrogantly as he looked down his ax of a nose. Darryl pressed his hands on his thighs—too much, he couldn't believe it—but his hands were shaking. Garber stepped forward, stood over his left side, planted on his stubby legs, his lips stretched over his dental mish-mash.

"We catch Pangbourne," he said, "we have a wedge into the org'ization."

Postlethwaite crossed his arms. "An egg tooth. We'll crack it open from the inside."

He looked up at them, towering over him. "What about my little girl?"

"We grab Blake Pangbourne at the swap. You get your daughter, keep your money, we don't prosecute."

"And if I don't?"

Postelthwaite pinned Darryl with his glance. "Murder charges for you and your son. Then what'll happen with your daughter?" He shrugged. "Play along, it'll work out, I promise. Scout's honor."

Darryl glanced up at the hard men looking at him and ran his shaking hands along his legs. His neck hurt, he couldn't breathe, he looked around, tried to think, something, anything, a way out, way back, Endwell, somewhere, anywhere. No, no way, nothing. Blood beat in his temples. Brittle silence. He squeezed his legs. His stomach churned. Postelthwaite said, "Darryl?"

"Yeah! Okay, you sonsabitches! I got no choice!"

"It's a go." Garber hurried out, footsteps clumping away in the hall. "Roust re-con! Move! Now!"

A disdainful twitch of Postelthwaite's lip. "He still thinks he's military."

Darryl sat simmering, flushed, and sweating. "Who's he calling, the Pentagon?"

"Re-con scouts the locale and positions agents." Postelthwaite leaned over and slapped Darryl's arm. He said, "Don't worry, Darryl. We'll have them surrounded."

"That's what worries me." Darryl glanced angrily at Binks. "You'll have me and Patty surrounded too."

CHAPTER 17

Kirk Bony hung in the shadows of the stoop, plucking at the scraggly hair on his chin. Won't grow, he thought. Naw shit, I'm ugly, isn' never gonna grow in to cover that phone.

Kirk had a telephone, a scar from his eyebrow to his chin. Dealer payback. His first bust, a know-nothin' ten-year-old, he thought he go to prison for five rocks, so scared shitless he ratted out Stevie Campbell on West 144th, a dumb kid move yo, and it got him a telephone gushin' blood on the sidewalk and his mama screaming. Taught him the best lesson he learn in seventeen years—don't rat out nobody—so now he protec' Big J, his main man, like he pure walking gold.

Whathefuck? 'leven p.m. and a white man pulls up in fronna Big Johnson's building like he own it, though Big J he run the whole building yo. Who this know nothin' white fuck, he gonna get freezer burn. So Kirk stick his hand in his pocket, slip his fingers round his piece...yeah, jus' like that...thumb off the little safety button, the pistol clit, step out, and stick it in white man's face.

"Dead fuck yo! White trash mothafuck, wrong place wrong time so I cap your ass!"

White man didn't react. He stop with one foot on Big J's first step, a gun barrel looking him in the eye, took a drag on his cigarette, and blew a smoke ring that floated right onto the barrel of Kirk Bony's piece. Kirk like to kill him right there, but he never shot nobody, so he shout it. "I cap your ass dead! What you doin' here? This Big J's territory."

White man had a glint in his eye like death hoping to happen. All he say was, "Shine my shoes, boy."

That death gleam in his eye, a snort comin' out his mouth, Kirk realize white man was a bad ass, uh-huh. Kirk squeeze his gun. Cap him! Now! White man, lookin' at Kirk Bony, snorted and took another step up. Kirk shouted, "Yo!" and squeezed the trigger.

Lucky for white man the peep in Big J's door snap open, eyes look out, the first of three locks clacked, chock-a-chunk rattle, and the door swung open. Kirk Bony ran upstairs, jammed the gun in white man's back and herded him into the dark, toward a shadow man. The gleam of one solid gold chain, young bossman always wore just one gold chain on the wrist, so Kirk Bony knew it was him.

"Yo, Phillip, lemme put him in a dumpster!"

"Back off." Phillip motioned with his chin. Kirk Bony slammed the door, the hall darkening. Phillip said, "In the front door, Pangbourne? You ill?"

Blake smelled burning rocks, crackheads grousing beyond a doorway, the glow of butane fire sputtering on the threshold. He said, "I'm not delivering tonight, am I?"

Phillip gestured up and down at Blake, looking at his stoop boy, and Kirk Bony did a shakedown, found the chrome-plated Browning, jerked it out of Blake's belt, and passed it over.

"Norbert's nine millimeter. How did you get it?" Blake looked back at Phillip and exhaled smoke. "Don't tell me. Big J, he'll tear it out of your ass anyway."

Kirk Bony gloated. "That right. Smoke comin' out his ears a'ready."

Phillip started up worn and grimy wooden stairs and Blake smoked his cigarette as he followed, the guns gleaming in Phillip's hands. Blake knew his story. Big Johnson found a baby in a garbage can, named him Phillip, and as if he was a good dad put him through Columbia. But really it was just grooming him to run Big J's telemarketing and pharmaceutical entertainment enterprises and conglomerate for online pornography.

"How did Norb get it?" Phillip asked. Pangbourne smoked. They reached a heavy wooden door. Phillip fit Norbert's gun into his pants and pushed his way into a carpeted hallway. He said, "Norbert was a good associate. Always completed his assignments."

Blake said nothing. They walked past a Spanish whore in a doorway naked but for panties, big messy black hair, bronze skin and nipples. She said, "Phillip, como fuck borracho en siesta?" How do I fuck a passed out drunk?

Phillip said, "I'll be back in a minute."

Through another door and they climbed a flight of stairs carpeted with money—lush shag between ornate wooden rails, varnished and gleaming. Jazz music grew apparent, Charlie Parker in a calmer mood, and they rose to a thick door with a gold knob. Phillip led them into a room with expensive leather furniture, a table like a glass top floating in the air with a blue swirl of an ash tray off center.

Phillip called, "Big J!"

Across the room, a door opened. An aging bull, Big Johnson ducked as he stepped through, filling the frame, heavy in the middle, thick in the arms, deep-chested. His afro was threaded with white, lines etched his forehead, the bridge of his nose broken crooked and scarred between raging red eyes.

"You ask for a little muscle, Pangbourne, but now my brother-in-law dead. Jesus H, what I tell my sista!" Big Johnson's hands clenched into lava rocks. "She screaming, his little girl wailing, mama's tearing her hair out and swearing how I am a scumbag. Jesus H! I gonna fuck you up!"

Blake put his hands on his hips. "Your brother-in-law? Is that why you let him wear dayglo sports jackets?"

"He for real?" Big Johnson's glance shifted to Phillip and back to Blake so fast his jowls shook. "You for real, Pangbourne? He dead and all you can say is...is... So what I say is, I gonna fuck you up!"

Phillip's level voice. "Big J."

"You shut up, I know!"

Phillip's mouth hardened, he turned his back and walked away. Big Johnson did the same in the other direction. He spun, grunting, and strode back to Blake.

"The only reason you still alive, Pangbourne, you supplyin' us with that crack product what everybody love. But god dammit to hell! What happen to him?"

Blake bent and purposely missed the ash tray, stubbed his cigarette out on the floating table top. "We were set up. They beat him to death."

"With what?"

Blake shrugged. "Pool cues and beer pitchers." Big Johnson suffered an involuntary shudder. Blake said, "The guy who set us up, Darryl Jones, he'll be here tomorrow morning."

His shoes rasping in the shag, Big Johnson lumbered back and forth, squeezing his knuckles, clicking three big gold rings.

"What he coming for? It serious? He won't dance around, will he?"

Blake watched Big Johnson pace, the muscles standing out from his shoulders as he clenched his fists. Blake said, "His daughter."

Big Johnson stopped. He looked over his broken nose at Blake, his lips pressed together. Even Big J. had his taboos.

"Cold blooded, Pangbourne. But it don't matter if you a reptile," he said, "my whole family want a piece of this guy. Quarter of six? Clements and 189th?"

Blake turned to the stairs. "The Jamaicans from Brooklyn lost a man too."

"They coming too?"

"Knowing them, with carving knives. Show up early, get a good seat."

He skipped downstairs, strode past the Spanish whore, then a home boy let him out onto the slate stoop. One end of Big Johnson's street was lit brighter than a fuse, so Blake saw Kirk Bony hiding in the shadows as he skipped down the steps.

"Boy," he said, "next time I'll make you my bitch."

"Next time I cap you!"

Blake chuckled, amused. He got into the SUV, got on the dog, drove like he was immune, stomped the pedal down to 125th Street and crossed Harlem on the wide, lighted avenue. He flogged the SUV south on F.D.R. Drive, the East River glittering in the moonlight. The Manhattan Bridge took him over the glittering chop, Blake passing that spot where he threw off a junkie girl once after he banged her—actually she jumped, but he told people it solved a problem—then he took an exit that curled down underneath the bridge into Red Hook.

Narrow cobbled streets littered with trash. Tiffany Place. He stopped in front of a sooty warehouse with boarded windows, broken bricks in the gutter, the air rank with the stink of the harbor, rotten wood pilings, and algae. He walked toward a steel door that swung open on shrieking hinges.

"Blake Pangbourne, my friend!" A Jamaican with a golden hoop in his ear smiled with perfect white teeth. He said, "You come in here."

"Hello, Raphael." Blake stepped past the skinny man with ropes of muscle in his arms, his branches of hair tied into a broom that stuck out a foot behind his head. "How's the bullet wound healing?"

Raphael motioned. "Fine. You come in here, right this way." A doorway, Blake stopped, but the tip of a knife sent a spike of pain up his back. Raphael murmured, "And pay for Eduard."

Two Jamaicans grabbed him, dragged him in, and eight more men, dark as coffee, came out of the shadows. Blake tripped on splintered floorboards as they pulled him by the arms.

"Raphael! No time for this. Raphael!"

Metal edges glinted in every hand, carving knives, throwing stars, a machete, box cutters, switchblades. A huge man turned on a lamp, light shimmering down a board with gouges and bloodstains. He said, "Man gotta pay for Ed!"

"You tell him, Pinchot," Raphael said.

Pinchot, wearing a denim vest with shredded edges, clamped a hand on Blake's throat and the three men slammed him against the bloodstained board. He said, "Don't move," and stepped around behind the board.

Blake gave Raphael a blistering look. "I don't have time for this nonsense."

"Man don't got time for nothing else." Raphael glanced at the other men. "On three. One...two..."

"Raphael!"

"Three."

Arms cocked and threw. Blake stiffened. It was an odd fraction of a second, the world taut, silent, time jerked to a stop. A machete streaked at him, the big blade glimmering once as it cartwheeled toward his crotch. Throwing stars became shimmering discs, a dozen points spinning, and knives glinted before the points and blades bit wood with a spattering of bites, stabs, and splintering sounds.

No pain.

Blake gasped, looking down. The machete pulled out of the wood and hit the floor with a clunk. No sound came from the Jamaicans as Blake looked to the side, turning his head, and felt the steel of throwing stars and knife blades against his temple.

His teeth clenched, anger hardening his stomach. "Very funny."

Pinchot stepped from behind the board. "Laugh like hell we do, puttin' a man to the board. We laughin' now, are we?"

The two men pinning Blake's wrists let go of him, he pushed off the killing board. "Any more bullshit and I'll make sure Immigration shows up at your door."

"Yah," Raphael snapped, "and you ask us for help and now Ed get killed. So you tell us, what he die for?"

"A man named Darryl Jones shot him."

Raphael pulled his knife out of the killing board, a bright white splinter left behind. He glanced at Blake and folded the blade into the handle.

"I sent him to see Jones at work," Blake said, "but he never came back. I don't know what happened, but I don't think he's alive. I told him to call if he had problems, but I didn't hear anything and I never saw him again."

Pinchot stepped forward and smacked Blake's shoulder. "You send Ed to do your dirty work? Alone?"

"No, to ask a few questions. And if you touch me again, Pinchot, they'll find you in the harbor."

Raphael stepped between them. "So what? This man Jones, he comin' down here?"

"I'm meeting him in six hours, in the South Bronx. Clements and 189th Street. You want a piece of him, be there." He glanced around at the Jamaicans, dark brown men, lean and tough. "I'm sorry about Eduard. I didn't think there was going to be any problem, but I was wrong."

"Yah man, you fucked up," Raphael said.

"Yeah, I did." Blake shrugged. "I was wrong, this Jones is a mean bastard. I heard bad things about him, that he likes to use his carpentry skills. He beats people in the head with hammers and cuts them up with electric saws. That's probably what he did with Eduard." A collective shudder rippled through the Jamaicans. "But Big Johnson lost a man too, and I lost a good friend, Escobido. We all lost someone, so now this Jones has to suffer."

Pinchot picked up his machete from the floor, the Jamaicans shifting on their feet, loosening up. Pinchot said, "What time we cut up this Jones man?"

"Sunrise. Quarter of six. 189th and Clements in the Bronx. Now if you'll excuse me..." He strode to the door, for the first time noticing two beautiful women, brown and white, observing from a sofa in a dark corner. He stopped in the doorway. "Anybody got a cigarette?"

"We cut this guy up," Raphael said, "we get a piece of him, right? Arm or a leg, feed it to the dogs. Okay?"

Blake nodded. "Get there early."

Out in the darkness, Blake inhaled the rank breeze off the harbor, smelled ashes as he rummaged in the ashtray. No long butts. Grunting, he yanked down the stick on the console and pulled out. He drove, busted a shock in a hole where thieves had stolen the old cobbles, drove onto the bridge, and beat the SUV over the arcing span toward Manhattan, the city towers standing like pillars of silver and light, an Oz without a wizard.

He cruised onto Canal Street, feeling strangely calm as he entered Chinatown. Asians were closing shop grates and stacking crates on the curb. Blake stuck his head out the window. "Chop chop!" He drove, karate chopping the steering wheel. "Sukie-yakie! Heee-yah!"

He laughed like crazy and almost ran over a papa-san. Young Asians strode the walks, the shops closed, sidewalks clear of vendors, the streets clear but for taxis and Asian boys cruising in dad's rice wagon. He wheeled onto Mott Street, the broken shock rattling as he turned down Bayard. He pulled over where a canopy hung greasy over the curb, an old Chinese man hosing sequins off the sidewalk, fish scales glinting in the gutter.

The old Chinese man sprayed elsewhere when Blake stood up out of the car.

"Hey. Old man, I need some fish." The old man, age spots on his cheeks and no eyebrows, sprayed the walk. "Hey! Fish!"

The old man let the hose go still. Blake swiveled his hands like a swimming fish and said, "Fish. Swim swim, I need."

The old man shrugged. "No speak Eng."

Blake pulled money out of his pocket and peeled off a hundred dollar bill. He handed it to the old man and said, "You speak English now?"

"Litta bit."

"I need a fish, about forty pounds."

The old man shrugged. "No big fish."

Blake jerked his chin at the closed grate. "Let me take a look." The old man hesitated. Blake pealed off another hundred.

The old man dropped the hose, stuffed the bills into his pocket, and rattled up the grate. They walked into the shop that stank of the ocean, filthy canvas laid over beds of ice, squid, and octopus, tuna chopped into red butterflies. The old man led him past baskets of mussels and clams, tanks of belligerent lobsters, into a cooler where big fish hung from the ceiling, hooked by the jaw and wide-eyed with the shock of death.

The old man said, "You want?"

Blake had ten fish to choose from—tuna, striped bass, a big goggle-eyed thing he couldn't identify. Couldn't take that one, so he pointed to two striped bass about forty inches long, twenty pounds each. "In a burlap bag so my trunk doesn't get slimed."

"Fitty cent a pound. Twenty dolla."

"I just gave you two hundred, gramps." Blake chuckled, he was feeling good. He pulled out his wad and said, "But what's a good hostage worth?"

CHAPTER 18

The South Bronx at night. Scary.

I squirmed on Binks' front seat, trapped, claustrophobic as he turned his copmobile into a canyon of old ugly buildings, sooty and beat, piled up off the sidewalks and tilted in over the trash-filled gutters. Binks pulled to the curb. No one anywhere, no street lights, no sign of life, but I was so hotwired on fear, dead tired, and scared about Patty, that I felt wasted on drugs, fuzzy, charged, paranoid.

"They're here?"

Binks nodded to a dark storefront. "Bring your bag. But as I said, I'd leave it here."

"You'd screw your next door neighbor too." I grabbed Paul's pack off the floor, heavy with money and dead Fisher's pistol, opened the door and got out. Old garbage smell. Binks pulled open the storefront door. The muzzle of a rifle looked at us. A Fed dressed in black, streaks of black grease under his eyes, jerked the barrel for us to come in. We walked a hallway, another Fed nodded to a doorway, and we strolled past holes smashed in the walls, broken plaster, graffiti, garbage, toward a light at the end.

My voice was shaky. "How many are here?"

"Agents? A dozen. I think that's a lot. Postelthwaite?" We stepped into a small room smelling of coffee and cement dust. A hazy photograph, blown up to three-by-four feet, hung tacked to an unplastered wall, handguns and boxes of shells on a table by a coffee maker and a can of Maxwell House. Binks asked, "What time is it? Is everybody ready?"

"Ten minutes," Postelthwaite said. The tall skinny son-of-a-bitch was still dressed in a business suit—he wasn't gonna get his hands dirty—and I realized his only connection to the action would be a quietly hissing scanner. He gave me a grin and said, "If this was a coon hunt I'd say we have the tree surrounded and the critter's about to climb it."

The hard little black man, Garber, stood by a back door. He said, "Go," and an agent in dull clothes and black boots ducked out into the darkness. "Thass the last. What's it look like?"

They turned to the infrared photograph, poster size, marked with red numbers.

"That was Rogers? He's going to be...here." Postelthwaite wrote "10" in red marker on the irregular grid of boxy shadows and blurred rectangles. I recognized streets at the top and bottom, a narrow alley along the left edge. He said, "This is an infrared photograph taken from a chopper two hours ago."

"Of the meeting place?" I asked.

"Three blocks north. Agents are planted where the numbers are. It's just a big patch of crumbling walls, no roof, but there are holes into the basement so watch your step."

Garber stepped in and thumped his finger on a red X in the center. "Thass where you two meet the goal, Pangbourne."

"My daughter's the goal."

A voice whispered from the scanner. Thirteen? Thirteen in?

Postelthwaite pushed a button. "Thirteen here."

Two here. We're not alone.

I stiffened. Garber pointed to a "2" a little below the middle, a few crumbling rooms and walls to the right of the red "X." Postelthwaite asked, "Goal's here?"

Negative. Goal may be here, but there's others.

Postelthwaite glanced at Garber, who looked up from his heavy gold watch. He was dressed in black clothes and boots fresh off the store shelf, but he did look startled. Postelthwaite pressed the button to speak, but it was Garber who asked, "How many?"

Two in position "A," twenty feet north at eleven o'clock, and one in position "B," fifteen feet north at one. But...I think there's more.

The air went taut. It was like a knife snapped open and we tensed, waiting to see if it would cut us.

"Hold steady." Postelthwaite marked the map with little x's north of agent 2, at eleven o'clock and one o'clock. I glanced at Binks. He looked well dressed in chinos, a dark button-down dress shirt, and a brown leather jacket. He also looked a little stout because under the dress shirt was a bullet proof vest. I had a flak jacket too, stiff and hugging my ribs.

Binks also looked uneasy, Garber too, and he broke the tension. "Pull 'em. He's right, we don't know what's out there."

"The hell we don't!" I startled them. "My daughter's out there, you son-of-a-bitch. You don't give a damn, but I want her back!"

"I'm going to let you get killed? No way, catfish."

"I got the money, and he'll kill her if we back out now, so we can't. We can't!" The three sons-of-bitches who set me up as bait for Pangbourne, who was using my daughter as bait for me, stood looking at me like I was crazy. True enough, they were driving me nuts. I said, "She won't get a second chance. How are you going to pull them out without tipping him off? Then he'll kill her!"

Postelthwaite pushed a button. "Units? Any traffic?"

Three red buttons on the scanner lit up. Nine here. It appears to be bums, sir. Someone's smoking marijuana. Looks like Jamaicans and— Postelthwaite pushed another button for another man's voice. Four here. Two unknowns, sir, climbed over the wall of the alley.

Postelthwaite pushed another red button. One here, I'm on goal. Goal's here, sir. Postelthwaite looked at Garber. Garber blinked. He's sticking wood in a barrel. Has a fire going.

Postelthwaite took his finger off the button. He said, "And then there was light." He shrugged his boney shoulders. "No choice. We have to go in."

Garber spoke from the doorway. "But Fred—"

Postelthwaite raised a hand, silencing him. He nodded to the door, looked at me, and his eyes wandered down to Paul's bag. He knew I was no fool, I had something planned, but he said, "Got your flak jacket? Then go. Go."

Binks followed Garber to the back door. "I'll be right behind."

Garber opened the door and peeked out. "I'll lead for haff a block, then you two go on 'head of me."

My stomach tightened, I felt sick, but then Garber stepped out and I followed him into the alley. Binks stepped out behind me, Garber striding ahead, the door slammed and the world went dark. By dark I mean dark, no light, so that's when I unslung Paul's bag from my shoulder. Garber halted. I bumped him, couldn't see, blind, breathing too loud, hands shaking, one hand in the pack. I stumbled as he shushed me quietly.

We filed toward a vague light, a street, my hand stuck in Paul's bag. Money packets, cloth, a sharp butt, I wrapped my hand around the grip of Fisher Pangbourne's pistol. I drew it out, stuck it in my belt, inside my jacket, zipped the bag as we reached the corner. Nobody saw. We turned north, our footsteps so loud they seemed to echo.

I'd already decided. Pangbourne would never leave us alone. I had to kill him. But only after he told me where Patty was.

Garber led us north. Empty street, no lights. A glowing crescent moon still hung in the sky, stars going pale in the west, but the tops of buildings burned with the faint red light of dawn. We walked loud in the dark. I glanced around and it all felt unreal. What day is it? The hard gun against my stomach and the fear made me nauseous.

For me? If my little sweetie didn't make it? It was a good day to die.

Garber halted in a doorway and motioned us on. I passed the Fed, set my jaw as I gave him a last glance, and let Binks come up beside me. I looked at him. He was scared, his lips set, but he saw me clearly. He said, "What?"

We kept walking. "I don't care about Pangbourne," I said. "I just want Patty. You hear me? You with me? We gotta get her back."

"Of course, yes."

"Bullshit. You sold us down the river so they could catch Pangbourne. Now I trust you, you son-of-a-bitch?"

Embarrassed, he looked at the ground. It was true, he knew it, but then he sighed and said, "I'm with you. Let's get her back. But..."

Uh-oh. He didn't sound cocksure of himself. "But what?"

"I heard them talking, when they thought I was asleep." He shook his head. "Something doesn't feel right."

"Binks?" We were at the corner, a wall of sooty brick across the street. The meeting place. I said, "Binks? What?"

Chain-link fencing had been ripped back from a crumbling brick corner, windows sealed with cinderblocks but the doorway open, trashy, the maze dark beyond the doorway, the weak flicker of firelight glowing over the broken tops of walls.

His feeling, the way he said it, spooked me.

"I think...Blake Pangbourne's been working for them."

"What?"

"Just a feeling but—"

"Bullshit! Total bullshit!" Used, toyed with, cornered, hot rage and terror, I snapped, I went ballistic, lost all caution. "Bull fucking shit! Pangbourne!"

Binks grabbed my sleeve. "Darryl?"

"Pangbourne!" I jerked free and marched across the street, kicked wine bottles out of the way, and stepped through the doorway. "Where are you, Pangbourne, you piece of shit?!"

A voice in the maze. "In here. Straight ahead."

I was boiling mad, terrified, panting, my jaw clenched. Do it. Do it!

I kicked garbage and strode in past an agent skulking behind a pile of rubble and timber. He had a rifle and wore a tiny headset, wire looped under his jaw, but I paid him no mind, stomped ahead, madder and madder as the light brightened.

Binks was hardly keeping up as I strode into a room littered with trash, bricks, and broken lumber. Two doors opened in the opposite wall, left and right. I was tempted to go for the left door but there was a hole in the floor, a pit of blackness, so I made a line drive to the right door and stepped into the light.

The infamous Blake Pangbourne stood beyond a rusty drum filled with burning wood. Black curly hair, grey eyes glinting with meanness, he needed a shave, but he was lean and hard as nails all the way down to his waffle-stomper hiking boots. His eyes held murder, his hand held a big pistol, and a pang of fear went through me.

"You piece of shit," I said, "where's my little girl?"

"Mr. Jones. Toughie." His eyes strayed off me as he said, "And Binks, your nice guy neighbor. We've had quite a running conversation, Mr. Binks."

The fire crackled. "Where is she, you son-of-a-bitch?!"

I bumped Binks aside and stepped past the barrel of fire. He snagged my sleeve, jerked me to a stop, but I yanked free. I ripped open Paul's backpack and dumped out everything, sweatpants, a shirt, a pair of socks and the house I wanted to build for my family, or at least the money for it. Thirty-two packets of cash hit the ground with little puffs of dust.

"There's the money." Pangbourne's eyes drilled me as I tossed away the backpack. I said, "Where is she?"

"Where's my brother?" He raised the pistol and aimed at my head. "What did you do to Fisher? You killed him, didn't you." The gun shook in his hand. Beyond the gun all I saw was the murder in his eyes and his bared white teeth. "You bastard! You killed him!"

"No!" I blurted and babbled. "No, I didn't. I don't, no I...I never saw him."

"Liar! He went to meet you, to get paid for all the junk you and your son stole!"

Binks said, "That's not what happened."

"Shut up!" He pointed the pistol at Binks, so I edged toward the barrel of fire. If I could get behind it I could pull the gun without him seeing it...or something like that. But Pangbourne swung his pistol over and froze me. He whispered, "I'll kill you right now."

"Where's Patty? You want him, I want her, that's the deal. So? Where is she?" He had the gun, but I couldn't hold it in. "You scumbag, where is she?"

A Rasta man popped up from behind a wall, his dreadlocks flopping. He shouted, "For Ed!" and threw a machete at me. It startled Blake, but Binks saw the guy, shoved me, and I fell behind the barrel of fire.

All hell broke loose. Binks pulled his gun and fired, the Rasta man fell back screaming, and guns started blasting all around us. World War Three. A big black guy on the wall, upper right, fired a pistol, dirt kicked up beside my head, and that's when I pulled Fisher's gun and whipped it up. Fired. The man toppled out of sight.

It was odd. Blake didn't kill me because I knew where Fisher was and I didn't kill Blake because he knew where Patty was. Binks didn't shoot him for the same reason as gunfire spit lightning over the walls, cracking like thunder. Bullets shattered concrete, men screamed, cursed, shouted, and close by I heard spent cartridges tingling on rocks. Binks wasn't protected. Blake's pistol jerked, crack! and Binks stumbled back, hit a wall and toppled down.

Metal whizzed past my ear and ricocheted off brick, but I was already jumping up. I charged, snarling. I tackled Blake, drove him back through a doorway, past a Rasta man with a knife. He took a swipe at me, cut a line of fire into my arm, but I finally had Blake, that son-of-a-bitch, and I growled, pumped my legs, drove him back.

I lost my feet. The ruined rooms and firelight rose away from me and I was still holding onto Blake but we were dropping down into darkness. Wham! We hit and went down. My knees slammed into something, I yelled into Blake's ribs—that pain was so bad—but my hand, holding the gun, took the weight of both of us. The shock of crushed joints was so sharp I saw spikes of red pain and yelled. Blackness, red streaks shooting through me, I rolled off him and pulled my hand out.

Pain, dust, coughing, dark. Blake still lay next to me in the rubble and I thought, What the...hurts...hurts! Then I saw the jagged hole in the ceiling and knew what happened. The floor, a hole, we ran into a hole. I was on my back, looking up, and above the hole a Rasta man was pointing a pistol at us.

"Blake! Which you? Blake!"

My hand, mashed and numb, was still holding Fisher's pistol. I raised it and fired. Shot him. The Rasta man stumbled back and hit a wall going down.

"Ah!" Something hit my wrist, Blake's boot maybe, my arm jerked and I couldn't hold the pistol, it disappeared in the dark. Rocks clattered as a black shadow, Blake himself, stood up and staggered. I reached for him and shouted, "Where!" I rolled over and dove, grabbed him by the leg. "Where is she?!"

"Where's Fisher!"

Blake didn't care as much as I did. He kicked me in the head—stars, pain, dizzy, but...can't...let him...get loose. Couldn't hold him. He stomped my hands, ripped his leg free of me, and stumbled out of the light shafting down from the hole in the ceiling. I scrabbled up, tripped over chunks of concrete, staggered into the blinding dark. Good thing too. Someone started shooting a machine gun down through the ceiling hole, a deafening roar of shots that drowned out the ricochet of bullets, the lead hitting steel beams over my head and sparking in the dark.

Smack, I hit a wall, rolled against it, fell through a doorway, and saw Blake in a column of pale light. He was at an outside wall, streetlight coming down hazy from a hole in the roof. He jumped, got a grip, and pulled himself up. I ran at him. Not possible. I tripped over something and fell—oomph!—rolled over, sat up, pushed off, knocked over a steel drum, clang! I staggered and grabbed his leg.

"Where? Tell me!" He kicked his hiking boots and I couldn't hold on. "Blake!"

A black shape over the hole. "Dead!"

"No! Blake!"

"She's gonna be!"

I leaped up and got a grip on the lip of the hole. All the pain I was in, I hauled myself up, boosted out, and rolled onto the blacktop of an alley. Ground level, he was running away. I spotted a gleaming shape. My eyes focused—pistol—a pistol lost beside an old smashed mailbox. I crawled over and grabbed it, swung it up, but Blake was already disappearing onto the street at the north end of the alley.

A scraping noise and I rolled over and pointed the pistol. A black kid popped up from behind the wall, a teenager with scraggly hairs on his chin, a long scar running from his chin up to his eyebrow. He swung a revolver over the wall and down toward me, so I shot him, the gun bucking in my hand.

One more grieving parent.

I found my feet and ran. Shotgun booms, screams, shouts beyond the walls. I ran for the street, sirens wailing somewhere far off. I rounded the corner onto a sidewalk. Blake was yanking open the door of a sporty black beast. I stopped, raised the pistol, aimed at the tires of the beast and fired. Click click, empty.

I chucked the pistol. "Pangbourne!"

Three Rastas backed out of the ruins, into the street, raising their hands over their heads. Two Feds stepped out from the building, rifles leveled, and shot all three, mowed them down, and the Rastas fell without a screech. Rifle shots, shotgun blasts, screams of pain behind me, the cracking of small caliber firearms, and I ran toward the black beast. Blake gunned the engine, tires spun, screeching, and I dove through the smoke of burning rubber.

He took off with me hooked to his bumper. Pavement blurred, my body sizzling over the tar, but it didn't hurt because of the flak jacket against my skin, my steel-toed boots zipping behind me. The Jag slid around a corner, wrenched my shoulders, one set of fingers ripped loose as I slewed sideways. My knees slammed against the chrome bumper. Pain, bolts of it.

Was I gonna let go? No way in hell. He dragged me up the street, hit a bump that slammed my knee caps, my fingers felt like they were getting sliced off at the joint, and I thought I was dead.

An intersection. The beast slid to a stop as three black-and-white NYPD squad cars blasted into the crossroads and slid around the corner. Apparently the Feds never notified the locals that something was going down. I was afraid to let go. Had to. My fingers bleeding, I gathered my legs and ducked around the car, along the curb. I swung my boot, the metal toe ground down to bright steel, and smashed the passenger window. It scared the hell out of Blake, so I grabbed the side view mirror.

The black beast leaped ahead, yanked me off my feet and almost out of my boots. Those boots rasped on the road like matches, the toes sparking, but that's not what worried me. The mirror was rankling and crackling in my hand, the screws ripping free of the door.

Crack! Oh shit. He was shooting at me!

Blake fired, crystals of broken window glass popping out past my forehead. The engine roared, we were flying past parked cars, and he fired again as I reached for the windshield well. I hooked my fingers into that groove as the mirror broke off. I let it drop, it shattered way back there on the street, and that's when Blake hit the electric window button. The shattered sheet of safety glass crinkled, chinked, folded, sheared off, and hit me in the ribs before it slid on the road and burst against a curb.

Didn't hurt, I had the flak jacket. Good thing too. Crack! Blake winged me that time and it felt like a fast ball beaned me in the ribs; but then he was out of bullets. "You fuck!" he shouted. "You stinking fuck!"

I dug my other hand into the window well and cranked a leg up. Clunk, my heel hit the engine hood and I hauled myself up in front of the windshield. He looked out at me, cursing, his teeth bared, but I couldn't hear him with the wind roaring in my ears.

I shouted, "Where is she?!"

I didn't give him a chance to answer before I swung my leg. Ka-shunk! The toe of my boot punched a hole through the windshield. That pissed him off, so he hit the brakes. My boot ripped out, slammed on the hood as I flopped, the momentum yanked me forward, my arm bones jerked out of my shoulder sockets, and I let out a yell. Fire in my fingers, no grip, I flopped and flew off the hood, hung in the air, still and disconnected, a moment of wild flight.

Uh-oh.

It felt like the whole planet slammed into me. I vaguely remember rolling end over end, pain over pain, until I hit something. Blank. I blacked out.

It couldn't have been more than a few seconds. I rolled onto my stomach and raised my head. The black beast was a hundred feet away. It was stopped, its brake lights glowing red.

Ah...god I...gotta...get up.

Couldn't. I squinted and saw Blake hop out from behind the wheel, the trunk open and the lid swinging up. He lifted out a burlap bag, heavy and squirming, and dropped it on the road. Thump.

Blake had a pistol. "You want her? Here she is!"

Patty? No...he can't, he...no! He could. He jammed a clip into the pistol, pointed and fired, the burlap perking, the bundle jumping.

"No! No!"

Blake fired four more times before he slipped into the black beast and took off. I scrabbled on the tar, every inch of me in pain, folded a leg, moaned, straightened, staggered up, swayed on my feet, suffering. My hands were on fire, sliced up and bleeding. I gazed dizzily down the street toward that still bundle of burlap.

Patty?

Walk. Get there. Move! The street cranked sideways as I stood up. I limped.

"Swa..." It stuck in my throat. I whispered, "Sweetie?"

No. Can't be. Smoke in the air, the stink of burnt cordite. Bloody holes in the burlap. She...can't be. No, she's...she's...

"Patty?" I dropped to my knees, my daughter not moving. I reached out and whispered, "Sweetie?"

No answer and there was blood. Blood on the burlap.

CHAPTER 19

She wasn't moving. My hands shook as I reached out to her. "Patty?" Can't be. I moaned. She was so...still. Dead? "No...please no!"

What...what's that? A sequin? A silver sequin glinted in the blood of a bullet hole.

Wait a minute. I grabbed the burlap and yanked it. The sequin was a fish scale. Pangbourne had shot them full of holes, two big stinky fish.

Oh my god...

Relief. I was so relieved it punctured me. I closed my eyes, my head sank, I tipped over and rolled on my back, the smell of dead fish in my nose.

She's alive! Not dead. Not dead!

Couldn't move. Too much pain to cry. Blake was gone, he beat me and I felt like it, beaten with a club, my shoulder crackling, my arm scraped bloody, and I was getting the drunken spins. Not dead, still alive, she's...she's...

I don't know how long I lay there, a minute or two. Cars droned past. Didn't want to move. I knew if I did it would split me with pain, my joints creaking, and my head ached. Just stay here, I thought. Be still. Tires rolled by, a foot from my head, but I didn't care.

Footsteps. A teenager's voice. "Yo man, you can't lay in the street. Get up before a car hit you."

Couldn't. Couldn't do it.

More footsteps, another voice, foreign, couldn't understand, so I opened my eyes. Huh?

Standing with the sky behind their heads was an odd couple. One was an old Chinese woman, her scalp showing through her grey hair, three yellow teeth behind old dry lips. The other was a black teenager in a purple tee-shirt with a bear cub on it, the mascot of some sports team. He was a bear cub, a big teen with fleshy arms, baby fat around his middle, big white teeth, and no beard. He also had a broom in his hand, way up there, the two looking down, pointing at me and talking Chinese.

The bear cub nodded, said something in Chinese, handed grandma the broom, and bent down. He hooked his hands under my shoulders. I moaned as he dragged me between two cars, thumping up the curb, across the sidewalk, and I grunted as my butt bumped over a threshold.

Grocery store? Racks of potato chips, candy, chewing gum, and beef jerky floated past. The bear cub dragged me into a back room, onto a futon mattress, and let me go, thump. I clenched my teeth and grunted. My entire right side felt pounded like a nail. Pain creased out from between all the little bones in my spine. My shoulder felt out of whack, pains rankling in the socket, my elbow had serious road burn, and my hip ached like it was getting stuck with a red hot pin.

Couldn't think, foggy, my eyes wouldn't focus. I was a mess.

The bear cub looked at the old woman. "Them fish too, Mz. Zhou? They shot fulla holes."

The old woman nodded. The bear cub slouched his baggy jeans out the door while Ms. Zhou, ancient and hunched, shuffled to a refrigerator. The store wasn't open yet, quiet except for the clatter of a mug she set into a microwave oven, and the beeps and hum as she turned it on. The bear cub walked in, clean chubby cheeks, a big silver fish hanging from each mitt. He spotted the Tupperware bowl on the counter and lifted his eyebrows.

"Oh man, Ms. Zhou, the good stuff?"

He lay the two fish, blasted with holes, into the refrigerator. I moaned. They turned and looked at me.

"So whassup with the fish?" the bear cub asked. "And who's Patty? Whassup, fallin' off the car? I saw that, yo, I knew it hadda hurt."

The old woman knelt beside me with a cup of hot steaming stuff that didn't smell like any tea I'd ever had. I shook my head. She picked up my hand and wrapped it around the cup.

"Drink it," she said. "You fee' betto."

It hurt to move. She wedged a pillow under my head, bending over me with the smell of black licorice.

"So whassup?" the bear cub said. "'sup with all them black an' whites? You wanted by the man?"

"You have to help me. I..."

I scowled, everything hurt, but after I got a sip of bitter tea I realized I was parched, hungry too, I slurped and started to gulp the hot tea. It felt so damn good, heat pooling in my belly, and in a moment I felt energy spreading through me.

There was something in that tea, something that woke me up and burned away the dizzy fog. Magical stuff, what I needed, but all I could do, still, was whisper.

"He kidnapped my daughter so...so you have to help me."

The kid shook his head. "No, man, we don't."

"I got money. I'll pay." I pulled money out of my coat, a packet of ten dollar bills. I held it out to Ms. Zhou, getting off her knees, but she looked at that five hundred dollars and shook her head.

"I gotta," I said, "gotta find him, but I don't know how. I don't know...this place. Can you help me? Please?" I looked at Ms. Zhou, her eyebrows gone, her lips rubbery and wrinkled. She knew enough English to understand. "My daughter, he stole her. Help me...please!"

The bear cub looked at Ms. Zhou. Some subtle sign passed between them. He said, "You know his name?"

"Pangbourne, Blake Pangbourne. You know him?"

"Of course, I know nine million people. You look in the phone book?"

I gulped the bitter tea.

"Yo stooge, duh." He slouched over to a thick yellow book and a cordless telephone. "Which borough he live in? Shit, busta." Ms. Zhou looked at her bear cub, he sighed and said, "Sorry." To me he said, "But yeah, busta, you gotta do information. Four-one-one, go ahead, but you gotta pay her for it."

He handed me the cordless phone. I pushed three buttons and pressed the phone to my ear. A woman's voice. City and state, please.

"New York, New York."

The bear cub snorted. "He Frank Sinatra."

What listing please? I told her, but after a moment the voice said, At the customer's request that number is unpublished.

I cut off the call and struggled to sit up. Damn, I was starting to feel like I could kick some major ass. I motioned for the telephone directory. "Gimme. Gimme it!"

Nothing else to do, I flopped the big yellow book open to the "P" section and found the Pangbournes, all twenty-three of them. I punched the buttons for Alice on 168th Street.

A groggy voice. Hello?

"I'm looking for Blake. Is he there?"

A pause, confusion. Do you know what time it is?

"Yeah. Is he there? If he is, I'll kick his damn ass! You tell him—"
Click.

I slammed the phone down and looked up at them. "She hung up on me."

The bear cub looked at Ms. Zhou. "You gave him too much."

I punched numbers and asked, "Do you have any guns?"

"No way! Chill, man. Smoke be comin' outta your ears."

A voice on the line. "Hello, is Blake there? No? How about Fisher? Fisher or Blake, you know either of them?"

I got answering machines, groggy voices, a perky young woman fresh out of the shower, a biker type who told me to go fuck myself. I punched buttons, crossed out names, scowled because I still hurt all over the place—my shoulder was starting to stiffen up—but I bent over the phone book, crossed off names, and dialed the next number.

I looked up at the bear cub. "I'll give you five hundred dollars for a gun. I have to get my daughter back."

The bear cub spoke to Ms. Zhou in Chinese. She shook her head and walked away. The phone rang. I tossed a packet of money onto the floor, pulled another packet out of my jean jacket, and tossed it to the floor.

"Tax free," I said, "fifteen hundred. Anything that shoots. Can you do it?"

I had him. The bear cub bent for the money, but I grabbed it. I met his glance and shook my head.

The phone clicked in my ear. An older woman's voice. Hullo? I was about to speak when the woman on the phone, a gruff voice, made me freeze. Fisher? Is that you? Honey?

I blurted it. "No, I'm looking for Blake. Is he there?"

The bear cub, looking at the packets of money in my hand, licked his lips. He whispered, "I can get you a gun. Gimme two K."

I slashed the air to shut him up.

I haven't seen Blake since last night. Who's this?

"This is...uh..."

Is this that man?

"What man? I've got a message from Fisher," I said, "for Blake. Have you seen him? Is he there? Who's this?" The phone book said her name was Dorothy. I said, "Dotty, are you Fisher's mom?"

I want to know who this is. Who is this? Who—

I cut off the call, dropped the phone and stuck out my hand. "Gimme a hand, champ."

I gasped through my teeth as the bear cub pulled me up off the mattress. The bruised muscles all over my body were clogged with dead blood, I was stiffening up, and I knew if I sat down again I'd never get up.

I leaned on the counter, wincing. "You can get me a gun? How much?"

"Two K. Good piece too, I'll make sure."

"Two thousand for something big? And shells?" He nodded, so I showed him another packet of tens and said, "Two K, here it is. Go fetch." He held out his hand. I shook my head. "Go get it and bring it back. Now."

The greed glinted in his eyes. He said, "Ten minutes," and jogged out into the store.

Grunting, I bent for the phone book. A pile of sales slips and a pen lay by the microwave oven. I copied down the address for Dorothy Pangbourne. Is that in Manhattan or...where?

"Ms. Zhou?"

I limped out into the store. My hip was banged up pretty bad. Ms. Zhou stood behind a counter that held the only new item in the store: the cash register. It was a computerized model with an L.E.D. read-out she was programming for the day.

"Ms. Zhou?" I said. "You know where East 238th Street is?"

She looked at me angrily. "You no get m'boy in trubba."

"Trouble? Uh-uh. All I want is my daughter." I glanced around. My daughter and some food. I grabbed a cheese danish, a muffin, a quart of milk, ripped open packages, wolfed and guzzled, burped.

Ms. Zhou looked at me disapprovingly. I said, "Excuse me," and lay a bill on the counter. She ignored it, and the next one too, but a hundred dollars got her attention. I nodded. "For the tea. It's got a heckuva kick."

A noise at the door. The bear cub hustled in, a hot looking black woman behind him. Jeez. She arched an eyebrow at me and sauntered into the back room, her heels clicking. I limped in after them, her hips swinging in shrinkwrap jeans, a nice bottom. When she turned around, though, standing before the microwave oven, she had a pistol in her hand, a chrome revolver with a carved wooden handle.

I reached for it. She pulled it back. "Cash."

I slapped two packets of twenties, two thousand dollars, on the counter. "Loaded? Show me."

She flipped open the cylinder, showed me the loads—.357 magnums—spun it, snapped the pistol shut, and grabbed for the money. I grabbed the gun, jerked it out of her turquoise claws, she sniffed indignantly but we both had what we wanted.

"Better get moving," I said, "it's time for homeroom." Up close, I could see she was the same age as the bear cub, all painted up at seven a.m. and ready for school. "Thanks...young lady."

She sniffed, raised her chin, and marched out into the store. "Cody, yo, you get your cut later."

I glanced at him. "Better get it now."

He hurried after her. "Yo! Shantel!"

I didn't know how good that pistol was, I thought it might misfire and blast my dick off, so I stuffed it into the back of my jeans and pulled down my jacket. I limped for the door. It was brighter out, people tramping along the sidewalk—but then I stopped.

I looked over at old Ms. Zhou, her bleached skin and the age spots on her hands, a tiny woman behind a big shiny cash register. She knew the harshness of life—that much was plain—so I made it clear.

"Thank you, Ms. Zhou. Thank you very much."

She flicked her skinny fingers toward the door. "Go fi' you daughter. Go."

I limped out, clenching my teeth, bad pain in my right shoulder and hip, and looked down the street. A hundred yards away Cody the bear cub had Shantel trapped against a doorframe and was slapping her arm for his cut. The City's a tough place all right and I didn't know where I was.

I stopped a black man in a business suit. "Excuse me. How do I get to East 238th Street?"

He was carrying a black leather briefcase the size of a postage stamp. No homework in there. He said, "That's Woodlawn, up near the golf course. Easy, just take the number four all the way to the end, then take a cab."

"The number four?"

"The green line, the subway, outbound. Catch it over that way about ten blocks. Or just catch that cab."

I spun around and almost fell down, a yellow taxi coming toward us. "Taxi!"

That cab pulled over like I knew what I was doing. I pulled open the front door and almost sat down on the cabbie's lunch. Most people sit in the back, I guess, but it was too late for that, and I was a little surprised to see that the cabbie was an Indian guy wearing a purple turban.

"Number four subway station northbound."

Seven dollars later I eased off the seat and looked up grimy black steel pillars to the subway platform. 176th Street? I gritted my teeth and climbed the stairs. No white people, everyone was black, brown, or Peruvian. I was the outsider, but I didn't feel like anyone noticed.

Everyone's a stranger in New York.

I stood in line at a token booth and stuck a fiver under glass. "How many will that buy?" Three. I plugged one into a turnstile and climbed up to the outbound platform. Across the tracks the inbound platform was crowded with people, but on this side it wasn't too bad, a college student, road workers, a few cleaning ladies.

The platform shook when the train rumbled up, I stepped on and stood there holding a pole. Didn't want to sit down, my hip ached and I knew that pistol in the small of my back would make it no picnic.

My fingertips were buzzing with Ms. Zhou's tea.

The trip took about twenty minutes, the cars ruckling and shaking, but it wasn't too many stops before the doors rattled open. A big sign—Woodlawn—so I limped across a crowded platform and into a madhouse stairwell, commuters rushing up.

The street, a crossroads. Big steel pillars held up the train tracks, traffic rushing underneath, crowded walks, streets, bus stops, pizza shop, Donut Heaven, pigeons, cans overflowing with garbage. I hobbled over to a taxi parked in front of a bar room. That cabbie was a skinny bronze Mexican guy with sunglasses flipped up on his head and a diamond earring.

"Where you go, choe?" he asked.

"East 238th Street. Move it."

He moved it fast as I sat gingerly on the seat, my hip aching and the gun hard against my spine. We followed a curve past a woodsy cemetery and in two minutes turned onto Katonah Avenue, another busy thoroughfare. Angelica's Bakery, Hosanna's Dry Cleaners, ornate black lamp posts, and we turned at P.S. 19, a big brick school with classrooms already lit up.

East 238th Street. It was a nice residential area, older houses with thick shrubs and old trees, but the street was too narrow and the houses close together, separated by a driveway but no lawn.

The cabbie said, "This the street, choe. Four dollar."

"The meter says three."

"Tip tip tip."

"Yeah, right, here's ten. And you see this..." I held up fifty bucks in a fan of tens. "You hang around until I come out, it's yours. Catch my drift?"

He shrugged and put the car in park. I climbed out and looked at the house. 364 East 238th Street was a flat-faced ugly house. Everything about it looked blunt.

One thought: Patty might be in there.

I limped up the front walk, my jeans dirty with road scrape, my boots scarred, one metal toe missing, the other steel toe ground down, dented, and bent. Not good, but the hell with it, especially since there was no welcome mat.

I pushed a button, an old fashion buzzer going off inside. I opened the screen door, the brass knob of the door worn to brown metal, and I gripped it. Vague shivers, someone was coming. I tensed. The knob turned.

I threw myself against the door and knocked her backwards.

"Ow! Get out!" A chunky woman, fifties, jowly, flailed at me. "No! Stay out! I'll call the police!"

I shoved her back, pulled the gun and stuck it in her face. "Where is she?!"

"Don't shoot!"

"Where's my daughter, you bitch!"

"Who?"

"My daughter!"

"I don't know, I...please don't shoot!"

I backed her up toward a kitchen door, a dachshund retreating into the corner.

"Tell me! Where she is! Where's my daughter? Dottie, now!"

"I don't know! I didn't!"

"She was here?" Mrs. Pangbourne's jowls shivered under her chin. I pointed the gun at her head, half turned, listened. Silent house. "Where is she? What did you do to her?"

"Last night? Made her supper, gave her a bath, and put her to bed."

"This morning?"

"He came and got her."

"How long ago?"

"Forty, forty-five minutes. He said she belonged to a friend."

"Yeah, right, Blake's a friend of mine. He got my son hooked on heroin, shot my babysitter, and kidnapped my daughter. Two hours ago he shot my next door neighbor, a state trooper." I shook my head. "Mrs. Pangbourne, your son is a real piece of work. Where'd he go?"

"Shot...who?" Mrs. Pangbourne, stunned, backed away, and settled heavily into a cheap creaky chair. The dachshund's toenails clicked on the kitchen floor. She whispered, "He shot somebody?"

"Your son is nuts but I don't care, I just want my Pattie back." She looked up at me and squinted. "Where'd he take her? Did he say?"

"He said he had one more person...to see." She put two and two together, looked up from the linoleum floor. "To see about Fisher. My other son. So...that must be you." Her face changed. She said, "What do you know about Fisher?"

"Nothing. Mrs. Pangbourne, he has my daughter. He's gonna kill her!"

She stood up, clenching her meat hooks, one mean bird.

"What about Fisher? What happened to him?"

"Mrs. Pangbourne, I—"

"Tell me." She grabbed my jacket, pushed me back to the frig, desperation in her eyes. "Where's my little boy? You tell me!"

"I don't know!"

"Tell me!" I grabbed her hands, the gun pointed at her head as I pried at her fingers. She shouted, "Where's my Fisher? Tell me!"

"Let go!"

"Tell me! Where is he?"

"Mrs. Pangbourne!"

"Where! Tell me, you bastard!"

"I...damn you!" I was afraid the gun would go off and shoot her in the head, yanking and twisting at me, so I shouted it. "Dead! He's dead!"

"No!"

"Yeah, you bitch, he's dead!" Her face puckered, but I had no pity. "Dead!"

Her eyes tightened, her lips trembled, and she hung on me like a big weight until I ripped her hands free. I pushed her away. She stumbled back two steps and sank onto the chair, stunned. Her mouth opened and closed. I had no compassion, I had Dottie Pangbourne pegged, one mean female bully, so I let her have it.

"How many more kids have to die? Blake too? Patty too? When is it gonna end, damn you? When!"

She let out a mewl of pain. "Fisher, he..."

"He's dead. Why? Blake got him mixed up in drugs. Fisher got my son hooked, he got all his friends hooked, and the whole thing blew up." I waved the gun over her. "My daughter, what about her? What about Blake? They don't have to die, do they? Where did he take her? Please, Mrs. Pangbourne. Please? Any idea? On the phone you asked if I was 'that' guy? Who? Blake's kingpin? Who is it? Any idea?"

Brows crumpled, her mouth fallen, she was wrecked. She stifled a gasp of pain, shuddered so only half a sob escaped her teeth.

"Blake," she mumbled, "he got involved with this man. His name is...boyfriend."

"Boyfriend?"

She looked at the floor, shook her head, choked. "An old word for it."

"For boyfriend? Beau? Honey? Squeeze?"

She shook her head. "He lives...um...I overheard them. Before Fisher left. He lives in...in Throgs Neck."

She pushed herself up to her feet and shuffled heavily into the dining room. She pulled open a small drawer in an old maple desk, pulled out trash, yellowed receipts, rubber bands, stamps, paper clips. The returning rage put an edge in her voice.

"He's always been a bad apple." She found a tiny scrap of paper and looked at me. "Blake's always been rotten. The man's name is Swain."

I snatched the paper and limped toward the door, kicked open the screen door, and hobbled toward the cab. Awful relief to get out of that house, the air of belligerence. Behind me Mrs. Pangbourne stopped on the threshold, tears leaking down her cheeks.

"Please," she said, "please don't hurt my Blake. He's all I have left."

I pulled open the door of the cab. "Only if I find him."

CHAPTER 20

Blake glanced up at the girders overhead, the underside of the highway splotched with bird dung, pigeons cooing a counterpoint to the buzz of morning traffic. A face of concrete slanted down to Blake's tires, tracks in fine sand, while across the road two seagulls stood motionless among the cigarette butts. They didn't blink as he circled his sports coupe, the black beast, and opened the door.

Patty, tiny on the bucket seat, looked at him. "Well, get out."

She slid off the seat. "I hate you."

"You're supposed to." He slammed the door and walked her to the back of the car. He unlocked the trunk, took out a roll of silver duct tape, and ripped off a six-inch piece. "Put this over your mouth."

"Why?"

"Because I don't trust you. You're going to squeal for your daddy and then I'll have to kill him." He held out the tape. "Put this over your mouth so I don't have to."

"Have to what?"

"Kill your daddy. Go ahead." Patty smoothed the tape over her mouth. "Hands too, but loose. I won't hurt you."

Blake ripped off tape and bound her wrists together behind her back. The fear didn't fill her eyes until he lifted her and lay her gently into the trunk. He knew those eyes. This time the female fear and venom didn't unsettle him, he just felt bleak. He reached for the top. She let out a sob, muffled by tape, her little blue sneakers thumping the carpet as she kicked.

He sighed. An emergency road kit lay by the sleeves of her blouse, edged with lace. He opened it, popped free a waterproof flashlight, turned it on, and put it by her head.

"Don't be scared, it won't be dark. And remember: be quiet or I'll kill your daddy."

He shut the trunk, and when she wailed he let out his breath slowly, trying to keep calm.

What now? he thought. Couldn't shoot the kid upstate, when we stole the ragtop, so what do I do with this one?

He got behind the wheel, stomped the gas pedal, rubber screeching as the tires spun and grabbed the blacktop. He knew she was crying but heard nothing as he drove up the ramp onto the Cross Bronx Expressway.

His shoulder ached from when he and Jones fell into the basement. "Tough bastard, that one." He shook out a butt, lit it, sucked, smoke burned his throat and he liked it, the burn, and when he coughed the stitch of anxiety in his stomach loosened. It came back, a knifing pain in his side, but it wasn't the worst. The worst was his brother's name.

Fisher? His face tightened, an ache over his eyes. He smoked a searing drag as the roof of his mouth cramped and he couldn't swallow past the clench in his throat. He whispered, "Fish?" He made the black beast fly past cars and delivery vans, people ignorant of him, his pain, the ache like he'd swallowed a hook. "Fisher? I...Fisher?"

A little voice...he's already gone...and Blake gripped the wheel and clenched his teeth against it, no, he isn't, he's...around, he's...he's here. Fisher? Fuck. What would Dad do? If he was here none of this would've...I never would've...

Blake flushed ugly with pain, squeezed the wheel to suffer the hard knotting of his arm muscles, squeezed to feel the bones of his hands crush the flesh inside them, tendons aching, his grip turning white on the wheel. Air rasped out of him, his shoulders shook, he was about to crack...but he began to gasp instead, the barb loosened out of his throat and he let out a single moan and downshifted.

Last exit before the Throgs Neck Bridge, the span arching over the channel ahead, he wheeled right into Swain's neighborhood. He drove slowly, wiping sweat off his cheeks. A neighborhood like he grew up in, neighborhood of flunkies for the corporate rulers. Sheep like his father, sacrifices, nothing more. Sacrifices for America, a pig at the trough. That's all they do, feed the pig.

Blake spun the wheel and turned into the driveway at Grandma's house, got out, and walked toward the back door. Shadows of the locust tree laced across the grassy lawn and over the tree's gnarly roots. The door buzzed, the locks releasing before he reached for the knob.

Bad sign. Too quick, they were waiting for him.

He walked into Grandma's kitchen. A design of blue flowers glowed on the new tile floor but the cabinets stood old and splintered along the bottom— didn't want Grandma to look too rich—the handles basic and the Formica countertop glowing pale to the backsplash, glass canisters standing full of cookies, uncooked spaghetti, Grandma's matchbook collection. A clock in the shape of an old milk can. 8:01 a.m.

Scratching. He turned to a door standing open six inches, white panels, a pink marble knob. Click, click, click, click. Stairs to the basement, he stepped down into the smell of cigarettes and menthol cleaner. Smoking a cigarette, one eye squinted, Ganz glanced up at him, his hair gelled into a dozen tiny blonde and brown thorns.

Ganz half-smiled, the cigarette bobbing. "Hey dude."

Swain still had his back turned. He was stirring a pot of crack soup, his peach-colored polo shirt bunched on his wide hips. Above him, the six security monitors displayed views of the yard and driveway.

Blake cleared his throat. "Swain?"

"How many did you kill?" Swain spun around and slashed the wooden spoon, spattering Blake with boiling cocaine slop. "You stupid fuck! How many?"

"Son-of-a..." Blake wiped his face. "He killed Fisher."

"Jones? Who cares?" Swain's lip kinked, his eyes vicious. "It's on C.N.N. Fourteen dead in four days? You ass, you should be the fifteenth!"

Blake looked at Ganz, who carried a .38. "Fourteen?"

"Oh, so you didn't do them all? What a good boy." Swain paced, spun, and stirred the bubbling white soup, a clear veneer on top. "They found Eduard in the trunk of a car. You dolt, how did that happen?"

"It was Jones, I sent Ed to see him. He's mean, he killed Fisher, I know he did. Swain? I—"

"Question is," Ganz said, "what's he look like?"

Ganz nodded toward the security monitors. A middle screen caught a view of the driveway, a figure sneaking past Blake's black beast. Blake's mouth opened. "Incredible."

Swain's spoon went still in his stirring. "That's him?"

The figure ducked into Grandma's detached garage. "Christ, this guy's a barnacle. I just got rid of him! "

"So you thought." Swain glanced at Ganz, then jerked his head toward the stairs. "Go take him out."

Ganz reached to a leather jacket draped over a pistol in a holster. Ganz said, "I'll dust him, then put him in Grandma's trunk."

"Put down some newspapers first." Swain shot a look at Blake, sarcasm in his voice. "Listen to me. It sounds like I'm taking care of puppies."

CHAPTER 21

"Pull over."

The Mexican cabbie stopped at the end of Revere Street, where this Swain guy lived. Blue collar neighborhood, little houses built in the 1940s, overgrown bushes, willow trees, economy Fords snug in single stall garages set back behind the houses. I got out and shut the door.

"Same as before," I said. "Fifty more if you wait for me."

He knew something was up. "You gotta pay the meter first, see."

I limped up Revere Street, the slate squares of the sidewalk heaved up by tree roots, and I didn't know where I was except we took the last exit before the Throgs Neck Bridge, a big span arching into the air half-a-mile away. Down at the end of the street was a yacht club, big iron gates standing shut, but I could see the water beyond, smelled it, green slime on rocks and wooden pilings. I tripped on a tree root, a shock of pain through my hip—that hip was in bad shape, I was in serious pain—so I stopped two houses away from Blake's machine, the black beast, parked in a driveway.

Swain's driveway. The kingpin?

I glanced up and down the street. Not a body in sight, worker grunts already gone for the office, but I hid behind a tree, shuffled my boots. Patty? I could feel she was close. In there? Gardener's heaven? Swain's house didn't look like a drug dealer's place, red roses on a white trestle, porch swing, window boxes, petunias, a front door with a brass knob. I ambled closer. A detached garage stood at the back of the driveway, a patch of grassy lawn back there, a sidewalk along the back of the house, a hoary old locust tree.

I stood before a house with a big weeping willow, hanging branches hiding me from Swain's. Clatter-bang of a screen door and a boy, ten or eleven, thick glasses and mousy brown hair, hustled out, late for school, his thumbs hooked under the shoulder straps of a big lunky knapsack. I backed away, almost tripped over a fireplug, but then I spun around as he reached the sidewalk.

"Hey." Jogging, he turned to look at me and his knapsack almost pulled him over. "You see that black beast there? The sports job?"

He was a skinny little guy. "Yeah, I gotta go, I'm late."

"You see it pull in here? Just a little while ago?"

The kid hitched up the straps of his knapsack. "Yeah."

"You see who it is, the driver?" He pushed up his thick glasses. "He take anyone inside? A little girl maybe?"

"Into Mrs. Swain's house? Naw, nobody, I gotta go."

"He didn't take anybody in?"

He jogged, throwing it over his shoulder. "Uh-uh!"

I turned toward Swain's house. She's not in there, but Blake is. So how do I flush him out? Tools. Tools where? My eyes lit on the garage at the back of the property.

I edged into Swain's driveway, looking around. Down at the end of the street a set of fancy metal gates were swinging open at the yacht club, a skipper towing his boat out, water splashing down around the wheels. Everything else was quiet. Birds chirped and the drone of the highway came over the trees.

I skipped past Blake's beast, ducking low.

I slipped in through the old side-hinge doors of the detached garage, their white paint peeling, past the fender of a little hatchback parked on a concrete floor broken up with grass growing out of the cracks. Oil stains, grass clippings, a work bench at the back. No light cord, I tripped over a gas can by a lawn mower that stank of rotting grass. The workbench: dusty window, splintered top, brushes soaking in coffee cans, paint trays, dusty jars, rags in a corner.

On the window sill: old Zippo lighter. Good enough.

I grabbed the gas can, a gooseneck spout, hoisted it to the bench and twisted off the top of a mason jar. I should've been careful, I sloshed gas all over the jar as I filled it, but then I grabbed a rag and spilled gas all over that too, for my wicks. With a screwdriver I stabbed a hole through a jar top, jammed the sloppy stinking cloth through the hole, and had it made, a fine molotov cocktail.

That'll flush him out. I set it aside, made two more, splashing and stabbing, gasoline splotching the workbench, screwing on covers and...

Behind me, a creak.

A silhouette—a man, prickly-haired—boom! His pistol spit granular smoke but I was already dropping for the floor, hit the oil stains with my hand wrapping around the .357 down my back, yanked it out and fired at the man's ankles. That's all I could see under the hatchback. I fired, pulled the trigger, missed, he was moving, sneakers skipping to the side, I fired, he fired—his bullet streaked the concrete in front of my nose—and finally I fired and hit him. His last shot brought a sprinkle of dust down from the roof but he was already yelling as he fell and slammed the wall. I dove past a front fender, firing, the pistol bucking, the man jerking with the hammer blows of bullets as they hit him.

I lay aiming at the door, waiting for the next guy to come. Couldn't hear, deaf from the pistol shots, I felt myself panting. I squeezed the gun. Nobody came. Tense, the gun shivered, I waited. The stinging stench of fired bullets. Nobody came.

I crabbed over to the guy kicking on the floor, blood all over him, and as I bent over him I heard the last animal sound he made as he died, eyes open, terrified, staring.

Faint blood smell. Killed him, I did. Holy shit. But...how'd he know I was here?

I spun for the bench. I stuffed the pistol into my belt and scooped up the mason jars stinking of gasoline, ran to the door, looked out. Nobody. Same quiet suburban street. Nobody heard us shooting? Apparently not, or they were ducking for cover.

I stepped out into the driveway, set down two of the jars, flipped open the top of the old-fashion Zippo, lit a flame, lit a sopping wick and lobbed the firebomb high at the house.

Decisive moments stretch long. The mason jar full of yellow sloshing gasoline trailed smoke from its flaming wick. The Molotov cocktail arced high and down and hit the roof, clunk. Bounced. Rolled. Dropped off the roof and smashed on the sidewalk, flames roiling up.

Dammit!

I grabbed another bomb and raised the Zippo. Click, click, I lit the wick.

Boom! The jar shattered, gas splashing, shit! It didn't blow up, I wasn't on fire, but I danced away from the burning wick, my jeans soaked in gasoline.

The house. An enclosed porch, a bullet hole through a pane of window glass. Blake Pangbourne stepped out the back door, pointing his pistol. Oh, a bullet, the shot, right, it was a bullet.

Blake looked disgusted. "You're not very good at this."

My hand went to the small of my back, my gun. He shook his head. Yeah, stupid idea. I pull the gun and I'm dead.

"On the grass," he said. "Now."

"Where's Patty?" I tossed the pistol, it thumped in the grass. I glanced to the street. Where would I run? Why? If anyone heard the shooting the cops would come, time was on my side, so I looked at Blake and his pistol. "You son-of-a-bitch, where's my little girl?"

"Where's Fisher?"

A voice from inside the house. "Get him in here, you fucking dolt."

Blake glanced over his shoulder, irritated, but motioned with the barrel. I hobbled across the grass to the walk, up onto the porch and into the kitchen, the gasoline fire dead on the walk and a patch of grass burnt black. I had to stop myself. It gripped me, the need to grab Blake and punch him in the head. My hands clenched, the shake of adrenalin, my jaw set, I tensed like a cocked trigger.

Don't. Find Patty.

A kitchen, I hardly saw it as Blake urged me downstairs into the basement. We filed down the creaky stairs, and at first the basement didn't look too odd, tools on a pegboard wall, camp stove on a bench, something cooking on the burners, toolboxes under the bench. Then I saw a bank of six mini-TVs that showed different views of the house.

That's how they knew. How stupid am I? But otherwise the place didn't look odd. Cement floor, boxes of Christmas bulbs stacked under the stairs, next to half-a-dozen dusty window screens.

The man, Swain, was different. Mid-thirties but too soft. Wide hips, no muscle in his arms, his cheeks shaved too smoothly, too carefully, his eyes too close together and glistening with too much hate. He looked at me and snarled.

"Trying to burn down my grandmother's house?" he asked. "Are you a pain in my ass, or what?"

"Where is she?"

He blinked. "Who?"

"My daughter."

Swain's mouth cracked open, he looked at Blake. "Don't tell me. Don't you fucking tell me."

Blake shrugged one shoulder. "He knows where Fisher is."

"God dammit! You kidnapped his...Christ! I can't believe it! And you brought her here?" Swain, throwing up his hands and cursing, turned away, and suddenly turned back. He looked at me, came to a decision, nodded to Blake. "Go ahead, shoot him. Now."

Blake looked at me. "He knows where Fisher is."

"Now!"

Blake was bigger, his muscles pumped, but there was a weird parent-and-child thing going on between them, as if Blake was a kid nervously facing down his mean parent. He stiffened. The tension pulled his head down to the side, then a spasm jerked his shoulder and his head straightened up again. He gripped his pistol and swallowed.

"No?" Swain barely held himself in check. "Why not?"

Blake's voice, firm but shaky. "Fisher, if he is...if he's dead, he has to be buried right. We're Catholic."

"So?"

"In a cemetery. Consecrated." We didn't understand. Blake looked at me. "Otherwise he goes to Purgatory. Forever. Because this putz killed him!" Wrath twisted his mouth and I actually felt the rage in his voice. "So? Where is he? Tell me, then I'll let her go."

I shook my head. "I don't believe you."

"That does it." Swain yanked open a drawer, hardware clattering. "As if this guy is responsible? For Fisher? Your arrogant little brother?" Swain grabbed a pistol, swung it around and aimed it. At me. "Who got him into this business, Blake? You did!"

Swain pointed the gun at me. The air caught in my throat. Holy God...

BOOM!

I flinched. Wasn't me, I wasn't dead.

Staggered by Blake's shot, Swain fell back and hit the bench. He knocked over the boiling crack, white slop splattered the wall, and the pot jangled as Swain fell to the floor. A dot on his shirt spread into a red blotch, he gasped, a startled look on his face, but he was on the floor and reaching, clawing for a grip on life.

Two steps and Blake leaned over him. "Who got me into this business? You did!"

Blake shot him again. A red hole appeared above Swain's eyebrows, the hand clutching at the bench dropped, his body slumped.

Holy God.

The ringing of shocked eardrums filled my head, but Swain was finished, his eyes open, staring. I looked at him, at Blake, the pistol shaking in his hand. Sirens in a shocked silence. The terrible stench of death and burnt gunpowder. Holy God in heaven. I reached out to a railing to steady myself. Swain's body, on the floor, shuddered weakly, a nervous spasm, his fingers twitched, and then he was still.

No question, that was the real thing. Murder.

Blake was unraveling and I was feeling sick. Honestly, the tension was making my stomach churn. Blood, violence, death, what did I know about them? Nothing. What I knew about was my family, how I felt about them, the love, the terrible fear for their safety.

That terrible fear was also tearing at Blake, and the guilt, so he was unraveling like a torn edge, desperate and ripping at himself. He kicked Swain's gun under the bench, turned to me and showed his white teeth.

"See what I can do? Now where is he?!" Nothing different. If I told him where Fisher was I was dead, I knew it, and Patty too. "You son-of-a-bitch!"

"Blake? Blake, please."

The look in his eyes, he was losing his grip. He pointed the pistol at my head and his finger tightened on the trigger. "Three seconds! One...two..."

CHAPTER 22

The muzzle of the gun stared at me, shivering, Blake scowling, a snarl seething through his teeth.

Holding onto the rail for dear life, I couldn't face him, it, that pistol. I whispered, "Please." I groaned, I was hurting, hung my head, and when I did I caught a glimpse of the stairs. Only way out. I connected with the thought and went with it, improvised, leaned over groaning, eased back, and let myself sink onto a stair.

One step closer to freedom. Lots of wear and tear, pains slicing down my leg and shooting up my back, every joint ached, I didn't have to fake it. I winced, hung my head and whispered, "Blake, please."

"Get up. Look at me!"

Couldn't. I leaned on my elbows, on my knees, and covered my eyes. I had to slow him down, someone would come, couldn't think, too much, too tight, the intensity, the shock of getting banged around, but I still had to think. One thought: don't look at him. I hung my head and stared at the floor. Speak. Say something. Couldn't think, but I spoke. "Blake...where?"

"God damn you!"

He grabbed me by the hair, my head on fire, I screamed and he jammed the gun into my ear. "Don't! Blake I...don't!"

"Piece of shit! Dead! I'll fucking kill you!"

He manhandled me down, I tried to get it out, the gun, but when my head hit the concrete floor I had to give, the muzzle gouging my ear, he was gonna jam it into my brain before he pulled the trigger. "Okay! Jesus, Blake, stop! Stop!"

He whacked me with it, the pistol, a second time for good measure, my brow ripped open so that blood dribbled onto my eyelash. I blinked, droplets dripping, I sleeved it away, cowed, I was totally played out, no juice left, and we both knew it. He stepped back, I heard him breathing. Blood spotted the floor, bright red in front of my eyes, a ringing in my ears.

Buy time. Buy time.

I felt my brow, tiny lips of flesh, my hand wet. "But Blake...Patty first." I kept looking at his boots. "I have to see her. See that she's...she's safe."

"You dictate to me?" He whacked me again, back of the head. "Fuck off!" Whack! Then I heard it, he whacked himself. Raving mad, he stepped back, stumbled over Swain's leg, and gave the body a vicious kick. "Stupid god damn...why the...how the...I'm gonna...fuck! Fuck!"

He swung the pistol. One of the little TVs exploded, glass tingling across the floor, and he heaved the camp stove off the bench. The stove crashed in the corner, clanging, grates cartwheeling, and the flames went out.

Silence. His breathing rasped loud. He opened his hands and looked up to the heavens, beyond the bare joists that held up the kitchen floor.

"Fisher?" He whispered it. "Fish, I just want you...you to be..." He was begging for something, forgiveness maybe, but after a moment of silence he gave up. He leaned over, settled his elbows on the bench, his head in his hands, and let out a cry. "Fuck me!"

He leaned panting into his arms. I held my brow, but it wasn't bleeding anymore. Silence. I settled back with a groan and looked up at the ceiling. Floor joists aged half-a-century to a mellow brown and blonde wood held up Grandma's kitchen floor, beautiful stock a full two inches thick, not like they cut it now, half-an-inch less, commercially grown, not as dense in the fibers, lightweight, not as good but...but what am I...

I came to my senses and found myself staring at the ceiling. Where is he? No murderous energy in the air, he was on the verge of tears, still leaning on the bench, but I sensed I shouldn't let him go too low.

"Blake?" I said it softly, gently, like a verbal nudge. "You don't want to hurt her. Blake? Think about it. She's just a little girl."

"Fisher was just a little boy. Little golden boy." Blake straightened, his back to me, and looked at the gun in his hand. "That's how she treated him, my mother, her golden boy, that's what he was. Me? I'm the family dog. That's all I'm ever going to be, I know it. No matter what I do, I'm the dog."

"I met her. She's...yeah. A bulldozer."

"And how could Dad stand up to her? Good dog, here's a biscuit, take the boys to church...until he got fired. Then she kicked him around too, poor guy. Christ almighty, he lived in the doghouse no matter what he did." Blake cleared his throat and shook his head. "One day he went on a job interview, had a coronary in somebody's waiting room and died by a magazine rack. In front of People Magazine. At John Wayne's fucking feet!"

He tensed, the muscles in his shoulders swelling. Uh-oh.

"You killed Fisher. And Ed. And now, if you don't tell me where he is, this dog is gonna kill you." He spun and pointed the gun at me. "Now! Sick of this shit. Blow your god damn head off!"

"Let her go!" I raised my hands. "She goes, I'll tell! I will!"

"Get up! You lousy stinking—"

He yanked me up, stiff and full of pains, shoved me gasping up the stairs. He pushed me into the kitchen. I fell down with a cry, a bolt of lightning ripping through my hip, but he kicked me so I scrambled to the back door, staggered out into the back yard.

Smell of burnt grass, oily tar. Birds chirped. Sunlight shafted down through the locust tree. Blake herded, I stumbled toward the black beast.

"Where we going? Where did you leave her?"

"Get in."

He popped the locks. I eased myself in, onto the passenger's bucket seat. Gorgeous car, the smell of new leather. Blake circled around, got in behind the wheel, and did something strange.

He stuck his finger in my face and shouted it. "Remember what I said! Not a sound! Make a sound and I'll kill you both!" Jeez. I looked at him and I was about to say okay, but he shouted, "Not a sound!"

He was shouting loud enough for Patty to hear, in the trunk. I didn't realize it. I nodded and swallowed the dryness in my throat. He gunned the engine and backed out onto the street.

The long hood of the black beast pointed south, the yacht club at the end of the street, the metal gates standing open. He looked at me and said, "Yes, that'll do it. That works for me."

He hit the gas. The tires screamed, we slewed sideways, straightened out, picked up speed.

"Where are we going?"

"Fasten your seatbelt."

"Where is she? Blake?" We started to fly, hit the end of the street. "Blake!" We blasted in between the gates of the yacht club. The launch ramp dropped to a corridor of water, choppy and dark between a cement wall and a dock. "What are you doing? Blake!"

"Where's Fisher?" The black beast roared. "Tell me! Now!"

Too late. I threw my boots up to the dash and braced myself. Eighty miles an hour, the engine roaring, we shot down the boat ramp and hit the water, a sheet of spray going up.

The steering wheel bent in Blake's hands like a wet pretzel.

The engine pulled us under. Black water gushed in the windows, frigid, shocking. I couldn't breathe, freaked out, struggled.

Blake was gone, swimming out his window. Panicky, I grabbed the roof edge, tried to swim out, couldn't, the seat belt around my hips. The car sank into dim submerged silence. Submerged, cold, the burble of bubbles. I fumbled with a buckle. The front bumper hit the bottom with a crunch. I popped the latch, got free of the seat belt, and struggled out the window.

A ceiling of air eighteen feet up, bubbles trickling up in columns, sheets of bubbles rising from around the edges of the trunk. That's where Patty was, but I didn't know it.

I kicked and swam up toward the underside of the textured mirror, the surface, broke through, and gasped for air. Doggie paddle. I splashed, heavy clothes, gasping, got my bearings. Blake was already climbing up a ladder to the dock. I thrashed over, grabbed the slimy plastic rungs, and started to climb.

Half-a-dozen South American waiters, dressed in white shirts and black bowties, were out on the deck of a restaurant terrace, up at the club, another six or eight club members, socialites, and boaters, watching us and pointing. I wasn't focused on them. Blake, soaking wet and homicidal, watched me climb the ladder. I dragged myself onto the dock, rolled onto my back and saw a blue sky.

He reached behind his back and pulled out a gun. The shock of the water cleared my head. Behind him, up on the terrace, the waiters shouted in Spanish.

I knew it: we were down to the wire. I said it again. "Where is she?"

"Where's Fisher? Tell me."

"So you can shoot me? Throw the gun in the water."

No question, we were at the end. I knew it, he knew it. He tossed the pistol over the railing, a splash.

"Where is he?"

"Where's Patty?"

"What happened to him?"

The moment of truth. I rolled over, pushed myself up. Groaning at the pain, I stood up, couldn't manage it, stumbled against the railing. I didn't want to tell him, it stuck in my throat, and he saw it.

"You killed him, didn't you?"

I'd done it, I was there, Paul too. I had to protect him, so what could I say? I clung to the railing. I never wanted anyone to suffer, I didn't, so I opened my one free hand.

"Blake, I...I'm sorry. It was an accident. Honest to God." His fists clenched, his chest began to heave. "He came up to the house, for when I get married, and he..."

"You killed him."

"He tripped, I didn't."

"Liar!"

"He fell. Blake, it's true!"

He shouted, "Liar!"

He charged. In a murderous rage, he hit me like a wet freight train, plowed me back against the railing, pain ripping across my back, and we fell jumbled on the dock. He rolled on top of me, bigger, and he was so blind raging angry that he went right for it, the kill. He grabbed me by the throat and squeezed. Crushing pain. I couldn't breathe, no air, I kicked, gagged, chopped at his arms.

Can't...let him...

Blake choked me and snarled, "God...damn...you!"

The sky blushed from blue to pink, went dark red, he was seething through his teeth. All I could see, white snarl, glint of gold swinging below his chin, I was passing out.

I clawed at him, his grip, crushing, I dug in, got inside one hook of his hand...his thumb, pry it loose...gotta...and ripped off a hand. I sucked air, clawed at his other hand, still clamped on my throat.

No mercy. He raised a rock of a fist way up into the blue and brought it down. Wham! I tried to block, deflected some of it, but his fist slammed a dull bruising pain into my mouth, the sweet taste of blood, and jerked my head to the left. Then I saw his left fist coming down, wham! My head jerked right and dizzy.

It was no Hollywood fistfight.

I got my hands up, blocked punches, he was pummeling me, his red wrathful face above me, cursing, spitting rage, red and hateful. I had to get him off. My legs were free. I kicked him in the back, no little thing with steel-toed boots. He let out a grunt but kept slamming his fists down at me, got through and jerked me, so I kicked him again, hard, and he yelled. It knocked him off balance, he landed on his hands, his face inches from mine. Bloodshot eyes, pure hate, clenched teeth, stubbled cheeks.

A small golden cross shivering on a fine chain.

He was that close. I swung a fist from the side and nailed him in the jaw. It jerked his head, stunned him, a moment's reprieve, so I swung both feet up and hooked my boot heels around his throat. I straightened with all the muscles in my body, cranked him backward, slammed him down, he hit hard on his back and shook the dock.

As I said, it wasn't Hollywood. I sat up, he was half on top of me, so I punched him in the crotch as hard as I could. He gasped and pulled in his legs, toppling off me.

"Where is she?!" I kicked him in the stomach. He yelled, but I was already crawling on top of him. "Blake!"

I belted him in the face. I hit him so hard a bolt of pain went up my arm. He moaned. The whole side of his face turned purple. I didn't care, desperate, wild, I grabbed him by the throat and squeezed until I felt the little gold cross he was wearing dig into my hand. I raised his head and slammed it down, bunk!bunk!bunk!bunk! "Damn you! You son-of-a-bitch!"

I tried to lift his head and slam it down again but my hands slipped free. Instead I tore the gold cross off his throat, the chain dangling, and he saw it.

"Where is she? Blake, for Christ's sake!"

Recognition. He could only see out of one eye, the other swollen shut, but I saw something in it, wild sadness, and he let out a cry.

"Where!" He growled, and about to hit him again, I hesitated. He fluttered his hand toward the railing. "Where? In the car?"

I looked at the water. No bubbles.

He grabbed my leg. "Fi...Fisher?"

No time. I threw away his gold cross, raised my boot, stomped it down on his face, and ripped loose.

I put a hand on the railing and vaulted over. I went in, water roaring up around me. Cool silence. The black beast was a dark shape eighteen feet below, resting at a tilt on the bottom.

I swam down. Where? Trunk? Only place possible. Door latch? I swam to the driver's door, opened it, pulled the trunk latch, and the lid popped.

A flash of weak light. I swam back and lifted the lid. No!

A flashlight spun slowly, lit and glowing, my little girl floating motionless, hands taped behind her back, silver tape across her mouth, yellow pigtails swaying lazily by her head.

Her eyes were staring. No blinks, no life.

No! I grabbed her arm and shoved off for the surface.

On the way up I passed Blake, floating motionless. His one good eye was open, blood staining the water around his head, but I didn't pause.

I burst through the surface. Thrashed for the ladder. "Patty!" Grabbed a rung. Got her head out. Ripped away the tape. Tried to breathe into her mouth. "Patty!"

Everything took an eternity.

Someone jumped in to get Blake, he was sinking out of sight, but I wrapped my arm around Patty and squeezed. I couldn't see beyond my child's blue face.

"Patty, it's me! Daddy!" In the water, clinging to the ladder, I squeezed her little body. "Patty! Dear god, please! Please!"

A South American guy, black hair and bronze skin, reached down the ladder. "Up here, gimme. Gimme."

"Sweetie! Wake up, it's me." I hoisted her up with my good hand, he grabbed her, her jumper crumpling, the blue jumper I gave her, that she put on one day and a lifetime before, and as he lifted her up and over and onto the dock I pulled myself up the ladder.

I almost lost it. She was laying on the dock, limp as a sodden doll, dead, I knew it, I wasn't in time.

"Patty? Dear God, please...please, oh God, please." I sank to my knees. "No! No!"

I pushed on her chest, one hand on top of the other, but nothing happened. A shadow fell over us, a woman in a big floppy hat.

She asked the waiter, "How long was she down there?"

"Sweetie? Jesus! Oh God, please no!"

"T'ree, maybe four minutes."

I took her up in my arms and hugged her. "Wake up! Patty!" I ripped the tape off her wrists, behind her back, and squeezed her. "Sweetie? Wake up. Wake up now. It's daddy. Patty, it's me!"

I squeezed. Her body felt so small and bony, fragile and...and what? I squeezed, squeezed her hard and felt...a tremor? I squeezed again and the little frame in my arms clenched, jerked, and I heard that miracle sound. A choke. My little sweetie coughed a hard spray of water and took in a ragged gasp. She coughed, water sprayed the South American guy, he backed away wiping his face, and she didn't open her eyes but she was gasping.

"No mort!" he shouted. "She come back! Si! She come back!"

I hugged my little sweetie, not crying, just breathing, but she was alive, mine, with me, alive, I had her.

God, oh God, thank you! Thank you!

I hugged her close, kissed her, staggered to my feet and stumbled against the railing. I wasn't thinking, had to get her someplace, somewhere, but I carried her limping up the dock, tape hanging off her wrists, as the woman in the floppy hat hurried ahead. She said, "I'll call an ambulance."

I limped past an old guy with a faded blue anchor tattooed on his forearm.

"What's the point, nobody will come," he said. He pointed. "They're all down there."

My little sweetie's hands clutched at me, her face tucked under my chin. Focused on her, I was only vaguely aware of other things, but that's what she needed, an ambulance.

I looked up. "Down where?"

He pointed south toward the city. A smudge of black smoke showed against the horizon. He said, "Two planes hit the World Trade Center."

"The what?"

"The World Trade Center. They're on fire, people trapped inside. All the fire trucks and ambulances went down there."

I didn't realize the significance. I knew I had Patty, she was breathing with a croupy sound, her lungs wet, and she stirred in my arms.

I whispered, "Sweetie?"

She mumbled one glorious word. "Daddy?"

"Yeah, sweetie, it's me. I'm here, you're safe." I kissed her and held her close and limped up the ramp toward the gates of the yacht club, my clammy wet boots crunching in the gravel. "Daddy's here, it's okay."

"Hey!" It was a black guy above us, on the terrace of the yacht club, managerial in a blue blazer. "What's going on here?"

I couldn't think of anything else to say. "Ask him. Back there."

"Can't." I turned and looked. It was one of the South American waiters, a short pudgy fella. Beyond him a few people stood around Blake, laid on the dock. He said, "He dead. Fell agains' the railing, broke his head."

Patty coughed into the hollow of my throat. I held her close. I hobbled up the ramp, past the gates to the street, spent, relieved, feeling all the pain but not thinking a word, and cradling my little sweetie like treasure.

Relief, blessed relief, oh thank you God.

I waved, signaling the Mexican cabbie. He drove his yellow taxi down the street. It stopped, he jumped out and opened the back door for me. I crawled with my little sweetie onto the back seat. I lay with her there as he shut the door at my feet. No energy left, no fight, I lay there with my little girl in my arms. She clung to me and I closed my eyes.

The seat hummed beneath us, we were moving. Patty, stuck to my side, stirred. She whispered, "Where are they?"

"Sweetie? Where is who?"

She opened her eyes, blue as a clear sky. She said, "The ones that came for me. The angels."

I didn't say, I didn't know. I only knew where the devils were.

AFTERWORD

August 11, 2002. Eleven months later, it's a hot Sunday afternoon.

In the forest around our new home sunlight is shafting down through the big elms and spruce trees, ferns and bracken dense under the low branches. I feel like Binks and I are strolling around a secluded party, kids playing tag on the lawn and folks drinking lemonade and beer in the shade, talking and laughing.

It's sad even though it is a birthday party. Patty turned seven years old yesterday and we're in the country house, so it's a housewarming party too...but there's a hole ripped in it.

Paul isn't here. He won't come.

Binks strolls with me. He says, "You're right, the trees make it peaceful."

Binks' beautiful wife, Sheila, sits on the lawn in a wreath of her own skirts, teaching someone else's toddler how to play patty cake. Kids run all over and roll around in the grass so freshly grown it still has that fluorescent green look. I say, looking at Sheila, "She wants one of her own."

Binks squints as we amble into a patch of sunlight.

"We've about given up on the natural method," he said, "but she mentioned adopting. Chinese babies, lots of people are doing it."

The pleasant laugh of women. We look over to the porch where Carla talks with Mudgie's wife, Marge. Marge isn't as big as before, she agreed to go on a diet, but only if Mudgie quit drinking. He sits in a folding chair next to her, gulps lemonade, chuckles, and crunches the ice. He sees me looking at him, grins, and lifts his glass in a toast.

Where would I be without him? Without her? Carla's glance connects with mine and I feel a charge. Nowadays you can't separate us with a crowbar. Patty clings to her too, so Carla feels like a part of the family. She's happy.

I'm not happy. I exhale slowly, trying to blow away my bum mood, and of course Binks notices. He says, "She'll want to have her own too, you know."

I shrug. There's been time to think in the eleven months since Patty and I were in New York, since the twin towers were bombed and collapsed and all those people died, thousands of them. That punched a big hole in America.

The drug terrorists ripped holes in Endwell too. Paul was the last one to see Cassie Green alive. Blake and his crew also sent six college kids to the Johnson City morgue, bodies that went back to Long Island, Islip, Oyster Bay, Douglaston, and Huntington, communities already stunned by losing people when the towers fell.

Holes punched in communities. Holes punched in families, in people, in lives, a million tiny holes punched in America.

Tell the truth, I'm not worried about America. She'll bounce back. Me, I'm worried about my family.

I swig beer, my eyes wandering to the side yard. Carla's boss, Frank Paganetti, smokes a cigar in the shade of an umbrella, never taking it out of his mouth, his wife Zelda puffing a Lucky Strike and croaking at the kids who run too close.

I think of Vincent Catalone, my old friend. Ah yes, you're not here either. They shot you at the Pine Inn.

Who's to blame for that? I am.

I still miss him, but the hoopla died down and we got past it somehow. There was some heavy financial damage—our lawyer cost us an arm and a leg—but the Feds recovered all my money in Harlem and covered up all the wreckage down there. It was a major embarrassment, so I'm sure they're happy the news is all taken up with the disaster at the World Trade Center.

No one knows I killed three guys in a shoot-out. I'm lucky to be alive. We're all alive and time is passing, pushing it farther and farther behind us.

Doesn't matter, I'm still sad. All that suffering. All that death.

We swish our feet in the grass, Binks is barefoot too, but he's a cop and still makes me feel like a fish in a barrel. He asks, "How is Paul doing lately? Sticking to the house rules?"

"Yeah. Finally."

Paul kicked heroin in his first visit to the hospital, but the District Attorney's office was bearing down on us, reporters calling, and two days after he was released from the detox Paul slipped out the back door. Two weeks later they found him on the banks of the Susquehanna River, thin as a Halloween skeleton, raving out of his mind in the October cold. Psych ward, rehab, shock camp. Binks called the D.A. and recommended shock camp, a jail like a boot camp, and it looks like it did the trick. He's been in a half-way house in Schenectady for six weeks, without any problems.

THE DESTROYERS

He'll never be the same. The cocky, carefree kid got smoked out of him. It makes me sad to think about that too.

My stomach feels heavy. I burp, the taste of a hotdog with mustard repeating on me. It's time to tell him and I don't want it to sound like a big deal.

"Dave," I say, "I appreciate everything you did. You took a bullet in the flak jacket for me, down there. I also get the feeling you ran interference for us, up here. So...thanks."

Binks shrugs it off. All those murders, they figured out what happened, which made everyone look at Paul and me. I kept my mouth shut even when they threatened to put me away. They grilled Mudgie pretty good too, but God bless him, he kept his lips zipped.

Binks says, "Has Paul been here to see the house? Since you moved in?"

"Not yet."

"Well...if it's any consolation, I was surprised he took the heat, didn't break down and tell us where the body is. He covered your backside." It hurts when he puts it that way. Binks stops and turns to face me, his back to the folks on the porch. His voice is low and quiet, just loud enough for me. He says, "Paul won't come here because Fisher is here. The body is here, isn't it."

I don't say, don't nod. I look around at the trees and squint. I can't look at Binks and can't lie to him.

"You were backfilling the foundation," he says, "the night Fisher disappeared. His body never showed up in the river. And there was the forensics, the tar on the seat of Fisher's car. So he's here, isn't he."

I chew my lip. Glance up at Binks. He would've nailed us already if he was going to, so I look at him and then I can't help it, my glance wanders over to a flower bed below a window on the back side of the house. Carla and Patty planted snapdragons and jonquils there, and now healthy blooms hang on their stems in beautiful pinks and whites, moist yellows and reds.

That was an anxious moment, watching them dig there, even though Fisher's body is at least four feet down. It's hard to explain. The foundation of my home, the ghost in it, the guilt, the sadness, I'm learning to live with it; but I'm still touchy about disturbing him, the newest member of the family.

I look at Binks. He understands, he's looking at the flowers. Sheila and the child sing, "Patty cake, patty cake, baker's man—"

I have to ask him, but hesitate.

"—bake me a cake as fast as you can."

"Dave," I say, "why didn't you nail us? You could've."

Binks glances around the yard, the trees whispering in the breeze, the house looking warm in the sunlight. There's a look on his face, as if he's seeing the world as it was, in a peaceful moment. He glances down at his wife, playing with the toddler.

"I just don't know how you do it," he says, "living with him so close. A constant reminder, isn't it?"

"Of what?"

"What you paid for the house."

"Honey?" Sheila looks up from her patty cake game. "Time to go."

The party is breaking up, Patty's playmates are going home with their parents, and Marge is eating fingertips of icing off the birthday cake. Time to get her out of temptation's way. I put my arm around Carla and say goodbye to Frank and Zelda Paganetti.

I look into the green eyes of my future wife and kiss her lips. "I love you."

"I love you too."

Mudgie and Marge are at his truck, getting in. He's much more serious now.

"Darryl," he calls, "I'll see you in the morning."

At work. He's more committed, more stable, but maybe Mudgie feels different because he killed a man with a two-by-four. We don't talk about it, but you can't look at yourself the same way after you do that. It does something to you. But we did that together, it's our secret, so now he knows he's a member of my family.

Patty, my little sweetie, slumps down in the grass, waving to a friend in a car pulling away on the dirt road. She looks like any other little girl, tired after her big birthday party. Then she looks into the grass and gets lost in thought.

What's she thinking about? She looks over at Carla and me, on the porch. She brightens up, trots over on her bony knees, a mosquito bite on her suntanned arm, clear blue eyes and blonde pigtails.

She puts her arms around my waist and clings to me. "I love you, Daddy."

"I love you too, sweetie."

The psychologist said she has post-traumatic stress disorder, separation anxiety, abandonment issues. What can I expect? What can I say about our little trip to New York City? September 11th damaged the little girl of my heart, who gets lost in thought and then a day later asks a question.

Once she asked me a really hard question. "Are they still there?"

"They who?"

"All those people who died in those buildings."

I thought about it. "No, sweetie. Their souls went up to heaven."

"What about the man who took me away?"

That was tougher. Blake, wearing the cross of St. Michael, good luck charm for a traveler, where are you traveling now? And who were the angels that Patty saw that morning, locked in the trunk and drowning? Some mysteries are too big to wrap my mind around, simple fella that I am, so I didn't know what to say.

I shrugged. "Some day he'll get to heaven too. Maybe."

The sun's going down, painting the ridge up past the driveway with orange light, and I'm not as sad as I was. Paul said he might come here for our wedding. I know he'll be okay. I'm just tired of thinking about it.

Too much, too much, it's time for bed. I straighten up from the front railing and turn to the doorway...and stop. I'm thinking about that flower bed. There's his body. What about the rest of him? I don't know, so I open the door to the house I finally managed to build, a home full of warmth, light, peace and hope.

And a ghost?

"Fisher?" I stand and listen. Crickets, wind in the trees, and a sense of that deep silence beneath all things. But no, he's out there, so I glance into the darkness and whisper it. "Fisher? Son?" No sign, no answer, but I know he hears me when I say it. "Good night."

ABOUT THE AUTHOR

Lawrence "Doc" Pruyne PhD has enjoyed careers as a contractor, a journalist and a poker player. As a college professor he taught writing and literature in the Albany, NY area, and in Boston. He is a trained film-maker and has been a consultant on literary and cinema projects for almost twenty years. He is the scriptwriter and cinematographer on films produced in partnership with his wife, Cheri Robartes. Together, they also raise rare ducks on a farm in western Massachusetts.

Made in the USA
Charleston, SC
03 May 2014